GUNNAR

NINA LEVINE

Copyright © 2020 by Nina Levine

All rights reserved.

No part of this book may be reproduced in any form or by any electronic or mechanical means, including information storage and retrieval systems, without written permission from the author, except for the use of brief quotations in a book review.

Editing by Becky Johnson at Hot Tree Editing

Cover Design by Letitia at Romantic Book Affair Designs

Cover Image by Wander Pedro Aguiar

This one's for my Stormgirls.

Girl, you already have what it takes.

Shoutout to some of my Stormgirls who I've watched claim their power over the years:

Jodie O'Brien
Diane Yoz
Missy Rafidi
Emily Montoya
Amanda Rockwood
Sam Evans
Heather MacCabe
Ruth Franklin
Jean Dewsbury
Angela Hart
Robin Mitnick
Rory Lampley
Rose Holub
Chasity Jane Williams
Karin Gesell-Miller
Bren M Hawk

Chanah Dickson
Melissa Meyers Winch
Nicole Lavu Lavu
Rachel Seeberger
Cheryl Norris
Sarah Jillain
Patti Novia West
Sharina Schwalger
Marg Munro
Line Norgaard Fallesen
Denise Jones-Blair
Sandra Galbraith
Lee Anna Dunk
Samantha Bainrot

PROLOGUE

Gunnar

I never imagined the woman I'd fall in love with would be a princess, but here I am. Fucking whipped by a woman who looks like she stepped out of a fashion magazine, who drips in diamonds, and who keeps me coming back for more even when she's being too fucking much for me to handle.

She's a fucking badass princess, though.

Attitude might be her middle name, but fierce is her first, and fuck if that hasn't grabbed my heart with some strong hands.

"Fuck, Mason," she cries as she grinds her pussy down on my dick and grips my hair so hard she's likely to pull it from my scalp. "I need it harder."

She's sitting in my lap, having planted herself there the second I arrived at her place after work. I've let her take charge. But if she wants it harder I'm gonna need her on her back so I can get the job done.

Taking hold of her, I shift her onto her back and spread her legs. Roughly, just how she likes it. Finding her eyes, I growl, "Tell me."

Her lips curl up into the sexy smile I would fucking die for. "I love you, Mason Blaise."

I thrust my dick inside her. "Yeah, baby, you fucking do."

She wraps her legs around me and brings her arms up so she can hold on. "Don't go easy on me."

I pull out and slam in again. "Babe, when your cunt is this wet for me, there aren't any plans to go easy." Even if I wanted to, I wouldn't be able to. From the very first time I fucked Chelsea, I haven't been able to hold myself back.

Her fingernails dig into my skin as her pussy squeezes my dick.

Fucking hell.

This woman was made for my destruction. I'm fucking sure of that. It's a good thing I made her mine; I wouldn't survive the carnage if she wasn't.

I keep my eyes firmly on hers while I fuck her how she asked me to.

And I don't go easy.

By the time she comes, I've fucked her so damn roughly and thoroughly that she'll find it hard to walk out of here tomorrow.

"I really do love you," she says afterwards as I pull out and roll onto my back. "But I *really* love that dick of yours."

I pull her close so she's resting her head on my shoulder. "Your mouth is getting filthier every day."

She brings her hand to my jaw and angles my face down so she can kiss me. "Are you saying you don't like it filthy?"

"No, so long as I'm the only one who hears that filth." It's fucking crazy to me how possessive I am of Chelsea. I've never been like this with a woman before.

She kisses me again, slow and deep. I feel the smile teasing her lips. When her eyes meet mine again, I see the pleasure she feels over my possessiveness. "You know you're the only one who'll ever hear that filth."

"Good. Keep it that way."

We turn silent for a beat while she traces lazy patterns on my chest. "I hate that it took us so long to get together, but I also think we wouldn't have worked before now. It feels like this is exactly how we were meant to be."

Chelsea talks my ear off non-stop about the universe and manifesting and shit. She's big on believing in the timing of life. Me, not so much. I'm more about forcing shit to happen, but I'll listen to her talk about this for the rest of my life so long as it means she's by my side.

"Why wouldn't we have worked out before now?"

She shifts onto her stomach so she can look up at me. "I was a hot mess before. I know I drive you crazy sometimes, but if we'd met before I got myself together, I don't think you would have stuck around for long."

"The words 'hot mess' don't belong anywhere near you, Mayfair. I think this is one of those times where the way you see yourself isn't accurate." I've never met a woman with her shit together as well as Chelsea has hers, but every now and then she shows me her self-doubt, and it's always over something she shouldn't doubt about herself.

She smiles. "No, I really would have driven you away. I was needy and jealous in relationships, and unable to manage those feelings. With you, I'm better at it."

I arch a brow. "Really?"

She smacks me. "Shut up. And trust me, I'm much better now."

I laugh. Chelsea's as possessive of me as I am of her. We've had a few fights over our insane jealousy. A few fights in three months is a ratio I can handle. "I wouldn't take you any other way. The minute you're not jealous of another woman or fucked off because I've said something insensitive, I know we've got a problem." I've watched my mother disconnect from my father over the years, so I know the signs of a woman who's no longer in love with her man. I'll take needy and jealous over that shit any day.

Chelsea drops her lips to mine and kisses me again before changing the subject. "Are you free on Friday night? I want you to come to a party with me."

I move onto my side, propping myself up onto my elbow. "You're moving us into new territory."

It's a statement, but she knows it's also a question. My family and club know about us, but we've kept our relationship away from her family these last three months. Chelsea's father has made it more than clear he doesn't want his daughter with me. My attendance at a party with her will gain his attention because it will gain the media's attention. Her father is the premier of our state. Everything Chelsea does puts her in the spotlight, however turning up to a party with a member of the Storm MC will shine that shit brightly. I need to know she's prepared for that before I agree. No fucking way am I throwing her to the wolves if I don't think she's ready.

She nods. "Yes, it's time. I'm done with us hiding away like we're doing something wrong."

I glide my hand over the small of her back and rest it on her ass. "And you want to announce our relationship at this party?" I don't know whose party she wants us to attend, but I know her world of privilege and wealth because it used to be mine too. I fucking hate everything these parties stand for. I'd rather splash this news around in other ways, but if this is what she wants, I'll do it.

Wiggling so she can move closer to me, she says, "I know you walked away from this world, and I don't expect you to come to every party I have to attend, but I need you by my side at this one."

I hear something in her voice that causes me to pay closer attention to what she's not saying. "You know I'll do whatever you need, but why? What is it about this party?"

Hesitation is clear in her eyes as she considers my question. She's slow to answer me, and when she does, I know why, and it pisses me off. "This is a huge fundraiser for Dad, and he's got a lot of people watching him, seeing who'll be at his side going into the next election." She bites her lip. "He'll also have Joe there. I haven't wanted to tell you this, but he's been pushing me harder the last two weeks over this. I don't know what's going on with him, but he seems more intent than he has been to make this marriage happen." She grips my bicep. "He needs to know you and I are together."

"Yeah, he fucking does," I say as I jerk up off the bed. Anger and a feeling of intense possessiveness are strangling me just thinking about the fact Chelsea's father is trying to marry her off to some fucking asshole who isn't me. "And I'm more than happy to make sure he understands once and for fucking all that you're mine and that he can't control you anymore."

"Mason," Chelsea says, coming to me as I pace her bedroom. "I don't need you to fight my battles for me. I just need you by my side."

"You've got a plan to take care of your father this time?" The question crashes down between us, harsher than I intended. But fuck, Chelsea gutted me eight years ago when she ended our friendship because her father threatened to destroy me if she didn't, so I need to know she won't do that again.

Her face creases with regret as she reaches for me. "You know I was trying to save you last time. Please don't let that always come between us."

Fuck, she's right. We've talked about this, and I promised her I'd let it go. We don't have a chance in hell of making this work if I can't do that.

I shove my fingers through my hair and suck in a deep breath before meeting her gaze and nodding. "Yeah," I say gruffly. "I know, baby, but you're gonna need to share your plan with me." I fucking hate how desperate I feel, but Chelsea owns my heart like no one ever has; I refuse to lose her again.

Her eyes soften. She reads me better than anyone, so she knows the depth of my feelings. "I have a plan. I'm just waiting on some information to come through, and then I'll share it. You just need to know that it's enough to get my father to leave us alone."

I look at the girl I've loved since we were kids and it

hits me that while I've spent the last three months falling deeply into this relationship with her, I haven't given her my complete trust. I realise there's a part of me still holding back. That needs to end so we can move forward together.

Exhaling the breath I've been holding, I say, "Okay."

"Okay as in you're on board with me taking charge of this or okay as in you're going to show up and try to bulldoze your way into getting what we want?"

I pull her to me and hold her tightly. "You know me too well, Mayfair." I kiss her, taking my time because kissing Chelsea is never something to rush. When I finally let her lips go, I say, "We'll try it your way, and if that doesn't work, we'll do it my way." I'm almost certain this job will require force to get done, but I'll give Chelsea the opportunity to try and get her father to see things her way. If he was a decent human being, he'd open his eyes to what his daughter wants, but Mark Novak is a piece of shit so I don't see that happening.

"I love you," she says, pulling my mouth back to hers.

I've got my hands all over her, ready to fuck her again, when my phone rings. "Fuck," I grumble. "I need to get that in case it's Scott." My president gave me strict instructions this afternoon to ignore his calls at the risk of death. Apparently he's heard rumblings of shit about to go down between the club and the cops. Fuck knows what for, but he seemed concerned, and if there's one thing I know, it's that Scott doesn't worry over nothing.

Chelsea nods and I locate my phone. "Pres," I answer the call when I see it is him. "What's up?"

"I need you at the clubhouse ASAP. We've had three

members arrested due to new legislation that's just passed so we've got some shit to go over."

"Fuck."

"Yeah, that about fuckin' covers it. Don't take your time, Gunnar, and watch your fuckin' back. These cops mean business."

After the line goes dead, I look at Chelsea. "I have to go."

She frowns. "Is everything okay?"

I pull on my clothes while my mind races, wondering what the hell is going on with the club. The last time I remember hearing Scott sound as concerned as he did on the phone was almost two years ago when all the shit went down with Rogue and Bourne. "No, but I don't know why yet." I grab my phone and keys before pulling her in for a kiss. "I'll call you later."

Chelsea follows me outside. I manage to keep my thoughts under control, but my gut is another story. It's telling me shit is about to hit the fan in the worst possible way. And my gut is usually right.

It's the flashing red and blue lights outside her house that tell me this time is no different. But it's the sight of her father exiting his car that tells me this is more than just club business.

Two cops come my way and start spitting words at me. Words that signal my arrest, but that I have trouble focussing on because the only thing I can focus on is the smug smile plastered across Mark Novak's face.

"Dad, what's going on?" Chelsea demands, but I know from the fear in her eyes that she knows exactly what's going on.

Her father knows about us and is going down a dangerous path in order to keep us apart.

The only thing I can fucking hope for now is that Chelsea doesn't cave and give him what he wants.

"Dad! Tell me what you've done!" she begs as he stares at me like he's won a fucking war.

It's that look that does it.

And the hysterical plea in my woman's voice.

History is repeating itself.

This time, though, I won't survive it.

I've given my heart to Chelsea this time. Every last piece of it. If she does what he wants, there's no way my body will ever accept it back.

"Chelsea." I demand her attention. "Don't do anything, baby. Not until you speak to me again."

She stares at me in silence.

"Chelsea! Promise me you won't let him fucking bully you into shit this time." When she doesn't respond, I bark, "Fucking promise me!"

She blinks, and it's in that hesitation that I fucking know.

She's going to fucking annihilate me, and there's nothing I can do about it.

1

GUNNAR
3 MONTHS LATER

I stare at the guy lying dead at my feet before looking up and meeting Griff's gaze. He didn't give me strict instructions not to kill the motherfucker, but by the look on his face, he maybe should have.

"Fuck," he mutters. "This complicates shit."

"Why?" I shrug. "He wasn't going to do what Moss wanted anyway."

"He's got a point," J says.

"Yeah," Griff agrees, "but I would have rather given Moss the opportunity to make this call. Now we have a fucking mess to clean up that we don't have time for." He checks his watch before looking at me again. "You and J wrap the body and clean the scene while I get the van. Work fast because we have another job to take care of tonight after we deal with this."

I nod and get to work with J while Griff leaves to swap his bike for one of the club vans.

Forty minutes later, I'm a sweaty mess after cleaning

up and getting the body ready to dispose of. October in Brisbane, in a house without air conditioning, is hell.

"You ready?" Griff asks when he arrives back.

J nods. "Yeah. Just give me a minute to finish wiping the room down."

Griff and I load the body into the van while J does the room. My vice president is pissed at me, but he's keeping it to himself. Griff's patience always fucking astounds me.

"You should get it out," I say as we close the back of the van.

He looks at me. "Get what out?"

"Your anger. I fucked up."

He exhales. "Yeah, you did." He pauses, watching me thoughtfully for a moment. "You've been fucking up a bit lately, brother. What's going on?"

The last thing Griff wants to hear is the truth, so I don't give it to him. "I've got a lot of family shit on my mind." This isn't a lie. I do have shit going on with my family.

"You need some time off to deal with that?"

"The last thing the club needs is me taking time off."

"That's the fucking truth, but what we really don't fucking need are dead bodies when the cops are watching us like they are. So if you need the time, take it."

J exits the house and joins us as I say, "I don't need time off. I'll get my shit together."

Griff's eyes bore into me. "Make sure you do." He looks between J and me. "We'll dump the body in the usual spot, and then we'll need to stop off and see Moss so I can let him know what's happened."

Since the cops cracked down on the club three months ago, Griff prefers to discuss as much business as possible with our clients in person rather than over the phone. Especially any business that has to do with Dwayne Moss. We've been cleaning up his messes for years now, but his connections to Premier Novak caused the club to sever ties with him just after the crackdown. Somehow, though, he's managed to worm his way back in, and here we are handling shit for him again. We're just a lot more careful about how we do that now. This time he asked us to strong-arm some government official who has been blocking an approval Moss needs to help push his mine development ahead. Fuck knows how he'll take the news the guy's dead, but it can't be a good look when one of the guys holding up a multi-billion-dollar mining project suddenly disappears.

∽

Two hours later, we're finished with the body and have made our way to Moss's home.

"You're fucking kidding me," J mutters, staring at the house that's lit up with a party. "The last thing we need is to be seen here."

He's right, there has to be hundreds of guests at this party.

"Moss told me to go around the back. He doesn't want to be seen with us either," Griff says.

Griff texts Moss to let him know we've arrived, and then we head around the back as directed. Moss's home is like a huge fucking resort with multiple residences, two pools, a tennis court, landscaped gardens, and a pool house, which is where he meets us, motioning us in.

"I take it from the fact you're here that we've had a hiccup?" Moss says, looking at Griff.

"That guy was never going to do what you want," Griff says. "We sorted the problem permanently."

Moss stares at Griff. "He's dead?"

Griff nods.

"Fucking hell." Moss rakes his fingers through his hair, looking anything but pleased. "I didn't fucking ask you to kill the asshole. I asked you to—"

"You asked us to handle the situation. We fucking handled it," Griff says darkly.

"No, you fucking screwed it up. This is going to cause me the kind of heat I don't need."

Griff steps forward and grabs a handful of Moss's shirt before forcing him back against the wall. Pushing his face close to Moss's, he says, "This is going to get you your fucking mine. All you need to do is stop fucking choking on your balls and have a little faith." He lets him go. "A fucking thank you wouldn't go astray either."

Moss pulls an envelope from his suit jacket and shoves it at Griff. He opens his mouth to speak but is interrupted when Mark Novak joins us.

"Griff," Novak says, walking our way. He's talking to my VP, but his eyes are firmly on me.

Every fibre in my being tenses with hatred as I stare at the man I despise more than I know what to do with. I want to wrap my hands around his neck and squeeze every last breath of life from him for what he's done to me.

"Mason," he says, fucking baiting me with that smug fucking smile of his.

Griff glances between Novak and me. He knows the

history there and is rightfully concerned about what I might do. Stepping in, he says, "What the fuck are you doing here, Novak?" He also can't stand the motherfucker, but is better able to control his emotions than me.

Novak continues watching me for a long moment before turning his gaze to Griff. "Who do you think you're working for here?"

"You've gotta be fucking kidding me," I say as my mind connects the dots right the fuck in front of me.

That smug smile of Novak's grows. "That's right, Mason. You'll do what I say going forward."

I jab my finger at him. "Like fucking hell I will." I swing my face around to look at Griff. "We need to get the fuck out of here and never take another job from these assholes."

Moss cuts in before Griff can respond. "That won't be happening. Not when we've got a fucking dead body sitting between us."

Novak's brows lift. "A dead body?"

"Yeah," Moss says. "Instead of threatening Jimmy, they killed him."

Novak whistles low and looks at Griff. "It looks like your club will be doing my dirty work for a long time now."

How Griff manages to keep his cool I don't fucking know, but he does. "You've been trying to shut us down for three months, Novak, and now you want to work with us? I'm not buying it."

"It seems I may have been hasty when I brought those laws in," Novak says. "I think we can come to a compromise."

Novak managed to push laws through when he

discovered my relationship with his daughter. Laws that threatened to tear my club apart. I was arrested, along with six other club members on bullshit charges that didn't land any of us in jail, but that fucked with us enough to be a constant reminder of what the state could do to us if they pushed the point. We've spent the last three months watching our back and being cautious as fuck in everything we do. I don't know what Novak's game is here, but it can't be anything good.

"What kind of compromise?" Griff asks.

"The kind where you take care of my dirty work and I make sure your club stays safe."

"That's the kind of compromise my president will have to okay," Griff says.

Novak nods. "I expect it is. You take it to him and get him to reach out." His voice drops low and threatening when he adds, "The only acceptable answer is yes, though. Make sure you tell him that."

Novak eyes me again before turning and exiting the pool house.

My fists clench by my side, itching like fuck to beat the hell out of him. One fucking day I will.

"I'll be in touch tomorrow," Moss says. "We've got a few things that need taking care of."

Griff works his jaw but doesn't respond. His ability to keep his mouth shut in times like this is why he's the VP. The rest of us wouldn't be able to fucking hold ourselves back.

I follow Griff and J out to where our bikes and van are parked down the street. I've almost reached my bike when I run into Joe fucking Hearst. He's standing beside a limousine talking on his phone. When he sees me, he stills and trains his eyes on me in the same way mine are on him.

This fucking night just keeps getting worse.

My stride slows as I take in the man who has everything I ever wanted.

Jealousy claws at me in ways I never knew until he entered my life.

It's eaten me alive for the past three months, but standing right in front of him is proving to be a whole new level of torment.

And then the limousine door opens and Chelsea exits, and my jealousy collides with hate in a shitshow of feelings I wish didn't exist inside me.

Her eyes meet mine, and the entire world falls away as I stare at the woman I used to love.

"Mason." My name falls from her lips in a hushed tone. It also falls by accident if the way her eyes instantly cut to her husband is anything to go by.

Joe's lips pinch together as he reaches for her hand. I don't miss the possessiveness in his action and struggle to take my eyes off her hand clasped tightly in his.

Fuck.

Forcing my attention from Chelsea back to what I'm doing, I stalk away from her and her fucking husband. No way can I afford to get tied up with her again. She made her decision three months ago and didn't stop to look back at me once.

Chelsea Novak is fucking dead to me and I don't ever intend to resurrect her.

2

CHELSEA

"Friday night is the fundraiser dinner for the Brain Foundation. Robyn will organise a dress for you. Just make sure you're available from six for an interview with *Society One*," my husband says over lunch the day after we ran into Mason outside Dwayne Moss's house. I've spent almost every minute since seeing Mason thinking about him, so I'm having trouble focussing on what Joe's saying. Something he doesn't fail to notice. "Chelsea, are you listening to me?"

My eyes snap to his. Joe doesn't handle it well when I don't give him my full attention. Usually I don't care to give him what he wants, but my mind is all over the place today and I'm feeling highly strung. That's making me do things out of character, like pandering to my husband. "Sorry, yes. Friday night. Robyn will get me a dress, and I have an interview at six." I frown. "What's the interview for?"

Joe's lips purse together, a sign of his displeasure. "You really need to focus on what we're trying to achieve here. Your father is preparing for re-election. This is a family interview."

Of course.

Dad has given my husband a whole range of responsibilities going into this next election. One of them is handling the media. Essentially, he's in charge of the spin, and he uses our family to achieve his and dad's goals.

I finish eating the sandwich Joe's assistant brought in and stand. "Right, got it. Friday night is all about playing happy fucking families."

"Fuck, Chelsea, what's with the attitude today?"

If Joe thinks this is attitude, he's got a lot more to learn about me. But then again, we have only been married for a month, so there's a whole lot of stuff he still has to discover about me. My fondness for throwing attitude when someone's being an asshole is only one of those things.

I don't bother to answer him. "I'm going to clean up and get going. I have a busy afternoon with clients ahead of me."

"You need to think about quitting your job," Joe says as I head towards his private bathroom. His office is practically a self-contained apartment with all its facilities. Maybe he'll choose to use it as an apartment one day. A girl couldn't be so lucky.

Shutting myself in the bathroom, I take a deep breath and rest my hands on the vanity.

You can do this.
You can do this.
You can do this.

I look at myself in the mirror, taking in the dark circles under my eyes.

I can't fucking do this.

I need out.

Oh, my darling, there is no out. You made your bed and now you shall lie in it.

The scream that's been trapped inside me for the last three months sits in my throat, desperate to be heard by the world.

I suck in another deep breath.

When I made my choice, I decided I would never allow myself to engage in pity parties. I won't ever be that girl who wallows in feeling sorry for herself. Shit happens, and we pick our path in life, and then we need to stick to it, standing strong every step of the way.

I retrieve my lipstick from my bag and reapply it. Russian Red. My favourite shade of red that always makes me feel able to take on the world.

I then tidy my hair and powder my face.

By the time I exit the bathroom, I've gathered myself enough to deal with my husband and his never-ending demands.

I'm surprised to find his office empty, but that doesn't bother me. I told him I have a busy afternoon, so I have a reason for leaving without waiting for him to return.

I sling my bag over my shoulder, straighten my suit jacket, and exit Joe's office.

I'm a few steps out of the office when I spot him.

Leather and jeans.

Attitude and ink.

Rolling in like the storm he is.

My breathing instantly slows.

Hell, my lungs stop working for a good three seconds.

Mason.

The man I never stopped loving even though all I want to feel for him now is hate for what he did to me after we broke up.

He's coming my way, his shoulders tense like stone, his eyes hard, and his expression closed off in the way it has been since the day I made it clear to him we were done. That awful fateful day I wish I could rip from my soul and never remember again.

Somehow I keep putting one foot in front of the other and continue making my way towards the lift even though this is bringing me closer to Mason. Seeing him last night killed me, but what truly slayed me was the way he looked at me and then looked away and kept going, like seeing me didn't affect him at all. I want to do the same to him today, but the way I'm finding it hard to even breathe, let alone not look at him, tells me I'm going to fail.

His eyes don't meet mine once.

He keeps them glued to something beyond me.

I know this because mine are on him.

It's like I'm begging for pain. Like I want the ache that sits deep in my heart to be dragged up and given a beating. If I didn't, I'd look straight ahead and keep walking. I surely wouldn't stop as he walks straight past me, turn to him, and demand, "Really?"

His legs falter, and after he takes a couple more steps, he finally stops and faces me. "Really what?"

His words are so cold they stab into my heart like shards of ice. Add to that the way his dark eyes stare at me with burning hatred and my own feelings of hostility rage to the surface. Feelings that make no sense to me after loving Mason for so long.

Mason is the boy I've loved since forever. Our families run in the same social circle, and we grew up together. I remember our first day of year one. I was scared and Mason sat with me and made sure I was okay. He looked out for me from that day on, keeping bullies like Samuel Hash away. In grade seven, when Samuel made fun of my chest still being flat, Mason got in a fight with him to shut him up. In grade ten, when Samuel spread lies about me sucking his dick on school camp (because I'd rejected him and he wanted to humiliate me like I'd apparently humiliated him), Mason once again got in a fight with him. And then when I was sixteen and he discovered my father hit me sometimes, he took on the role of my protector in a whole new way.

I'd planned to tell him I loved him when I was seventeen, but that plan went out the window the night Mason and I were at a party that got busted by the cops for drugs. Neither of us were found with drugs, but the publicity wasn't great for my father at a time when he was getting everything in line to one day run for premier. When my father threatened to ruin Mason after that party, I knew he meant it, so I'd done the only thing I thought I could do: I cut all ties to the boy I loved and pretended I didn't want him in my life anymore. I'll never forget the hurt in Mason's eyes every time we passed each other at school after that. Most people would have only seen hate, but I knew it was hurt that sat deeper and more keenly.

Looking at him now, I see that same hurt, but what I see more is next level hate. Twice burned, he'll never forgive me for what I did to him.

"You're really going to walk past me without even looking at me?" I say.

He closes the distance between us, bringing a hurricane of anger with him. "I'm not sure what the fuck you expect from me, Chelsea, but you broke your fucking promise to always fight for me, so as far as I'm concerned, you don't deserve for me to even acknowledge your fucking existence."

It's like he's punched me without laying a finger on me. The thing is, he's right. We're done. I'm not sure why I stopped to speak to him, but the pull I feel is too great to ignore. It has a life of its own and I'm helpless to do anything but go with it.

"God, you are so fucking cold. Three months ago, you—"

"Three months ago, I fucking gave you everything I had to give and you threw it all back in my face."

"I gave you everything I had to give, too. I don't know why that's so hard for you to understand."

"No." He stabs a finger at me. "You fucking gave up on us. You didn't even come close to giving everything you had to give."

My chest squeezes with anger and hurt, and all the things I never had the chance to tell him. "Don't you dare say that to me again. You have no idea how much I tried to save us."

"I know you never gave *me* the opportunity to save us."

My eyes widen. "You were arrested, Mason, and charged with serious crimes. You were dealing with club stuff. And we both know my father was determined to ruin you. There wasn't anything you *could* do."

The vein in his neck pulses as he leans his face close to mine. So close I swear I can taste his rage. "You keep fucking telling yourself that, princess. We both know you gave up on us. Again." He pulls his face away. "I'm better off without you. I need a woman by my side who has some fucking grit in her, and that's something you don't fucking have."

I slap him. Hard enough to redden his face. Ignoring the surprise in his eyes, I spit out, "Fuck you. At least I didn't fuck your friend to hurt you."

His eyes glitter with hate. "No, you just suck another man's dick every fucking night after promising that to me. It turns out you give away promises like you give away your lips."

I can't breathe.

Mason's hate is too much to endure.

And mine is twisting my heart all over the place.

"You're right: we're better off without each other. I don't need an asshole in my life."

With that, I spin on my heel and walk away from him a hell of a lot more confidently than I feel on the inside. I'll be damned if I'll show Mason Blaise just how much he's hurt me.

3

GUNNAR

Fuck.

Chelsea was the last person I expected to run into today, and now that I have, I'm ready for the day to be done so I can drink myself into oblivion. I'm staring at about eight more hours of work before I can do that, though, so I need to pull my shit together and get on with it.

"Gunnar," Griff calls out as he catches up to me. "You found him yet?"

We're at Joe Hearst's offices, trying to locate him and having trouble doing so. The guy's business takes up three levels of this building, and we've been given the run around from his staff as to where he might be.

I jab my finger at the office I'm standing outside of. "This is his apparently, but he's not in there." I checked after Chelsea left. That was after I kicked myself for watching her walk away until I could no longer see her.

Fuck, she pissed me off when she asked me why I refused to look at her. She has no fucking idea how much

I crave the sight of her. But looking at her, let alone being fucking near her, is too hard. Not when I can't have her.

"Christ," Griff mutters. "We don't have time to be fucked around like this."

"Tell me again why we're doing this."

"We need to keep these assholes close while we figure out the best way forward."

I know Scott's not keen on working for Novak. I also know we don't have many options where he's concerned. The legislation Novak managed to get passed put so many restrictions on motorcycle clubs they practically strangled us. After the initial arrests were made three months ago, the cops haven't done much but let us know they're watching us. That's frustrated the hell out of us and gotten in the way of some of our cleaning jobs. It's also cut our cleaning jobs down because assholes who need their messes cleaned up aren't fucking keen on hiring a club who are being watched by the cops. Keeping Novak onside by doing his dirty work is something Scott couldn't pass up at this point. Un-fucking-fortunately, Novak and Moss have declared Hearst our point of contact, meaning I'm going to be seeing more of the motherfucker than I ever wanted.

Griff and I head back out to reception. On our way, we finally locate Hearst, who's watching me with hawk eyes.

"We've got less than five minutes before we have to be out of here," Griff says, his tone letting Hearst know he's less than impressed to have been screwed around.

"This'll only take two," Hearst snaps back, striding like the asshole he is to his office.

After I discovered Chelsea's engagement to this guy, I dug up as much information on him as I could. He comes from old money; he's run his own highly successful financial management firm for five years; he's been engaged once before, but she ended it when he cheated on her; he likes to fuck prostitutes; and he practically sucks his father-in-law's dick.

We follow him back to his office where he hands over a thick envelope of cash and says, "There's a list of names in there; you need to pay them all a visit and remind them of their agreement with Novak over the mine." He pauses and looks at me. "We need them all alive so perhaps only send members who can follow instructions and get the job done properly. I take it you were the one who fucked up."

My hands are on him before I can stop myself. "You fucking asshole," I bellow, gripping his shirt and shoving him backwards.

"Fucking hell, Gunnar. Stop!" Griff yanks me away before I can do any damage. Pushing me towards the door, he orders, "Wait for me outside."

I barely hear a word he says. My focus is on Hearst, who's watching me with a feral expression.

"No," Hearst says. "I want a word with him. Alone."

Griff's brows arch. "You sure about that?"

Hearst keeps his eyes on me. "I'm sure."

Griff forces out a harsh breath and mutters, "Fuck," before walking to me and saying, "Try not to kill him."

A moment later, Griff exits the room and I'm alone with Hearst.

He comes closer to me. "It seems we find ourselves in a difficult situation."

I scrub a hand over my face. "You're shitting me,

right? What, you wanna clear the air and shake fucking hands?"

His face darkens. "No, I want to tell you in no uncertain terms to keep your eyes and hands off my wife."

I plant my feet wide and cross my arms. "You can save your breath, Hearst. I don't intend to ever fucking touch her again."

"Good, because if I find out you've touched her, I'll fucking kill you."

I drop my arms and move into his space. "You need to be careful who you're threatening. Just try to fucking kill me and see what that gets you."

"Don't underestimate me, Mason."

Fuck him. "Are we done here?" If I don't get out of here soon, Griff will rip my balls from my body for what I'll do.

"So long as you understand what I've said, we're done."

I can't stop myself. My fist is in his face before I know what I'm doing. The fucking patronising prick. He stumbles back, but the look in his eyes tells me he was expecting this punch, and the way he comes at me with one of his own makes me think this is exactly what he wanted.

I dodge his punch and land another one on him, the crack of my fist connecting with his cheekbone satisfying as fuck. He comes back at me, this time more determined and manages to smash his fist into my face.

We spend the next few minutes trading punches, each one growing more savage than the last. His office chairs go flying, and the books in one of his bookshelves end up all over the floor as we crash into shit. The sound eventually draws Griff back into the room, and he steps into the fray, yelling at me to stop.

I'm fucking jacked up on adrenaline, and the blazing need to make this asshole hurt, so it takes Griff wrapping his arms around me and physically pulling me away from Hearst to stop me.

"Jesus fucking Christ, Gunnar," Griff says once we're out of Hearst's office. "It'd make my fucking day if for once you managed to control your urge to punch people."

Blood roars in my ears, fury races through my veins, and a whole fucking range of emotions I can't even begin to understand threaten to consume me. It's taking everything I have not to go back into Hearst's office and finish what I started. Images of Chelsea with that motherfucker slice through my heart, adding to the bullshit in my head.

"Fuck!" I roar as I put my fist through the wall.

"Jesus fuck!" Griff eyes me, his own anger surfacing. "You about fucking done, brother? The last thing we need is trouble with this asshole."

I suck in oxygen and work on clearing my thoughts.

He's right, and I need to get myself under control. The last three months have been a mess of me doing whatever the fuck it takes just to get through my days. Fighting, drinking, and fucking, but mostly fighting. None of it is working, though. I'm still as fucked up over Chelsea as I was when this all started.

I look at Griff and nod. "Yeah, I'm done. Let's get the fuck out of here."

One of the things I respect about Griff is his ability to let shit go. He always makes it clear where he stands and what he thinks, but he doesn't hold onto shit. He does that now and doesn't bang on about what I just did in

Hearst's office, but I know he's looking for me to make some changes. My club and my brothers are everything to me, so I'll try, but fuck me, working with Hearst is going to make that hard as hell to do.

∼

I THROW some beer down my throat as I listen to my sister go on about the long day she had at work. Alexa helps our brother, Calder, manage our family's chain of hotels around the world, and today they had problems with the computer system that crashed and caused havoc with the reservations. It's shit I have zero fucks to give about, because I want nothing to do with my family's business, but I love my sister enough to listen to her have a meltdown over it.

"Seriously, Calder can kiss my ass if he wants to treat me like shit over this. It wasn't my fault the system crashed. I told him weeks ago it needed updating." Alexa narrows her eyes at me. "You're not really listening, are you?"

I suck back some more beer while thinking I'm going to need some stronger liquor than this. "I'm listening. Calder's an asshole. I think that about covers it."

She slides onto the stool next to mine at her kitchen island. Motioning at my face, she says, "Dare I ask who you punched today? I'm presuming that if you look like this, the other guy took a beating."

"You can ask, but you won't like the answer."

"God, Mason, who?"

"Joe Hearst."

Her eyes widen. "You're not being serious?"

I move off my stool. "I'm gonna need rum for this. You still got that bottle I left here last time?"

She nods and points at a cupboard. "In there."

I locate the rum and pour myself a glass. After I drink some, I rest my ass against the kitchen counter and look at my sister. Out of all my siblings, Alexa's the one I'm closest to. There's only one year between us and we were inseparable as kids. She might be younger than me, but she doesn't act like a twenty-four-year-old; she's far more responsible than I am. "I have to see Hearst due to club stuff going on, and he pushed my fucking buttons today." I take another sip of rum. "He wanted to get into it with me."

She shakes her head. "I don't understand men. Why is it so hard to walk away instead of getting your fists out?"

"And I don't fucking understand women." I drain my glass and pour myself another drink. "Because I'm sure she'll tell you and you'll bust my balls for not mentioning it if I don't, I also saw Chelsea today."

Alexa frowns. "I spoke to her about an hour ago and she didn't mention it. But then again, I've noticed she's stopped talking about you to me. I think maybe she's worried about our friendship now that you two aren't together."

Alexa and Chelsea have been friends for years, but became really close while I was with Chelsea. I encouraged it at the time because while Chelsea knew a lot of people, she didn't have the kind of friends she could rely on when she needed someone by her side.

"Fuck, you women worry too much about shit that you shouldn't."

Alexa purses her lips. "For the record, we don't. Also

for the record, most men could afford to worry about shit a little more. Now tell me you two didn't have another fight today."

"This is the reason I wasn't going to mention it to you."

"So you did have a fight."

"We had a discussion."

"When you say discussion, that means something vastly different to almost everyone else."

"A fight involves yelling and screaming. There was none of that."

She rolls her eyes. "Don't you think you guys did enough fighting three months ago? Why couldn't you just walk on by and ignore your burning desire to have another go at her?"

"I fucking tried. She initiated it this time."

"Oh." That shuts her up for half a second. "So, what happened?"

"Nothing new. It was the same old shit."

"Okay, wait, let's back this up. You walked past her without saying anything to her?"

I take a gulp of rum. "Yes."

She grins. "This is good news because it means you should be able to get through my birthday party without losing your shit."

"What birthday party?" My gut's not feeling good about where she's going with this.

"The one I sent you an invitation to this morning. Check your emails."

I shove my fingers through my hair. "I take it you've also invited Chelsea." And her fucking husband.

"Yes, she'll be there, but there will be so many people

at the party that you two won't even need to be in the same room or see each other."

"Fuck." If it were anyone else, I'd say a flat out no, but it's Alexa, and I can't do that to her.

"Also, Mum and Dad will be there."

I'm not sure which is worse, having to see Dad or having to see Chelsea with Joe.

"Right," Alexa says as she slides off her stool, "I'm ordering Thai for dinner, and we're going to watch the new episode of *Yellowstone*. Oh, and"—she smiles sweetly—"I need you to please clean my air conditioning filters and fix the tap in the kitchen."

"Of course you do," I mutter, but I wouldn't care if she wanted me to renovate her entire fucking apartment. I'd do it without complaint. I might not be close to my parents these days, but I love the hell out of my brothers and sister, and would lay down and die for them if I had to.

4

CHELSEA

Eight hours after seeing him at Joe's office, I'm still thinking about Mason. I'm beginning to wonder if I'll ever stop thinking about him. God, I'm beginning to wonder if he'll send me crazy.

"You've been quiet all night," Joe says, joining me in our library.

During our whirlwind engagement, we bought this house after inspecting twenty-three other houses. Joe is the kind of man whose attention to detail is so great it's actually infuriating. He found the smallest things wrong with each house we looked at, so when we found this place, and he didn't have any problems with it, I didn't bother to tell him I hated it. I couldn't take another house inspection. We moved in a week later after he rushed the sale, and I've since become adept at lying to him. Joe thinks I love this library and the furniture he filled it with. I don't; I detest everything about it, especially the brown leather armchairs. Who wants brown furniture? Not me, and yet here I am with a whole fucking house full of it.

I look at him. If this wasn't an arranged marriage and I wasn't in love with another man, I'd admit to the fact my husband is one of the best-looking men I've ever met. Tall and fit with dark hair that's always perfectly styled, a strong chiselled jaw, and piercing blue eyes, Joe turns many heads, just not mine. That could also have something to do with the fact he's a cold and ruthless man who in just a month I've learned to always be on guard with.

"I've got a lot of work stuff on my mind," I lie as I take a sip of wine and note the bruises on his face. I don't know who he got in a fight with, and I don't want to know, so I don't mention it.

"Stuff you don't need to fill your mind with." God, I hate how condescending he is.

"My mind likes being filled with my work."

He sighs. "How many times are we going to have this argument, Chelsea?"

"As many times as you keep initiating it."

"There will come a time I won't initiate it. I'll simply make it clear I've reached the end of my patience." The way he says this scatters goosebumps over my skin, not the good kind.

I sip some more wine. "Let's not discuss this tonight."

He appraises me for a long moment before granting my wish. Sitting in the armchair across from me, he says, "Your father is pleased with the way the campaign is coming together."

Shoot. Me. Now.

I don't want to be bored by the details of my father's re-election campaign. However, what I'm slowly figuring out is which battles to fight with my husband and which to walk away from. This is one to stay far, far away from. So I play the dutiful wife and say, "That's good. Are you happy with it too?"

I can tell by the slight lift of his lips that this question pleases Joe. "I am. We really need you to come on strong in this interview on Friday, though."

"Come on strong? What does that mean?"

"It means that since you're insisting on keeping your job for now rather than taking on extra social engagements that would benefit the family, we need you to be extra enthusiastic about what your father's doing." He pauses. "And about our marriage."

This is the real reason he's in here talking with me. Joe usually spends his nights working at his office or in his home office unless we're out at a social function. He doesn't casually join me in the library for a chat.

I take a bigger sip of wine. I'm going to need it to get through this conversation. "What would you prefer I say about our marriage, Joe?"

"Chelsea," he starts, low and with warning, but I cut him off.

"Should we mention what my father threatened me with if I didn't marry you? Or perhaps we could talk about how our union has cemented his future with your family connections? Or wait, should we discuss more intimate details of our marriage?"

His lips pull into a thin, disapproving line. "I don't know what the fuck has gotten into you today, but it needs to end. I didn't agree to this marriage simply to put up with this kind of attitude."

I cock my head, feeling extra frisky tonight. Joe and I

didn't spend a great deal of time together before our wedding a month ago and haven't spent much time having deep and meaningfuls since, so there's some things I'd love to know about him. "Why *did* you agree to this marriage, Joe?"

"We both know the benefits of a Hearst aligning with a Novak."

"Right, but there are plenty of other women out there from families like mine. You're a good looking, well-connected guy; you could have taken your pick."

"You're not giving yourself enough credit, Chelsea."

I don't know what he means by that, and I'm not sure I want to. As far as I'm concerned, this marriage is nothing but an arrangement. Joe, on the other hand, has said and done a few things that make me wonder if he wants it to be more. I don't want to open up a conversation about that.

"Fine," I concede, "I'll play the good girl and be enthusiastic about our amazing marriage. Both you and my father will be more than happy with my performance."

That thin line of displeasure doesn't disappear from Joe's face as he stands. "Good."

With that, he leaves me in peace. I stare after him and guzzle the rest of my wine. It's going to be a long week of psyching myself up for that interview and fundraiser. It's only Tuesday, so I have three long days ahead of me. Oh, God, and then I have Alexa's birthday party on Saturday night. She hasn't told me she's invited Mason, but he's her brother so of course she's invited him. After our run-in today, I'm apprehensive about seeing him there. Actually, really fucking stressed is more like it. If I could rely on my brain to make some good decisions when he's near, I'd be okay about it, but since I can't, I'm not. And bringing this up with Alexa is something I've been nervous about doing, so I haven't. I've stopped talking to her about her brother full stop. She's become my closest friend over the last few months, and I don't want to lose her. However, the way my stomach twists in on itself every time I think about this party makes me think I need to talk to her. Maybe it'll help me prepare if I know whether he'll be there.

I reach for my phone and tap out a text.

Me: Quick question: Is Mason going to be at your party this weekend?

She rings me instantly.

"God, I'm sorry to ask you that and put you in the middle," I say.

"Babe, no. Stop apologising and stop avoiding talking to me about him, okay? I've noticed you're doing that and I'm not into it. The minute we have an elephant in the room is the minute our friendship is doomed. I know this stuff with Mason is hard, but we don't have to let it affect us."

I exhale a long, relieved breath. "I'm so glad you said that. It's been getting weirder every time I hold myself back from saying something."

"Now that we've got that out of the way, yes, he'll be at my party. But I will give him strict instructions to leave you alone, okay?"

I love Alexa. Like, it's crazy to me how close we've become over the last few months, and how I would miss her if she was no longer in my life. I've never had a friend like her.

"Please don't do that," I say. "We're old enough to fight our own battles. I just needed to know so I could prepare myself."

"He told me about today," she says softly, like she's concerned she's bringing up a touchy subject.

"That surprises me." Mason isn't much of a talker unless he's forced into a conversation.

"You and me both. I mean, he didn't give me any real specifics of what you guys talked about, but he told me he saw you."

"Trust me, you don't want to know what we talked about today. God, it was a fucking debacle. One that should never have taken place."

"Because we haven't talked about him for a little while, how are you doing? Like really doing?"

"I'll tell you in a sec, but first I want to say I've missed this." With all my skirting around Mason over the last few weeks, our conversations have been a little shallow.

"I have too. Now tell me how you are."

"Not great, as you can imagine, but I'm working on that."

"Hmm, what does that mean?"

"It means I'm spending far more hours at yoga than ever, drinking more wine than ever, and considering taking up archery or maybe joining a shooting club."

"Oh, babe, I'm sorry I haven't been there for you."

"You have been. I just haven't let you fully in. But you can come all the way in now and see the wreck I've created of my life. I'm warning you, it's not pretty."

"I can handle not pretty."

"You know what?"

"What?"

"I think you should come to yoga with me."

"Umm, how did we go from me telling you I can handle not pretty to you inviting me to yoga? You know I'm no sporty spice."

I laugh, and it's the best sound I've heard all day. Talking with Alexa never fails to make me feel better about whatever I'm dealing with. "You don't have to be sporty for yoga. Please come. There's this weird woman there who keeps asking me to have tea with her after class, and I'm running out of reasons to say no."

"Oh, so you're just using me."

"Yes. Absolutely. You don't really need to do the poses. You just need to show up and pretend to do them and then save me from tea with her."

"It's a hell yes from me then."

"Your sarcasm is noted but not acknowledged, my friend. You're coming. First class is at 6:00 a.m. tomorrow."

"The fuck?"

The way she says that reminds me of her brother and my heart squeezes with pain as his face floods my mind. It takes my breath away, and I fight the tears that threaten to fall. God, am I ever going to get over him?

"Chelsea," Alexa says, "are you still there?"

I take a deep breath. "Yes, sorry, you just sounded like Mason and it caught me off guard."

"Shit. I'm sorry."

"No, don't be sorry. I only told you because of our new no-elephant-in-the-room agreement."

"I'm glad you did."

"Me too. Okay, so I'll text you the address and see you in the morning. I'm excited you're coming."

"I'm sure I am too, but I'm yet to locate that excitement."

I laugh again. "I love you, Alexa. Thank you for calling."

"Love you too. Now I must run because I need some fucking sleep since I'm getting up at the crack of dawn tomorrow."

We end the call, and I stare at my phone for a long moment. Thank God for friends like Alexa. Not that I have any other friend like her, but since I know what it's like not to have any good friends, I know the blessing she is. I may be stuck in a marriage I never wanted, but I'm not going to let that dictate my happiness in life. I'll find other ways to be happy, starting with lots more Alexa time. First, though, I need to get through this birthday party.

5

GUNNAR

"How the hell did she get you to wear a suit?" Hayden asks when I join him and our brothers in Alexa's kitchen on Saturday night.

I shrug. "She asked. I said yes." I haven't worn a suit for years, but I'm not against wearing one.

Our older brother, Adam, shakes his head and drinks some of his scotch before saying, "If it was anyone else who asked, you would have told them where to go."

I grin. "Highly fucking likely." I accept the beer Calder hands me and down some before glancing between all three of them. "How long are you all in town for?"

Adam and Calder divide their time between Sydney and New York while Hayden lives in Los Angeles.

"I leave tomorrow," Adam says. "I've got a deal we're pushing through in New York that I need to be there for."

"I leave on Tuesday," Hayden says.

"You're starting a new movie soon, aren't you?" Calder says.

Hayden nods. "Yeah, in two weeks. Although, there's an issue with the contracts, so fuck knows what'll happen there. That might hold us up a bit."

"It's so fucking difficult being a movie star," Calder says, his voice dripping with sarcasm.

Hayden grins. "Fuck you."

Calder returns his grin. "Maybe you could hook me up with a job. It's gotta be easier than dealing with the shit I've had to deal with this week at work."

"Oh really?" Alexa says, joining us. "Maybe if someone had listened to me about that system upgrade we needed, your week wouldn't have been so hard." Her eyes land on me and she smiles. "Oh my God, you actually did it. You wore a suit for me."

I hook my arm around her neck and pull her close for a hug. "Happy birthday, sis."

She snakes her arm around my waist and rests her head against me for a beat before looking up at me, "This is my birthday present, isn't it?"

"You know me too well."

She lets me go. "Maybe one of these days, one of you will actually remember to buy me a present when it's my birthday or Christmas or hell, for any random occasion."

"I bought you coffee yesterday," Calder says.

Alexa rolls her eyes. "That was an 'I'm fucking sorry I'm an asshole' coffee."

"I prefer to think of it as an 'early birthday present' coffee," Calder says.

Alexa jabs his bicep. "You suck." She looks around at the four of us. "You all suck."

We all laugh, and I realise it's the first time in months I've fucking laughed. It's the first time I haven't felt the crushing weight of devastation that I've carried with me since that fucked-up night shit exploded with Chelsea.

"Alexa, darling," our mother says, entering the kitchen.

"Mum." Alexa hugs her.

Mum hugs all her sons before making her way to me. It's only been a week since I've seen her, but before that, it was a good six months. I cut all ties to my father because I want nothing to do with him; time with Mum was a casualty of that decision. She might look elegant in her fancy dress and expensive jewels, but my mother hasn't been well. When Alexa called me last week to tell me, I didn't hesitate to visit her.

"Mason," she says with a smile as she places her hand to my cheek. "A suit looks good on you, darling." She wraps her arms around me, and I can't help but notice again how frail she feels. Cancer has done this to her, and from what I've been told, she's still got months of treatment ahead of her.

"How are you feeling?" I ask when she lets me go.

She keeps hold of my arm. "Don't worry about me. I'm fine."

Alexa and my brothers carry on a conversation while I say to Mum, "I do worry about you."

We're interrupted by my father when he cuts in. "You have a funny way of showing that."

My eyes cut to him, finding his cold gaze zeroed in on me.

Before I can reply, Mum removes her hand from my arm and wraps it around his. "Please don't start something, James. I don't want Alexa's party to be ruined."

He barely pays attention to her. "Your mother has been ill for some time, son."

I don't miss what he's not saying, but I'm not copping the blame for not knowing. "I came as soon as I knew." He's full of shit, too. She may have been ill for some time, but she kept that from all her children until last week. I wasn't the only one who didn't know.

"Not good enough. A son shouldn't be distanced from his mother like you have been."

My mother squeezes his arm. "James, please."

"Cherise, he needs to accept that what he's done is wrong," Dad says, not taking his eyes off me.

"I'm not getting into this with you now, Dad," I say, my tone as hard as his is cold. "I'm here for Alexa tonight, and like Mum, I don't want to ruin her party."

"A real man doesn't walk away from his family," Dad says, carrying on with his agenda.

"A real fucking man puts his family first," I snarl, instantly fucking wishing I didn't always let my father bring the asshole in me out. But here I am, the man my father made me, and I can't fucking stop myself. Stabbing my finger at him, I carry on, "Don't fucking come here and lecture me on how to be a man when you don't know the first fucking thing about it yourself."

Mum's sharp intake of breath is the only sound to be heard as my siblings tune into the conversation taking place between my father and me.

"Fuck," Adam mutters. "Do we really need to do this now, Mason?"

I glare at him. "He wanted to get into it."

Alexa looks at me, pissed off. "And you always fucking take the bait."

"Good Lord, Alexa, must you really use that language?" Mum says.

Dad shakes his head like he's disgusted by me. "Alexa, your mother can't stay long tonight. She needs her rest. We'll be out on the balcony; make sure you come and see us before we leave."

After they exit the kitchen, Alexa slaps my chest. "God, you are so frustrating! Why do you always have to argue with him?"

"It's my specialty." Fuck, I'm an asshole, just like my father. I told myself I wouldn't get into it with him tonight, for Alexa, and here I am already screwing shit up.

"Ugh! I love you, but, man, you're hard work."

I hold up my hands. "I'll keep out of his way. I'm on my best behaviour for the rest of the night."

She rolls her eyes. "You don't even know what bad behaviour is, so I don't know how you expect to figure out what good behaviour is."

I grin. "I never said I'd be good."

Hayden slaps me on my back. "I'll keep an eye on him, Lex."

"Jesus, that's the blind leading the blind," she says. Then, pointing at us, she directs, "Keep away from our parents and your exes, and I'll accept that as my birthday present."

Hayden frowns. "One of my exes is here?"

"I wouldn't doubt it," Alexa says. "You have so fucking many of them one can never be sure when they'll pop up." She reaches for her glass of wine. "Right, promise me you'll all behave. I have to go see one of my friends and then I'm coming back to do our shots."

Adam steps forward and places his hand on her arm. "Before you go, we have something for you."

Alexa's eyes widen a little. "Oh God, what? Please tell me this isn't like that time the four of you got me that stripper who turned out to prefer Mason to me."

We all laugh, remembering that birthday. I'd never experienced a lap dance until that night; it was a fucking shame I ended up with cock in my face rather than pussy.

Calder hands Alexa an envelope, and she opens it while eyeing us like she doesn't trust us. She opens the birthday card inside and reads it, her eyes widening a hell of a lot more than a moment ago.

"Holy shit," she says, looking at us again. "You guys. I have no words."

"Just tell us you'll be there," Hayden says.

"Of course I'll be there. I just, I can't even. Gah. Since when do you four listen to anything I ever say?"

"All the fucking time," I say. "You never fucking shut up, so we're forced to listen."

She bursts into tears before opening her arms and saying, "Get in here. Group hug."

Alexa's the only person we know who can make us do shit like this. She's also the only person we know who can make us figure out our schedules and align them so we can organise a week away for the five of us. Trying to make that shit happen might be one of the hardest things we've ever done, but we locked it in and booked rooms at a Port Douglas resort as her gift because we know it's the one thing she actually really wants: everyone together for an extended amount of time.

"Okay, boys, I'll be back soon," she says when she pulls out of our hug. "I love you all for this gift. And you"—she looks at me, her eyes softening—"I love you for coming even though I know this is hard for you."

I cup the back of her head and pull her close. Pressing a kiss to her forehead, I say, "I wouldn't be anywhere else."

With one last smile at me, she heads out of the kitchen in search of her friend. My mind instantly circles back to the fact Chelsea and her husband will be at this party, something I'd almost managed to forget while hanging out with my family.

Adam and Calder follow Alexa out while Hayden says to me, "You got any free time over the next couple of days? I thought we could take the bikes out. Maybe take a ride down to Byron."

"Yeah, sounds like a plan. How about Sunday?"

"Works for me." A text comes through on his phone, distracting him.

"Come over first thing. I'll have your bike ready." Hayden left his bike with me when he moved to LA a few years ago. We usually take it out every trip he makes home.

He nods, busy with whoever's texting him.

I grab another beer and wander out of the kitchen. Alexa's apartment is huge, with four bedrooms and multiple living areas. Fuck knows why she needs such a large place, but she declared it the perfect home when she bought it a year ago and has managed to fill every available space in it with her shit. My sister is a hoarder, not that she'd call it that. She prefers the term "collector," but fuck me, between the shoes, clothes, handbags, books, make-up, perfume, plants, and artwork, there's not one empty spot in this place. I'm not sure how fifty-odd people have squished into the apartment tonight, but they have. And they're fucking rowdy. I can hardly hear myself think over the music blasting, the chatter, and the laughter.

"Mason!" one of Alexa's friends calls out. "Oh my God, I feel like I haven't seen you in ages!" She throws her arms around me and kisses my cheek.

Fuck, what was her name again? Debbie? No, Josie. Fuck, maybe it's Sarah.

Before I can say anything, the blonde with her shoots me a sexy smile and places her hand on her friend's arm. "Jess, nip slip, babe."

Fuck. Jess. That's right.

Jess keeps one arm around me, settled across my ass, while fixing her top. "Thanks, girlfriend. Seriously, this top is the worst for that." She looks up at me and grins. "Not that I think Macon would care."

Memories of the night we fucked flash through my mind. Christ, I remember now, this chick was clingy as fuck after that night.

"So, Mason," the blonde says, "the last we heard, you were single again. Is that still true?"

I suck back some beer, wishing like hell I wasn't trapped with these two. As the beer slides down my throat, movement near Alexa's front door catches my eye, and Chelsea comes into view.

Time fucking stops.

My lungs fight for breath.

I practically fucking choke at the sight of her husband putting his fucking hands on her.

"Fuck." The word drops from my lips. It tastes as bitter as looking at her feels.

Jess's arm tightens around me as Chelsea's eyes lock with mine. "Are you okay?" she asks.

Chelsea's gaze shifts to Jess and then back to me. I don't miss the jealous flash in her eyes. And I sure as fuck don't hate it.

I glance down at Jess, putting my arm around her shoulders. "Yeah, I'm good."

I briefly catch her smile as I look back at Chelsea, who's still watching me. I've no fucking idea what game I'm engaging in here or why, but I can't stop myself. I fucking want her to hurt like I am.

Hearst bends his mouth to Chelsea's ear and says something to her. She nods and turns to him, bringing her hand to cup his cheek before standing on her toes and fucking kissing him.

It's like the fucking world is sitting on top of my chest.

Pressure like I've never known presses down on me.

"Mason, did you hear what I said?" Jess says.

I try to drag my attention from Chelsea, but fail. She's a fucking train wreck I can't look away from.

"Mace!" Calder says, joining us. "It's time for our annual shots."

I finally look away from Chelsea and meet Calder's gaze. "Yeah," I agree. "It fucking is." I can't think of anything I want more right now. "Alexa's ready?"

He nods. "Hayden's rounding her up."

The five of us always do shots of Alexa's choice on her birthday. Last year, she made us do multiple four horsemen shots; fuck knows what she'll make us drink tonight.

Hayden and Adam make their way through the crowd

with Alexa, who grins at me and says, "Are you ready to get fucked up, big brother?"

"You have no idea. Hit me."

She looks at Adam. "Adam's making them this year."

I arch a brow and eye my brother. "She's letting someone else take over?"

"We're going old school," Alexa says.

Adam's mouth quirks. "She's requested some Aftershock."

"Fuck me," Hayden mutters. "I should have known this party would be a two-day affair."

Adam heads to the bar Alexa has set up for the night and pulls a bottle of blue Aftershock out, along with five brandy sniffers and five tumblers. He fills the brandy sniffers with Aftershock, lights them up and lets them sit for a beat. He then pours the Aftershock into the tumblers, placing the sniffers over the tumblers to seal the fumes in. While he does that, I set up the straws we need—one each, poking through a serviette.

Alexa looks around at us, reaching for her brandy sniffer. "Go."

We all remove our brandy sniffer from the tumbler and place it upside down on our serviette over one end of the straw, and then down the Aftershock. Then, we suck the straw, dragging the fumes in from the glass sitting on the other end of the straw.

Alexa's eyes light up. Hanging out with us is one of her favourite things, and since we don't get to do that often these days, I know these moments mean a lot to her. She motions at Adam. "We need more."

He shakes his head, but he's smiling. He might be a fancy fucker these days with his suits and penthouses and yacht, but he'd do anything for Alexa. Fuck, we all would. She's our baby sister.

We end up doing four rounds. I'm not fucked up by the last one, but it's a good fucking start. I intend to find myself a bottle of Beam and slaughter all the thoughts of Chelsea screaming through my mind.

"You good?" Alexa asks as I narrow my eyes on the alcohol behind the bar.

"Yeah, but I'm gonna need one of those bottles of Jim."

"You're staying here tonight, right?"

I pull my keys from my pocket and pass them to her. "Yeah."

She lifts her chin at the bourbon. "It's all yours, but you need to promise me you won't go near Chelsea."

"I have no fucking intention of going near her."

She looks at me like she doesn't believe me, but she doesn't stop me from taking the bottle.

Twenty minutes later, I'm feeling a hell of a lot better after planting my ass on one of Alexa's couches and keeping to myself while slowly knocking myself out.

That is until I hear Chelsea's laughter behind me.

Fucking hell.

I down some more bourbon, trying to scratch her laughter from my brain.

"Yes, the wedding was magical," she says to whoever has cornered her to talk about her fucking wedding.

"I heard he took you to Paris for the honeymoon. So romantic."

Fucking kill me now.

"It was amazing. I told him we need to go back there

for every anniversary," Chelsea says, and I see fucking red.

Pushing up off the couch and turning, my eyes collide with hers, and I send her a signal to fuck this chick off and to do that fast.

She places her hand on the girl's arm and says, "I'm sorry, Anna, I just saw someone I have to say hi to."

"Oh, no worries, Chelsea. It was good to see you. Tell Joe that we need to do dinner soon, okay?"

Chelsea nods while I try like fuck to hold onto the small amount of patience for this shit that I have.

Anna walks away, and Chelsea stares at me like she's never seen me before. She's seen me wild, but the level of wild I'm feeling isn't a level she's ever experienced.

"The fuck was that?" I demand, moving closer to her against all good reason.

She continues staring at me, not saying anything.

"Well?" I say. "Was that shit true?"

Chelsea shakes her head. "No, we're not doing this, Mason."

"Yeah, we fucking are, princess."

"This is your sister's party. And my husband is here. We're not doing this here." With that, she turns and walks her ass away from me, pissing me off more than she already has.

Chelsea's wearing a short green dress that barely covers that ass of hers that's never stopped featuring in my fucking dreams. The dress has long, flowing sleeves that I know from listening to Alexa bang on about clothes are meant to be the "star" of the dress, but for me, the star of that dress is the way it shows off her cleavage by dipping low in the front. If she was mine, no fucking way would she wear a dress like that in public.

Unable to stop myself, I stalk after her, catching up with her halfway down Alexa's hallway. Taking hold of her arm, I pull her into Alexa's bedroom. There's no way we're not finishing this conversation.

"Mason," she hisses, trying to fight me off. "What the hell are you doing?"

I slam the door closed with my boot and back her up against it. The only lighting in here is what's coming from outside. It falls across Chelsea, illuminating her face and chest, giving me an eyeful of the beauty that steals my breath every fucking time.

"I want an answer to what I asked you," I order.

"No you don't."

"Yeah, I fucking do."

"Mason, no. Please."

I work my jaw, trying to keep my shit together. The problem is, there's too much alcohol in me now, and between that and the boiling rage I feel over what Chelsea said, there's no hope of me being able to hold myself back. I'm hurtling towards a fucking mess here and I can't save myself even if I try.

Gripping her face, I growl, "Fucking tell me."

Her eyes search mine. I know her well, so I see the anger brewing in them. I also see the moment she snaps and breaks. And fuck me, as much as I hate her and everything she says, she's fucking fire when she's like this. "You wanna know how my honeymoon went down? All the ways I fucked my husband in Paris? How many times I sucked his dick?" She leans her face close to mine. "Is that what you're looking for?"

My mind explodes.

It's a fucking wreck of thoughts that never ease.

Images of Chelsea with Hearst, doing all the shit she just threw in my face.

I let her go and stumble back, jamming my fingers through my hair while emotions I don't know what to do with assault me. "Fuck! Fucking hell!" I stare at her as the world crashes down around me. "You're a fucking piece of work."

Her eyes flare as she pushes off from the door and comes at me with her hands. Smacking them against my chest, she yells, "*I'm* a piece of work? You fucking asshole!" She pushes me. "It's all right for you to say shit like that to me when you fuck my friend, but *I'm* a piece of work when I say it to you? Fuck you!"

"I'm not the fucking asshole here. You're the one who fucked this all up."

"Well, it looks like I made the best decision of my life if this is what our life together would have been like."

I grab both her wrists with one hand and shove her up against the wall. "Our life would have been more fucking *magical* than anything Hearst will give you. But you'll never fucking know because you didn't hang around long enough to find out."

She continues trying to fight me off, but I'm holding her so tightly that she hasn't got a chance in hell of making that happen. "You know what? My marriage was arranged and you know that, but you still give me shit over it, and there *you* are all over Jess McDonnell. Don't fucking come at me with your bullshit, Mason. I'm not taking it anymore. Not now that you've moved on."

I let her go and move my hands to press against the

wall either side of her, forcing my body against hers to hold her in place. "I don't know anything about your marriage, Chelsea, and I don't fucking want to know. And as far as me and Jess go, yeah, I'm fucking moving on. I'm finding pussy that won't fuck me over."

She jerks against me, as wild as I am, her eyes stormy, her expression fierce. "Fucking let me go!"

I don't know what the fuck possesses me—except I do, this fucking woman in front of me blazing with everything I both love and hate—I crash my lips down onto hers. Fuck, I practically inhale her while forcing my tongue against hers and taking what I want. She tastes like home, and I fucking hate that, but I can't not kiss her. Hell, I want to tear her clothes off and fuck her, but somehow I manage to restrain myself.

She groans as I deepen the kiss.

I growl in response, my hands moving to her body.

Fucking hell, I've missed her. Missed this mouth and this body. But more than anything, I've missed being with her.

Her leg slides up and hooks around mine as she presses herself against me.

I reach down and grasp her ass under her dress, still kissing her.

We're all hands and mouths and lust, and before I know what's happening, she's in my arms with both legs wrapped around me, and my dick grinding against her cunt.

"Fuck!" I pull my lips from hers. "We're not fucking doing this again." I let her go before I change my mind. Before I fuck this up more than it's already fucked up.

She glares at me, straightening her dress and trying to get herself together. "Don't ever touch me again!"

With one last glare, she pushes past me and stalks out of the bedroom.

Jesus fucking Christ.

What the hell was I thinking?

I wasn't, and that's the problem.

I never fucking think with Chelsea. I feel.

And that shit needs to stop.

6

CHELSEA

Staring at myself in the mirror at my dressing table, I touch my lips and think about kissing Mason last night. He was savage. Possessed. And I loved every second of it even though I wanted to hate it.

I've never seen him like that before. Well, except for that time after he slept with my friend Samantha and threw it in my face. He slept with her after he saw the news of my engagement to Joe on the news. That was my father's doing, not mine. If I'd had my way, I would have broken that news to Mason myself, but my father engineered a lot of things back then in such a way as to inflict maximum pain on Mason. To this day, Mason thinks I chose for everything to go down the way it all did, but none of that is true. My father is to blame for everything I've taken the blame for. In the end, I decided to let Mason think what he thinks; it'll be easier to keep us apart if he hates me. But good God, I never imagined his hate would hurt like it does.

I take a deep breath and reach for my earrings while

carefully tracking my husband's movements in our bedroom. We're getting ready for Sunday lunch with our families. Joe has been especially testy this morning, making all kinds of demands I want to say no to. I've no clue what's caused him this mood, but for once, I'm grateful our parents are coming over. It'll give me a reprieve from him.

I've just finished securing my earrings in place when he moves behind me. Placing his hands on my bare shoulders, he meets my gaze in the mirror. "Your father is going to ask you today to take a couple of weeks off work at the beginning of his campaign in a couple of months so you can be by his side. It wouldn't pay for you to decline."

I stare at him, my chest filling with anger. Anger at both my father for thinking he can ask this of me and at Joe for the arrogant way he talks to me. "He can ask all he likes, but I'm not saying yes."

Joe's lips press together. "Chelsea, this may start off as a negotiation, but you know it won't end as one."

I stand and face him. "I'm done negotiating with him."

"No, you're not. Especially not when it comes to his premiership."

God, I hate my husband when he's like this. He's infuriating in his lack of ability to actually engage in a discussion. He likes to simply state how things will be. Well, not this fucking time.

With a shake of my head, I walk away from him, towards our bathroom.

"Don't walk away from me when we're in the middle of a fucking conversation," he says.

I spin back around to face him. "We weren't in the middle of a fucking conversation. We were in the middle of you being the dictator you like to be, and I'll always walk away from you when you're like that."

He closes the distance between us as I turn to continue on my way to the bathroom. His hand snaps around my wrist as I turn. Pulling me back to him, he warns, "Careful, Chelsea. I've been more than patient with you over the last month, but I only have so much patience to give."

I attempt to pull my wrist from his hold, but his grip is too strong. Glaring at him, I say, "Let me go."

He contemplates that for a moment before releasing me. "This was me giving you a heads-up so you can prepare yourself. I suggest you take what I've said under consideration."

"I've taken it under consideration, dear husband, and I've given you my answer. Perhaps you could take it back to my father and give him a heads-up so he's prepared for our conversation." I know I'm playing with fire here, but I can't hold myself back. Joe brings this side of me out.

When he doesn't respond except to look at me with his signature look of displeasure, I make my exit and lock myself in the bathroom.

Deep breaths, Chelsea.
You can do this.
You can do this.
You. Can. Do. This.

It's crazy how often I have to chant that to myself these days. I used to practice manifestation. Now, I spend my days chanting this over and over. In its own way, this is my new form of manifesting things in my life. It's just a shame the only thing I'm trying to manifest is success in getting through my days.

I spend a good ten minutes in the bathroom, which I suspect is the amount of time Joe's patience will last before he comes looking for me. Slipping out, I'm relieved not to find him in our bedroom. I spend another few minutes psyching myself up to face the afternoon and then make my way out to the kitchen.

Joe's parents, Andrew and Rachel, have arrived. I hear them talking with Joe in the formal living room. Knowing Joe won't be happy if I don't say hello, I join them.

"Chelsea," Rachel greets me, a smile fixed on her face. It's a fake smile, the one she gives every person she comes in contact with. Joe's mother doesn't like many people, especially not me. She tolerates me because of what my family can do for hers, but I don't think she wants to share her son with any woman. As far as I'm concerned, we don't need to share him; she can have him.

I air-kiss her. "Hi, Rachel. How are you?"

"Oh, you know, dear, as well as I can be."

That's code for "my husband's an utter prick and I hate my life." I know this because I've observed them when they don't think anyone's watching, and he is an utter prick, and she hates him as much as I suspect I'll hate her son one day.

Andrew doesn't move from the armchair he's sitting in. He simply rakes his gaze over me and says, "Chelsea."

"Andrew," I reply, moving to sit next to Joe on the sofa.

Joe extends his arm across the back of the sofa and pulls me close to him. I allow this because I feel safer being near him when his father's around. The only time

I'm more than happy to sit next to Joe is when his father's in the same room.

"Joe tells me you celebrated a remarkable success at your job this week," Andrew says, referring to the financial analysis and subsequent advice I gave one of the companies I work with that helped them double their profit this year. I received a huge bonus from my company for my work on this.

I look at my husband. I wasn't aware he cared enough about my work for this to be something he'd share with his family. Smiling at him, I say, "Yes, I did."

Joe returns my smile and takes my hand in his. Placing it on his thigh, he keeps his hand over mine. This is all so weird and unexpected that it stuns me into silence. Joe doesn't do displays of affection, especially not ones that feel real.

"Congratulations," Andrew says, drawing my attention back to the conversation.

"Thank you."

Andrew shifts back to discussing business with his son while Rachel and I fade to the background and stare into space, waiting for them to finish.

When a lull hits the conversation, I look at Joe and say, "I'm going to check the roast." Sundays are the only day I cook because our staff all have the day off, and I always cook a roast for our family lunch.

He nods and lets my hand go.

I excuse myself and hurry into the kitchen, desperate to distance myself from Joe's family.

The roast is ready, so I pull it out of the oven. I spend some time fussing with it and the roast vegetables before reaching into the fridge for a bottle of wine. I've just poured myself a glass and taken a gulp when Rachel joins me.

"I'd love a wine, Chelsea," she says, surprising me. Rachel doesn't usually indulge in alcohol.

I smile and grab the bottle back out of the fridge. "Absolutely."

She takes the glass I offer her, looking more grateful than I've ever seen her. "Thank you." She guzzles half of it, and I have to restrain my eyes from popping out of my head. Placing the glass on the kitchen counter, she says, "I'm just going to pop to the bathroom, dear."

I watch her leave and wonder what's going on with her. I've never seen her like this. She actually seems like a normal person like this. Maybe even like someone I could get on with.

Joe's phone, which is sitting on the kitchen counter, sounds with a text, so I grab it to take it into him. He handles a lot of high-level investments that often require immediate attention, so this could be an important text.

I slow as I draw closer to the living room. Joe and his father are arguing, and when they're doing that, I don't want to be anywhere near them. It doesn't happen often, but when it does, it's nasty.

"I'm not doing it, Dad," Joe says, his voice harder than usual.

"You will do this, Joe, and you'll fucking do it tomorrow." His father's voice slides through my veins like ice. And poison. That's the best word I can use to describe how his father makes me feel: like I'm being poisoned just by being in his presence.

"Christ. Do you have any idea what you're fucking asking of me?"

I frown. I've never heard Joe sound torn like this. Like he genuinely doesn't want to do what his father is ordering him to do.

"Yes, I'm asking you to step up for your brother. For your family."

"No, you're asking me to commit a crime."

"We both know it wouldn't be the first time you've done that, son." Andrew's voice drops low as he threatens, "If you refuse to do this, you could find yourself in hot water over some of those previous crimes."

Joe turns silent before spitting out, "There are days where I wonder whether you're actually my father."

"Trust me, boy, I wonder the same fucking thing sometimes."

Oh, God.

The doorbell sounds, and I rush to the front door to answer it. I don't want to hear any more of Joe's conversation with his father. Andrew is toxic, and I fear my husband will become like his father one day, which is something I don't even want to contemplate.

"Chelsea, darling," my mother greets me when I open the door to her.

"Hi, Mum," I say, stepping aside to let her in. She air-kisses me as she moves past me, but we don't embrace. We never embrace. It's not the Novak way.

Dad follows her in with a "Chelsea" as his greeting. Already, he's all business, and I have to admit that I'm grateful for Joe's heads-up earlier. I may not have enjoyed the conversation with my husband, but at least I'm prepared for what my father is going to ask of me.

We all head into the living room where Joe is still with his father. Rachel has rejoined them, sipping her wine quietly as the men talk business again. Andrew stands as soon as he sees my father, greeting Dad with more enthusiasm than he did his own son.

I assess Joe. His shoulders are like stone. His eyes are hard. He has the look on his face I've come to associate with the likelihood of him demanding sex from me later. He's never forced himself on me, but he made it clear on our wedding night what his expectations are, and they involve regular sex. I say no as often as I can get away with, but when he looks at me the way he is now, I know that word is off the table.

I take a deep breath before handing him his phone. "You received a text. I thought it might be important."

"Thank you." He checks the message and stands to exit the room.

I glance around the room, and to no one in particular, I say, "I'm going to check on lunch."

My father surprises me when he says, "I'll come with you. We need to talk." Usually, he waits until after lunch to approach me with his demands.

When we reach the kitchen and I take a good look at him, I note that he appears anxious to have this conversation. Odd. My father is never anxious about anything to do with me. He just takes what he wants or pushes me until I give him what he wants.

He cuts straight to the chase. "I want to talk to you about my re-election campaign and the fact I need you to appear by my side with your mother at certain functions."

I nod. "I realise this."

"Yes, but this is going to be a tight race, Chelsea, so you'll need to take a few weeks off work so you can travel with us throughout the state rather than just coming to the Brisbane and Gold Coast functions."

"No."

He was expecting that and doesn't even blink at my refusal. "That's not the answer I'm looking for."

"I know, but it's the only answer you're going to get from me."

Dad's eyes snap to Joe as he joins us. "Good, you're here. Maybe you can talk some sense into her."

Joe looks at me. "The Liberals have a strong candidate. Your father needs you with him for this."

"He doesn't," I say. "He needs better policies."

My father's eyes darken with anger. "Why don't you leave the politics to the men and focus on what you're good for?"

"See, when you say things like that to me, it doesn't make me want to help you, Dad."

He clenches his jaw. "You think you have a choice here, Chelsea?"

My heart races at what he's not saying, and I do my best to ignore it. Surely he won't make more threats against Mason to get what he wants here.

"I've given you everything you asked for. I married Joe. I do interviews and tell anyone who'll listen how happy I am in my marriage. I show up to all your fundraisers on Joe's arm. I'll keep playing happy families for you, but I won't do this. I won't ever give up my work."

Joe steps in, doing the thing he does when there's tension between Dad and me. "Perhaps Chelsea and I can talk about this some more tonight, Mark?"

Dad doesn't take his eyes off me. He's all anger and control, and I brace myself for what I know he's about to say. "You *will* do this, Chelsea, or else I'll go after Mason. You think he's seen the worst of what those new laws can do? He hasn't, not by a long shot."

I can't breathe.

"You said he'd be safe once I married Joe." I'm disgusted with myself for sounding so desperate in front of my father and husband. I promised myself I'd never beg them for anything, and here I am doing just that.

Dad's eyes glitter with victory. He knows that regardless of where this conversation goes now, he's won. He knows that all he ever has to do is pull the Mason card out and he'll always win. "You honestly thought your marriage would protect that boy and his club forever? My girl, you have a lot to learn about the world. Your marriage saved them all once. Your choices going forward will determine their futures."

My legs turn to jelly.

I reach for the kitchen counter to steady myself.

I should have seen this coming.

How did I not?

"Well?" my father demands. "What will it be? A few weeks off work for you or jail for Mason?"

I swallow my hatred.

I swallow my resentment.

I swallow my fear.

"I'll take a few weeks off."

"Good girl."

My eyes meet Joe's as Dad leaves us and I suck in a breath at what I see there.

"You're mine now, Chelsea, and it would do you well to remember that." The darkness in his voice matches the dark flash of his eyes.

"I know that." My voice betrays me, wobbling with the same dread pooling deep in my belly.

"It doesn't appear that way to me."

"It's only been one month, Joe. You need to give me time."

He moves close to me, bringing his finger to trail along my jaw. "I'll give you time, but you're going to need to give me a lot more than you currently are."

I stare at him, trying not to lose the little courage I have left after this entire confrontation. Only my father and Joe are able to reduce me to this person I don't recognise. I hate myself for not being stronger, but when they threaten the one person I would die for, I'm unable to do anything but give them what they want.

I nod, the agreement taking all the breath from me. "I understand."

His fingers trail over my lips. "Good." He pauses before adding, "The next time your father asks you to do something for him, I don't fucking want that asshole to be the deciding factor in your agreement."

I watch in silence as he exits the room, my heart in my mouth.

If I thought the last three months were hard, I had no idea what was in store for me.

7

GUNNAR

"You look like you could do with this," Wilder says late Monday afternoon, sliding onto the stool next to me at the clubhouse bar and placing a schooner of beer in front of me.

"Yeah, I could. Thanks, brother." I take a sip. "It's been a long fucking day. How's shit at Trilogy?" The restaurant the club owns has grown busier over the last few months, and that's because of Wilder's efforts there. He was a good choice for manager.

He drinks some of his beer. "Busy. You still good to work security there this week?"

I nod. He asked me to cover some shifts on Wednesday and Friday night. "Yeah. And just let me know if you need me for more. It'll keep me out of trouble."

He grins. "Nothing'll keep you out of trouble."

I throw back some more beer. "Well, something fucking needs to." At the rate I'm going lately, I'm about to skid off a fucking mountain of bad choices into a pit of hell.

"Wilder," Madison says, joining us. "Have you got a minute?"

He looks at her. "Yeah. What's up?"

She smiles at me. "Sorry, Gunnar, this won't take long."

"All good, babe," I say. I've got a lot of time for J's old lady. She can take as long as she wants.

"So," she says to Wilder, "I've been planning Harlow's baby shower and we've had a problem come up with the venue we booked. They're being assholes so I've told them to cancel our booking." She smiles sweetly at him. "I'm hopeful you'll be able to squeeze us in at Trilogy."

Wilder grimaces. "When?"

"Not this weekend, but next. Saturday afternoon."

"Fuck. I really want to say yes, but I think we're fully booked that day."

"What about out on the back deck?"

The deck's a new addition to the restaurant and has only just been completed.

Wilder shakes his head. "No, we've been booking it out from this weekend, so it's all gone for next weekend."

"Damn," she says. "Do you have any suggestions for where else we could try? I know you're up with all the local venues more than I am."

Before Wilder can answer, J turns up. Sliding his arm around his wife's waist, he drops a kiss to the top of her head and says, "You giving Wilder a headache, babe? He looks pained as fuck."

Madison looks up at her husband and pulls a face. "No, we're discussing possible venues for Harlow's baby shower. You should make yourself useful and get me a drink."

I grin. This is one of the reasons I like Madison so much. She never gives J an inch.

J eyes me. "I caught that, asshole."

I continue grinning. "I'll have another beer while you're at it."

"You don't suck my dick. You can get your own fucking drink," he says before leaving us.

Wilder and Madison go back to discussing the baby shower, and I tune out, thinking about my plans for the night. At this point, I don't have any, but I'm all for that changing.

"Hey, you," a sexy voice I know well purrs in my ear as her hand slides over my thigh and rests on my dick.

I turn to look at her. "Tiana." She's fucking gorgeous, but my dick's not even registering her. Not when there's only one woman my dick's after and it isn't her.

She presses herself against me, stroking my cock. "I haven't seen you for a couple of weeks. Where have you been?"

I drain my glass. "Around."

"You're always so cagey, Gunnar." She frowns. "And what's going on with your cock? I know I haven't lost my touch, but you're not even semihard."

"Story of my fucking life lately," I mutter, willing my dick to get to work, but knowing it won't. Some days I can get it up, but increasingly not.

"Oh good, so it's you, not me."

I chuckle. "Yeah, it's definitely not you."

She removes her hand and pulls up the stool next to

me. "You should buy me a drink. Maybe you need to talk tonight instead of fuck."

"Babe, not even talking can fucking save me at this point, but I appreciate the offer."

She stares at me. "Damn, you're really into this chick, aren't you? Is it the one you just broke up with?"

I stand. "I've gotta go."

"Yeah, I get it. You're not much of a talker." She jerks her chin at me. "Call me when your dick starts working again. I miss you."

As I walk out of the bar, I fucking curse the fact I'm now thinking about Chelsea. Fuck her for ruining my sex life. I should have fucked her the other night just so I could fucking get some. Because my dick was sure as shit fucking working then.

"Gunnar," Scott calls out from down the hall. "Need you for a minute, brother."

He reaches into his desk once I'm in his office and pulls a USB out of the drawer. Handing it to me, he says, "I need you to drop this off to Joe Hearst tonight."

Fuck. No.

I shake my head. "I can't."

"I know you've got a difficult history with this asshole, but I need this done tonight, and you're who I'm trusting to make that happen."

Fuck, when my president says shit like that to me, I can't refuse what he's asking. I take the USB. "I'll get it done."

"Text me once he has it."

I agree and exit the office to head out to my bike.

Clearly Griff didn't share the news with our president

that I got into it with Hearst last week. I owe my VP a drink for that.

∾

I END up at Alexa's for a few hours and have dinner with her and Hayden before doing what Scott asked. Hayden's leaving to fly back to LA tomorrow, so it's good to catch up before he goes.

"When will you be back?" I ask as we kick back on Alexa's couch after dinner.

"He'll tell you sweet, sweet lies," Alexa calls out from the kitchen. "Add a month onto whatever he says."

I look at him. "What's she going on about?"

He shakes his head. "She's been harassing me for days about when I'll be home again. Won't fucking leave me alone about it, so I threw out December to shut her up. She clued on that I was full of shit."

"She misses the hell out of you guys."

"Yeah, I know. Thank fuck you never moved away."

"It's looking like a good option lately."

Hayden frowns. "Because of Chelsea?"

"Yeah."

He leans forward, resting his elbows on his knees. "What the hell happened there, brother? I thought you two were tight."

"I did too." I exhale a long breath. "Her father got in her ear, convinced her to break it off with me and marry some asshole he thinks is better for her. I should have known we wouldn't last. It wasn't the first time she dumped me because of her father."

He continues frowning. "You guys dated before? How did I miss that?"

"No, we weren't dating. That was back in high school after that party I was almost arrested at. You remember how we weren't friends after that?" At his nod, I say, "That was because of her father. He decided he didn't like me as her friend and forced her to end our friendship."

Hayden leans back against the couch. "Wow, okay. How did he convince her to end it this time? She's an adult now, not a teenager scared of her father."

"He was gunning for the club because of me. Chelsea ended things so he'd give up on that. Not that it really fucking helped; the cops haven't stopped watching us."

"Fuck. So why'd she marry this other guy?"

I shrug. "I don't fucking know and I don't wanna fucking know. All I know is she keeps insisting it was arranged by their fathers, but whenever I see them together, she's all fucking over him." And telling her friends how fucking magical shit is with him.

"It sounds like you're better off without her, Mace."

"Yeah, I fucking am."

The worst thing about lying to yourself is you buy that shit when you say it, but in the dead of night when you're alone, you know those lies are a pile of shit because you'd do anything to get her back. The one thing I know for sure is that I would have rather stayed in jail knowing I had her to walk out to one day than being free and knowing she'll never be mine again.

"Okay," Alexa says, collapsing onto the couch in between us, "we're going to watch some *Big Bang Theory,* and neither of you are going to argue with me over this."

I groan. She loves that show and has subjected us to it for too many years to remember.

Hayden laughs at me. "You're outnumbered, brother."

"Fuck, you like it now?" He used to hate it like I do.

He nods. "Yeah, this chick I was dating for a while got me hooked."

"Fucking women," I mutter. How they get us to do shit we never fucking imagined doing I'll never know.

∽

It's around 9:00 p.m. when I pull up outside Hearst's place. He and Chelsea live in Hamilton on the river. Their house reminds me of my parents' home, the house I grew up in. Fucking huge and opulent, designed for status.

I knock on the front door, agitated and pissed off about being here. About having to deal with Hearst. I'd fucking choose dealing with Chelsea's father over this motherfucker.

A woman who I presume is their housekeeper lets me in and tells me to wait in the foyer while she lets Hearst know I'm here. She returns a few minutes later and motions for me to follow her, leading me down a long, wide hallway to his office. Advising me he's in the middle of a meeting, she points at a chair against the wall of the hallway, indicating for me to sit and wait.

Jesus, I'd be just as happy to shove the USB at her and tell her to give it to him, but I know Scott wants me to personally hand it over, so I sit and wait.

Hearst takes his sweet time coming out, stepping into the hallway looking as angry to see me as I am to see him. "I take it you have the USB."

I hand it over. "Yeah."

He holds it up. "This is everything I asked for?"

"Fucked if I know. I'm just here to deliver it."

He clenches his jaw. "I fucking knew relying on your club was a bad idea."

I step closer to him, my fists ready to meet his face again. "I might not know the details of what's on that USB, but my club always comes through with the goods, so if you fucking asked for something, it'll fucking be on there."

"Perhaps you should have said that."

I ball my fists, trying like fuck to keep them by my side. "Fuck you."

Something flashes through his eyes, something dark and fucked up. "You seem on edge, Mason. Not having much luck replacing Chelsea and that talented mouth of hers?"

I reel.

My mind stretches.

Snaps.

Fucking reaches breaking point.

"The fuck did you just fucking say to me?" I snarl.

He looks fucking satisfied at that question, but before he can throw more shit at me, the door to his office opens, and Chelsea's father appears. Glancing between Hearst and me, he says, "Joe, you done here? We need you."

I step back, keeping my eyes on Hearst. "Yeah, we're fucking done here."

Hearst jerks his chin down the hall. "The exit's that way. Don't fucking touch anything that's not yours to touch on your way out."

With that, he and Novak disappear back into his office, slamming the door in my face.

Motherfuckers.

I suck in a deep breath, steadying myself, but mostly steadying my fucking thoughts. I have an intense fucking desire to smash his place to shit, but I remind myself why I'm here: for my club. We do not need any more problems with these assholes or the law they can bring down on us.

Fuck.

Shoving my fingers through my hair, I stalk away from his office. I'm about ten steps down the hall when I hear Chelsea's voice.

My feet stop working all by themselves and I turn in the direction of that voice.

She's sitting in the room down the hall from her husband's office. A library from what I can see. How fucking convenient, she sits here and fucking reads while her husband works in the next room. My brain conjures up a mess of images of her fucking him in here, in there, in the fucking hall.

She stares at me, her phone to her ear, and says to whoever's on the other end of the call, "I'm sorry, I have to go. I'll see you tomorrow."

Dropping her phone to the couch, she stands, her black dress hitting her knees as she straightens. "Mason," she breathes, her chest rising and falling rapidly.

I take in her long brunette hair that used to be mine to pull.

I take in her full red lips that used to be mine to kiss.

I take in her beautiful blue eyes that used to only look at me.

And then my gaze shifts to the Monopoly board

sitting on the coffee table, open, in the middle of a game, and I lose my fucking mind.

Entering the library in a gush of wild, angry energy, I jab my finger at the Monopoly game. "You're playing our fucking game with *him*?"

Her lips part and she glances at the game before bringing her eyes back to mine. She looks thrown, like she can't think straight, so I say, "I know you've moved the fuck on, but I thought I meant something to you. That was ours. Not yours and his. *Ours*, Mayfair. From when we were fucking kids, it was *our* thing."

"Mason—" she starts, but I don't want to hear it.

"No," I snarl, bending and smashing the game off the table, scattering Monopoly money, cards, and game pieces all over the floor. "Don't fucking say it. I don't want to hear it."

She comes to me, so close I can smell her, touch her, fucking taste her. Grasping my shirt, she begs, "Please don't do this. You need to go."

Anger unfurls through me. She's telling me to go when I was supposed to be the one person she never told to go.

If I thought my mind snapped earlier, I was wrong. It snaps now.

Grabbing a handful of her hair, I yank her head back and bring my nose to her neck so I can inhale her scent. Fuck, that vanilla perfume she loves shoots need through my veins. My dick wakes the fuck up, and the mess in my mind tangles to the point I don't know what the fuck I'm doing.

I let go of her hair so I can lift her into my arms and

back her up against the wall. The wall that joins this room to her husband's office.

Pressing her against it, I find her eyes for a moment. I can't read her thoughts anymore, and that pisses me off.

"Mason," she says shakily, her legs around me and her hands gripping my shirt, "what are you doing?"

Taking hold of her hips, I place her down and reach for her belt. Undoing it, I throw it on the floor as I rake my gaze over her. Over the body I've loved too many times to count. Over the body I haven't had enough of. Then, without warning, I rip her dress down the middle, wide fucking open so I can see that body that should be mine.

She gasps and her eyes go wide as she tries to push me away. "Fucking hell, Mason, you need to fucking leave," she hisses.

"I'm not leaving, Mayfair." I nudge a leg between hers and press myself closer to her, "I'm staying right the fuck here and I'm going to fuck you." I slide my hand into her panties and my fingers through her wet cunt. "Fuck, you're so fucking ready for me."

Her eyes cut to the library door, filled with worry, while her hands try desperately to push me away. "Joe's right next door."

I grip her wrists and pin them both to the wall above her head while fingering her. Bringing my mouth to her neck, I growl, "Yeah, and it's getting me hard knowing that I'm going to fuck you against this wall while he's sitting right fucking there."

"Oh my God, you've lost your ever-loving mind."

I lift my head and look at her. "No, baby, I lost that three months ago." I reach my fingers deeper inside her.

"Tell me that doesn't feel good. Tell me you don't still love my fingers inside you."

She writhes against the wall, fighting me. "I don't. It doesn't feel good."

I work my jaw, squeezing her wrists harder. "Bull-fucking-shit. You can't just switch that shit off, Chelsea."

"Please don't do this, Mason. Please leave before he finds us. God, the door's wide open and you're not being quiet. He's going to come in here any minute."

I keep working her pussy. She's soaking my fingers while trying to tell me she's not feeling any of this. She's so full of shit.

"Do you think I give a fuck if he comes in here?" I dip my face and bite her neck, sinking my teeth in so it marks the fuck out of her. I've never felt such a primal need to mark her like this. "I fucking don't. I'd fucking love him to watch me take your cunt."

"Oh my God," she moans, her eyes fluttering open and shut, her body arching, her pussy pulsing as her orgasm shatters through her. After she comes, she opens her eyes, panting, and crashes her mouth to mine.

Fuck.

I let her hands go and tear her bra off while she works my belt and jeans to undo them.

Her tongue forces its way into my mouth and she kisses me like she's never fucking kissed me.

We're frantic.

Violent.

Reckless.

"Holy fuck," she gasps, taking my cock in her hand. "I need you inside me right now."

I fucking need that too. In ways I don't even care to understand.

Pulling her dress off, I spin her to face the wall and grip her hips. "Tell me you're on birth control," I demand. I might have lost my fucking mind, but there's no way I'm getting her pregnant.

She nods furiously. "Yes, just fuck me already."

I slam inside her and the entire world shuts down.

It's just me and her.

Together.

Chasing bliss.

I fucking hate her, but I fucking love being inside her.

I fuck her harder than I've ever fucked her.

I bite her and mark her.

I'm brutal and give no fucks about any of it.

She took my fucking heart; I'm taking this.

"Oh, God, Mason," she cries out, instantly biting down on her arm to silence herself.

I grip her harder, slamming harder into her, trying to end her silence.

I fucking want her husband to hear all of this.

"Fuck," I growl as I empty myself into her. "Fucking hell."

Pressing my body to hers, I stay inside her for a minute more before pulling out and zipping myself back up.

Chelsea turns to face me, her skin marked to shit by my hands and teeth. Her clothes lay strewn at her feet, her dress in tatters. She's fucking beautiful like this, her lips swollen and her face alive with desire.

Fuck, it all crashes down around me.

She's not mine anymore.

And when she looks frantically at the door again, that fact is thrown in my face.

Without another word, I turn and stalk out of the library, out of the house, out of her fucking life.

I might love being inside her, but I need to remember that's not my privilege anymore. She has a fucking husband for that now.

8

CHELSEA

Flicking off the shower, I reach for my towel and step out to dry myself off. I'm grateful I woke earlier than usual this morning because my mind isn't with it, and everything is taking me longer. The reason for that is the six-foot asshole who crashed into my life again last night. I can't stop thinking about him. I haven't been able to since he strode out of the library looking more pissed off than he ever has, and that's saying something because I've seen Mason display extreme anger on more than one occasion.

Goosebumps scatter across my skin as I think about the fury he arrived with last night. He was furious when he saw the Monopoly game, instantly assuming I'd been playing with Joe. That is so far from the truth it isn't funny. I haven't been playing it with anyone; I play it by myself, imagining I'm with Mason. It's the time I spend allowing myself to remember being with him, to remember how good he made me feel. Joe would never play fucking Monopoly with me, and I wouldn't want him to.

I glance at the mirror as I finish drying off, catching sight of the marks Mason left on my body. Bite marks on my neck and bruises on my hips. The bruises can be covered with my clothes. I'm not worried about them so much. It's the damn bite marks that are going to be a problem. If Joe sees them, all hell will break loose. It's a good thing my husband likes to rise early. He's already downstairs in his office, which gives me the space and time to figure out how I'm going to cover these marks up. It would be a lot easier if it were winter and I could wrap a scarf around my neck, but since it's October, that's not an option. Spring practically bypasses Brisbane; it's far too hot for a scarf.

Half an hour later, I'm dressed in a midi dress I've chosen intentionally to draw Joe's attention to my body rather than my neck. It's not really appropriate for work, but that's the least of my concerns today. The sleeveless black dress features a super high neckline and a figure-hugging fit. I've teamed it with strappy heels that I know always catch his attention, and I've applied layers of concealer to cover the bite marks still peeking out from my dress.

Joe frowns as I enter the kitchen. He's sitting at the kitchen island sipping coffee while our housekeeper, Maria, serves his breakfast.

"Good morning, Maria." I glide in, all smiles and sweetness while preparing myself for my husband.

Maria smiles. "Good morning, Mrs Hearst. Would you like some breakfast?"

Maria always calls me by that name even though I

didn't take Joe's surname when I married him. That pissed him off, but I refused to budge. I gave him my life and my body; I wasn't giving him that.

"No thank you, Maria. I'm just going to have a coffee this morning."

"You need to eat," Joe says, still running his gaze over my dress, still looking perplexed.

"I'm not hungry."

Maria finishes serving his breakfast and exits the kitchen. She knows our conversations can get heated and is always quick to leave us alone.

"What have you got on at work today?" he asks, thankfully leaving my appetite alone. It's a point of contention between us. I've lost my appetite since marrying him, and he's always trying to force me to eat. The last time he pushed the point, our fight ended with me refusing to talk to him for a day.

"The usual." I stand across from him, willing him not to take this further. I'm careful not to change the subject, though. Joe's a smart man whose mind works in ways most don't; he'll know I'm hiding something if I do that.

"You're a little overdressed for the office, don't you think?"

I look down at my dress and then back at him. "Maybe, but I remembered we have dinner with Nicholas and Pam tonight, and since I have a late appointment with a client, I decided to wear this in case I have to go straight from work to the restaurant."

His lips press together. "You could take the dress with you rather than wear it."

I sigh. "Are we really going to begin our day with an argument over my clothes?"

"I wouldn't tolerate my staff wearing a dress like that, Chelsea. You need to change."

"It's a good thing you're not my boss then. I'm not changing."

"I am your husband, though." His eyes say everything he doesn't, but I choose to ignore his unspoken warning. The risk associated with him seeing Mason's marks is greater than the risk of ignoring that warning.

I sip my coffee, keeping my eyes on him, not showing an ounce of the anxiety I'm feeling down to my bones. Fuck you, Mason, for putting me in this position. But oh God, it was worth every second of worry and fear over Joe discovering what I did. To have Mason one last time, and to have him so recklessly and passionately, was everything I didn't know I wanted. He might have marked me, ruined a favourite dress of mine, and caused me this argument with Joe, but I wouldn't take any of it back.

"I don't want to argue with you today, Joe," I say. "Please just let me wear this dress. If you must know, it makes me feel pretty and I need to feel pretty today."

That slows him down. Confuses him. I see it in his eyes, and I silently high five myself. I must remember to say stuff like that to him in times of need like this.

I endure a long silent moment while he decides which way to go, and then finally, he says, "If you must." He eats some of his bacon before starting a new conversation. "I have to go out of town on Friday night for the weekend. I'll be home Sunday afternoon."

I work hard not to show how happy this makes me. Casually, I enquire, "Where are you going?"

"Sydney. I have work meetings all weekend."

"Okay." I nod, thinking about all the free hours I'll

have. Joe likes to pack our weekends with social engagements that bore the hell out of me. He also keeps me on my toes on the weekends simply because he's home and always watching me.

He finishes eating his breakfast while I scroll my work emails. When he's finished, he moves around the island to make a coffee to go. This is our standard routine every morning before his driver drives us into the city for work. I'd prefer to make my own way, but Joe insists we drive together. It's just another way he can control me. I'm fully aware of that and allow it because I have other battles with him that are more worthy of fighting.

I finish with my emails as his hand slides over my hip, and he moves in close behind me. Unease prickles across my skin, and I still when he says, "I want you ready for me tonight." He drops his lips to my bare shoulder and kisses me. "You were asleep by the time I came to bed last night."

Oh God, no.

He'll see the bite marks and bruises if we have sex.

I place my hand over his. "I'm on my period."

His fingers grip my hip, digging into my skin. "I don't give a fuck."

The unease of a moment ago slithers all the way through me.

"I do." I turn to face him, desperately wanting his eyes as far away from my neck as possible. "I don't like to have sex when I have my period."

The vein in his neck pulses. "That needs to change. Tonight."

With that, he reaches for his coffee and strides out of

the kitchen, leaving me with no doubt as to what he intends to make happen tonight.

∼

"CHELSEA." My boss sticks his head in my office just before lunch, looking irritated. "Have you finished with those files I asked you to look at this morning?"

Shit. I grimace. "Sorry, I'm still going through them. Can you give me another half hour? I'll make sure they're done by then."

"Fuck," he mutters. "Okay, half an hour. Get it done."

I lean back in my seat after he leaves and throw my pen down on the desk. It's been a shit of a morning so far, and I don't see the day improving anytime soon. My boss is usually the most patient man I know, but he's been on edge today; I've had client after client call me with issues they need fixed straight away; and on top of that, Brielle, one of my colleagues, has been the biggest bitch to me simply because she thinks I get special privileges at work due to my father being the premier. That's been going on for weeks, and I've let her catty remarks slide, but I'm ready to tell her where to go today. I don't get anything at work due to Dad being the premier. If anything, I have more to prove and have to work harder than everyone else.

My phone sounds with a text.

Alexa: Wanna go to yoga tonight?
Me: I knew you enjoyed it the other day!
Alexa: Well?
Me: Ugh, I can't. I have a dinner with Joe's friends tonight.

Alexa: How come I never get invited to dinner with you and Joe?

Me: Trust me, that's not an invite you want.

Alexa: He's your husband now, babe. You can't keep me from him forever.

Alexa knows the same story Mason knows about my marriage. She thinks I walked away from Mason so he wouldn't go to jail. She thinks I married Joe to help my father's political career. While those things are true, they don't come close to being the whole story, but that's a story neither of them can ever know.

Me: I won't. But be careful what you wish for is all I'm saying. Joe's dinners aren't as fun as our dinners.

Alexa: I bet. I can't imagine you getting smashed with him like you do with me.

Me: I don't. Shit, I gotta go. I promised to get a heap of work done for my boss in the next half hour. See you in an hour xx

Alexa: See you then xx

We're having lunch together today. Well, I won't be if I don't get these files done for my boss, so I block out all distractions and spend the next twenty-five minutes finishing work on them. I drop them on his desk with one minute to spare.

"Thanks, Chelsea," he says. "I appreciate this and I'm sorry if I was snappy earlier."

I wave him off. "All good. Let me know if you need anything else."

He nods and gets back to work.

I head to the bathroom and run into Brielle in there.

She's applying lipstick as I enter and shoots me a filthy look in the mirror.

I tell myself to keep walking, and I do for a second, but then I stop. My nerves are shot today thanks to being on high alert this morning with Joe, and then dealing with all the things I've had to today while also trying to figure out how to keep my husband away from me tonight. At this point, I'm not above poisoning myself so I end up in hospital, far, far away from him.

I'm also done with Brielle's bullshit.

"Are you a bitch to everyone or is it just me?" I ask.

She glares at me as she takes her time finishing applying her lipstick. With a smack of her lips, she turns to face me. "I don't like you, Chelsea, and I don't like the fact your surname opens doors for you. You're no better than any of us, so you shouldn't be treated better."

"Are you fucking kidding me? I'm not treated any better than you or anyone else."

"Yeah, you are. And that was before you married into the Hearst family. I mean, I'm surprised you even bothered coming back to work after your wedding. You have a gorgeous husband with millions in the bank. Why don't you just do us all a favour and sit at home and let him take care of you?"

"Ah, because I'm not the kind of woman to rely on a man like that. And because I have goals and dreams in life that don't revolve around a man."

"Yeah, well you being here takes up a spot at the firm that someone else could have. Someone who really needs the job."

I jab my chest, my anger rising. "*I* really need this job."

"Until you start having babies, and then all this time you were here will have been a waste of time for someone else who had to wait for you to leave." She leans closer. "Just fucking quit and spend your days shopping and sucking your husband's dick. We'll all be a hell of a lot happier."

I slap her without thinking.

Her eyes widen as her hand moves to her cheek. "You did *not* just do that."

My breathing has sped right up. I can't think straight I'm so mad. "Yeah, I did just do that, and you deserved it. Don't ever say anything like that to me again."

"Or what? You'll run to the higher-ups and let them kiss your ass for fear of upsetting your daddy or your husband?"

My chest rises and falls harshly as I stare at her. I'm stunned by everything she's said. She's even more poisonous than I thought. "I don't know where you're getting these ideas from, Brielle, but no one kisses my ass here because of who I'm related to."

"You really have no idea, do you?" She shakes her head and looks at me like she pities me. "The Novak's and Hearst's of this world run it, which means women like you get a free pass all the way through. Anything you've achieved is because of the men in your life, honey, not because you're any good at what you do. The sooner you understand that the better off we'll all be."

With that, she breezes out of the bathroom, leaving me feeling like I've just taken a beating. I've worked hard getting my degree and then this job, and I know the work I do at the firm is good, so I don't believe her that my success is because of my connections. But it's hard when someone like Brielle, a bully, gets in your ear. You start to question things you shouldn't, and I know that as much as I'll try not to, I'll stew over every single word she's said to me today. I'll do my best not to buy into any of it, but the things bullies say always leave their mark in some way. I should know; my father has spent my entire life teaching me this.

I finish in the bathroom and head back to my office, checking the Facebook notification I receive on the way. Alexa shared a link for a new hairdresser she's thinking of trying out, and I'm about to tap it when I see a post featuring a photo of Mason. It's crazy that we're still friends on Facebook, that neither of us has unfriended the other. Mason's hardly on Facebook, so I get that he hasn't bothered to remove me, but I'm on here every day, and I can't bring myself to do it. He didn't share the photo I'm looking at now; he was tagged in a post from Harlow, his president's old lady. I really like her, but what I truly like is that she shares photos of the guys, which means I stumble across Mason every now and then when I'm not expecting it.

God, I'm supposed to be leaving him behind and moving on, but here I am, desperately craving a piece of him. Desperately craving a piece of the man who I want to hate for how fast he moved on from me. I know he thought *I'd* moved on, and that's why he did it, but it still cut deep. Alexa told me it meant nothing to him, but that doesn't matter; it meant something to me. He didn't just sleep with her. He broadcast that fact everywhere to make sure I knew. To make sure I hurt me.

I exit out of the app as a text comes through from Joe.

Joe: I need you at the restaurant half an hour earlier than dinner.

Me: Why?

Joe: I've lined up a quick interview for a piece on your dad. They want a photo of us and a few questions.

Me: I can't guarantee I'll be finished with my client in time.

He switches from text to a call.

"Make this happen, Chelsea," he says, his voice dropping into warning territory. "Tonight's the only night they can do the interview."

"My work's important to me, Joe. I don't think you understand that."

"And I don't think you understand my level of care about that. Your father put me in charge of publicity; I'm making sure I deliver what he needs."

My hand squeezes around my phone as I take a couple of deep breaths. "You can be a real prick, do you know that?"

"I'm aware. I'll see you tonight. Make sure your hair is out. It photographs better like that."

The line goes dead and I stare at the phone.

I fucking hate him.

I send a text to Alexa.

Me: Joe's away this weekend. We need a girls' weekend down the coast.

Alexa: Oh God, yes! With all the girls or just us?

Me: Invite everyone.

Alexa: On it!

It's been too many months since I've had something to look forward to; I intend on forgetting my life for a few days and having the best weekend doing all the things my husband hates me doing.

I MAKE it to the restaurant with five minutes to spare. I had to cancel my lunch with Alexa and work like a demon all afternoon so I could bring my last client meeting forward in order to keep Joe happy. I'm pissed as hell over this fact, but I've got a lot of balls in the air where Joe's concerned, and this is not a battle worth fighting with him. Not when the biggest thing I need to focus on right now is keeping him away from my body and Mason's marks.

He's sitting at the bar when I arrive and tracks every step I take to him. Standing, he slides his hand around my waist and kisses my cheek before moving his mouth to my ear and saying, "Good girl."

The display of affection is for show.

The greeting is to remind me he's in charge.

Asshole.

I smile tightly up at him as I bring my hand to cup his cheek. "How was your day, darling?"

He works his jaw. "Careful, Chelsea. I'm not in the mood tonight."

I drop my hand and glance around the restaurant. "I'm on time. It'd be nice if the journalist was too."

Joe looks past me. "I have to take care of something. I'll be back in a minute."

I turn and stop breathing for a second when I find Mason watching me from the doorway. He's with Griff and he looks pissed to be here.

Joe leaves me, heading in their direction and ushering them out of the bar. I watch them until I can no longer see them. I then collapse onto a barstool and order wine. I fucking need it after the day I've had. I also need it after seeing Mason. We've managed to go months without running into each other, and now he's everywhere. I have no idea why, but it seems his club is doing some work with Joe. I make a mental note to find out why. I need to know how much longer I can expect to be seeing him every damn day.

The journalist turns up before Joe returns. I've just ordered my second wine, after guzzling my first, when she arrives. Not a bad thing; it means I've taken the edge off enough to dazzle her with engaging conversation and laughter.

"Oh good," Joe says when he comes back, "you two have met."

I shoot him a big, wide smile like a real wife would. "Darling, come and tell Susan all about how you proposed to me." I look at Susan and wink. "He's such a romantic. He made me swoon so hard."

Joe watches me carefully. No one but me would note the assessment going on in that brain of his. They would only see the love he's taking care to project. But I see the way he watches, and right now, I've had enough to drink to play with him.

He moves to my side, casually placing his arm over my shoulders as he recounts our fake proposal. We didn't come up with this story together. I made it up during the first interview he forced me to do, and I've embellished it every time I've told it since then. The last time I told it, he pulled me aside after and told me in no uncertain terms to fucking stop adding extra layers to it. I took that as a win.

"So when can we expect baby Hearsts?" Susan asks.

I almost choke on the sip of wine I'm taking as she throws that question out.

Joe squeezes me tightly. "Soon I hope." He looks down at me, a cautionary glint in his eyes. "We're working on it."

I place my hand to his chest. Lovingly. So very fucking lovingly. "Darling, let's not start a rumour. That's not fair to anyone." I look at Susan and smile sweetly. "He's being silly, Susan. It's a joke between us. I mean, we want kids for sure, but I'm only twenty-five and just at the start of my career, so it's going to be a few years before we think seriously about children."

Joe's fingers dig into my arm. "I'm sorry, Susan, but we need to wrap this up now. Our dinner guests have just arrived."

"Oh, of course!" Susan exclaims. She's been flustered since Joe arrived. Most women who meet him have the same experience. If only they knew his devastatingly good looks don't match his soul. "Thank you so much for this interview. I'll send a copy through as soon as it's written up."

Joe reaches for his scotch and takes a sip as he watches her walk away. He then looks at me. "Don't ever fucking do that again."

His tone crawls all over me. Even the wine I've had doesn't dull the effect his voice has. I hate that I swing between wanting to go head-to-head with him and wanting to run away. Joe handles me in such a way that some days he lets things slide, while other days he doesn't give an inch. There doesn't seem to be a rhyme or reason to which things he refuses to ignore, so I don't have a playbook figured out yet.

I drink some wine, doing my best not to show how much he's affected me. I then take a risk I'm not fully feeling, but damn him, I can't keep allowing fear into this relationship. When I agreed to marry him, I did not agree to give him all the power. "I'm not having children soon, Joe. That was never part of our agreement, and I don't appreciate you telling people that."

The displeasure he feels is splashed all across his face. So much so that anyone looking at him right now will see it as clearly as I do. Gone are all the pretences of a moment ago. "Our agreement was for a marriage. Marriages produce children as far as I'm concerned, Chelsea. You'll do well to remember that."

I'm in a mood today. It's the only reason I have for saying, "And you'll do well to remember I actually hold the power when it comes to having a baby. It's my body, not yours. Don't push me on this because you won't like being childless."

Before he has a chance to respond, I drain my wine glass, pick up my clutch, and stalk away from him. I shake all the way to the bathroom. From anger mostly, but also a little fear. This marriage is a battle zone I was not prepared for.

I take my time in the bathroom. I need to in order to calm myself down enough to make it through this dinner. When I exit back out into the hallway that connects through to the bar and restaurant, I find Mason leaning against the wall, arms crossed, eyes narrowed at me, still with that pissed off look on his face.

I'm surprised, but only momentarily because my anger takes over. It's all the emotions carrying over from last night with him, today with Brielle, and this morning and tonight with Joe, all rolled into one that explodes out of me when I spit out, "Fuck you!"

He keeps his ass against the wall and his arms crossed as he lifts a brow and says, "I did that last night and it did fucking nothing for me."

I take a step closer to him, my whole body lit with the need to fight this battle with him. I might be ignoring most of the battles in my life with Joe, but there's not one part of me that can walk away from Mason. "That wasn't the impression I got."

His nostrils flare. "You misread the situation, princess. I was just showing you what you're missing."

"I'm not missing anything." Lies, lies, lies. They're littered all through my life these days.

His features darken. "Yeah, you looked real fucking cosy with your husband and that reporter."

His jealousy sparks feelings in me I'm ashamed to admit I like. "What do you want, Mason? I have to get back to him."

"Of course you fucking do." His jaw clenches and he looks away from me for a moment. Then, swinging his face back to mine, he reaches for the neck of my dress. Pulling it down, he rubs his thumb over my skin and settles his eyes on my neck. "I don't know what the fuck I wanted."

He lets me go, pushes off from the wall, and strides down the hallway to the restaurant exit.

My heart races as I watch him leave, both wishing he'd come back and that he'd never set foot in my life again.

I spend a little too long staring after him before I come to my senses. I need to get back to Joe, but first, I need to double-check my neck and make sure Mason didn't expose any of his bite marks. That's the last thing I need to deal with today.

∽

"You were quiet during dinner," Joe says on the drive home from the restaurant.

I glance across the car, finding him watching me while he waits for the red light to turn green. Rain gently falls, droplets of water trickling down the windows, providing the soundtrack to a night I wish I didn't have to live through. "You and Nicholas spent all night discussing business. I didn't have anything to contribute to the conversation."

"Chelsea, at any point in the conversation, you could have spoken up. Changed the subject." The light turns green, and he directs his attention back to the road. "Contrary to what you may think, I want this to be a partnership between us. I want you involved in our marriage and our life."

I stare out my window. I don't know what to say to that because everything that's gone down between us today hasn't led me to believe a word of this.

After I returned from the bathroom earlier in the night, after seeing Mason, Joe was foul with me. That lasted for half the dinner. I'd expected it, though, after I told him I didn't want children anytime soon. The second half of dinner wasn't as bad, but on a scale of one to ten, with ten being him at full asshole level, this dinner rated as an eight. Maybe that's because I was already in a mood with him going into it, but either way, it was a night I never want to relive. And now I have to get through the rest of the night, fending him off so he doesn't see Mason's marks on me.

Joe places his hand on my thigh. "Don't ignore me."

I look back at him, avoiding thinking about his hand on me. It burns through my dress, increasing my worry over what will happen when we arrive home. "Trust me, I'm not."

His grip on my leg tightens. "I'm fucking done with this attitude. Perhaps we need to spend more time together so you can learn to read me better. I'll get my assistant to clear some room on my calendar. We'll go away for a weekend here and there."

Oxygen ceases to make its way into my lungs. I can't spend weekends away with him. It's bad enough spending them with him in Brisbane, but at least we're surrounded by other people here. Weekends away signal time alone. And sex. God, weekends away are *all* about sex, and that's the last thing I want more of with him.

"You don't need to clear your calendar. I know how busy you are. I'll work around your calendar and schedule in extra time for us when you're free." I hate every word coming out of my mouth, but I hate the alternative more.

He looks at me. "I appreciate that."

When he looks ahead again, I exhale the breath I was holding.

Fifteen minutes later, we're home and I've locked myself in our bathroom while Joe takes care of some work things that cropped up during the night. He told me he'd be up soon, so I'm now commencing my final freak out before he potentially discovers that I fucked Mason last night.

"Chelsea," he calls out, coming to our bedroom much sooner than I expected. I thought his work would take at least an hour.

"I'll be out in a minute," I say, willing the fear in my veins to calm the fuck down so I at least don't look stressed. That won't be a good look, and it will draw his attention in all the wrong ways.

A minute passes.

Two.

Five.

I open the bathroom door and exit into the bedroom, where Joe is nowhere to be found.

Oh God, this game is my least favourite game I've ever played.

"There you are," he says, coming back.

I almost jump out of my skin I'm on such a fine edge.

Turning, I collide with him, not realising he's so close. He slides one hand around my waist and the other through my hair to take hold of my head. His lips are on mine in an instant and his tongue demands my submission.

I kiss him back while frantically contemplating my next move. When his hand goes to the zip of my dress, I pull my mouth from his. Meeting his gaze, I say, "I meant it when I told you I don't like sex while I have my period."

I try to move out of his embrace, but he tightens his hold on me.

"And I meant it when I told you that needs to change." His voice is dark, flashing warning bells in front of me.

My heart practically beats out of my chest as I push my way out of his hold. "It's not going to change, Joe."

His jaw clenches, and I see the battle he wages on the inside. He doesn't like my lack of obedience, but I'm unsure if he'll force it. I have no doubt that at some point in our marriage he will. I just don't know if we've reached that point yet.

He undoes his belt, his eyes firmly on mine.

The sound of it sliding over the fabric of his pants as he removes it ratchets up my fear.

He drops it on the bed and moves his fingers to the button on his pants. Flicking it open, he reaches for the zip.

"You will learn to enjoy sex at all times, Chelsea. I will make sure of it."

I'm going to vomit.

My hand absently moves to my neck.

I was kidding myself thinking I could keep these bite marks and bruises from him.

He slides his zip down and reaches for me.

His hand curls around my neck, touching the marks he doesn't yet know exist.

Bringing his mouth to mine, he kisses me again.

It's rough. Demanding. Cold.

It's a reminder of his power.

A promise of what's to come.

When he's done with my mouth, he moves his hand to the top of my head. Pushing me down, he says, "If you won't fuck me tonight, you can get on your knees instead."

As I take my husband's cock into my mouth, I imagine it's Mason's just so I can get through this. As I suck it, I still think of Mason. And after, when I curl into a ball on my side of the bed, I think about the day far, far in the future when I never have to share a bed with this man again.

That day can't come soon enough.

All I can hope is that I haven't lost myself completely when it arrives.

9

GUNNAR

This week can go to hell. It's been fucked up from the get-go. Now that I'm staring at a long afternoon taking care of Joe fucking Hearst's bullshit, I'm more pissed than I was when I woke up. And that's saying something, because I went to bed angry after seeing Chelsea and Joe last night, and woke up with that anger still sitting deep in my gut.

I couldn't fucking help myself, hanging around after Griff and I finished club business with him. I watched Chelsea with him and that reporter. Watched him put his arm over her and pull her close. Watched her laugh when he said shit. When she put her hand to his chest and looked up lovingly at him, I was done. Fuck, I thought I was, but no, I still chose to torture myself by waiting for her in the hallway outside the bathroom when I saw her slip in there.

I'd told her that fucking her did nothing for me. That was a load of fucking shit. It stirred my need for her to new fucking levels, and I've spent nearly every second since, thinking about her. Hell, I wanted to fuck her again outside that fucking bathroom. Especially when I saw my bite marks on her neck.

"Gunnar," Griff says as we enter the office building of the first asshole we have to see for Hearst this afternoon. "You think you can hold your shit together for this? 'Cause I'm looking at you, and I'm not seeing any semblance of calm in you."

"That's a big fucking word, Griff."

He comes to a halt, his eyes flashing with irritation. "You wanna be a smartass, I can work with that, but we're gonna need to take that shit outside."

Fuck.

I exhale a long breath. "Sorry, brother. I'm good."

He watches me silently for a beat. "You fucking sure about that, because I don't need you to go in there and fuck shit up. I don't need Hearst or Novak busting my fucking balls like they have been."

"I'm sure." I'm fucking not, but I'm not telling him that.

He stabs a finger at me. "If you screw shit up, this'll be the last job you come on with me. I'll fucking put you to work at Indigo instead."

Christ, that's a fucking threat, and he knows it. Working at Storm's strip club isn't something I like to do. Fucking ever. Some of those strippers are whiny bitches who do my head in.

I follow him up to the office of the guy we're here to see. He lets us in with hesitation that soon turns to anger when Griff tells him why we're here.

"Just a friendly reminder to keep supporting Novak," Griff says. "You withdraw that support and he'll have your application blocked." An application for zoning the guy needs to push his commercial development through.

The guy's face puffs up red. "You go back and tell Novak that if he screws me in the ass, I'll screw him right back."

"No," Griff says more calmly than I'd be saying it, "you just tell us now that your support is guaranteed, and we'll take that back to him. He'll play nice after that, and you'll get your development."

"I'm not guaranteeing anything. Not with the current policies it looks like he's bringing in."

Griff moves towards him, and the guy flinches while trying like fuck to appear unaffected. "You wanna revise that statement?" Griff's voice takes on a darker tone; he was just getting warmed up.

The guy shakes his head. "No. And it's time for you two to leave."

"We're not leaving until we get what we came for," Griff says.

"Well, we've got a problem then."

Jesus, this shit could take all fucking day at this rate.

I walk to the guy and grab him roughly by the shirt. Yanking him to me, I growl, "That's not what we wanna fucking hear. Try again."

His eyes flare with fear. He's a suit-wearing, desk-riding dickhead. This kind of force is what men like him need to respond in the way we want them to. "You're going to threaten me to get what you want?"

I grip his shirt harder. "I'm gonna do whatever the fuck it takes to get what we want." My eyes land on the framed photo of him with a woman on his desk. Jerking my chin at it, I say, "That your wife?" I'm not big on threatening innocent family members, and wouldn't go through with it, but it works every fucking time.

Real fear fills his face and sweat lines his brow. "Leave her out of it."

I shove him back so he lands on his ass. Moving so I'm standing over him, I say, "That's gonna require you giving Novak your support." Just fucking saying Novak's name pisses me off, let alone making something happen for him that he wants. This is the worst fucking job I've ever had to take on for my club.

The guy stares up at me, torn with his choice. I know I've moved him closer to where we want him, so I apply a little more pressure. I walk to his desk and grab the frame. Holding it up, I say to Griff, "We got an address for her?"

Griff nods. "Yeah."

"Wait! Stop!" The guy pushes up off the floor and comes at me, madly reaching for the photo of his wife. "I'll fucking give that asshole my support, but if you go anywhere near my wife, I'll do a fucking interview with the press and tell them everything I know about Mark Novak and his dirty deeds."

Fuck, I would fucking love him to do that. But that option doesn't work for my club anywhere near as well as it would work for me, so I let him have his precious frame back and say, "It looks like we have a deal."

Griff holds up his phone at the guy. "We'll send you a copy of this."

The guy scowls. "You fucking recorded that?"

"We're not fucking idiots," I say before shaking my head and exiting his office.

Griff follows me out, and when we reach the lifts, I

look at him and say, "People always fucking underestimate us."

He nods. "Yeah, and it makes our job a hell of a lot fucking easier."

"It fucking pisses me off is what it does."

We step into the lift when it arrives and Griff selects the ground floor. "Once you figure out how to switch your thinking, brother, your life will be a lot fucking easier."

"How do you figure that?"

"Look beyond your first assumption. Look for what you're not seeing on that first glimpse of a situation. The whole fucking world will open up to you." He pauses. "And maybe you won't be so ready to punch people all the damn time."

Griff talks some deep shit sometimes. I respect the hell out of him, but I don't always agree with what he says. "I'll take that under advisement," I mutter. I'm not sure why he thinks I go around punching innocent people. The only people I want to punch are those who fucking deserve it.

∼

IT TAKES us four hours to get through everyone on Hearst's list, and by the time we're done, I'm ready to fucking drown myself in a bottle of Beam. We're on our way back to the clubhouse when a call comes through from Hearst.

Griff takes it while I drive. When I hear him say, "We'll be there in about half an hour," I want to fucking stab myself.

"We have to go see him?" I ask, gripping the steering wheel like I'm trying to strangle it.

"Yeah."

I keep my annoyance to myself while pulling into the left lane so I can change directions. Working at Indigo is starting to sound like a good fucking idea.

"You wait out here," Griff says as he exits the ute once we get to Hearst's place.

"Happy to." I flick the radio up and kick back while I wait for him.

Five minutes after he leaves, a black Range Rover pulls into the driveway at the same time that Hearst comes out of the house. I watch as Chelsea exits the Range Rover and waits for Hearst to meet her. They have a conversation during which she rips her sunglasses off and begins arguing with him. I turn the radio down and hear his raised voice.

"Cancel your plans. We're having dinner with my parents tonight," he says. His tone is one I know she despises from the arguments we had.

"I'm not cancelling, Joe. I made my plans yesterday, long before you decided we were going out for dinner. Besides, your parents won't miss me." She practically spits that last sentence.

Hearst grabs her bicep, hard enough that she winces. I sit forward. What the fuck? "I told you I was fucking done with your attitude."

She glares at him before pulling out of his hold, reaching into her bag, and retrieving an envelope. "Here's the paperwork you wanted." She shoves the envelope at him. "I have to get back to work. The next time you need something so urgently, organise for your assistant to deliver it. I don't have time to run around for you."

She gets back in the Range Rover and slams the door while he turns and stalks back into their house.

The fuck was all that?

A couple of minutes pass and then Chelsea exits the vehicle again. She's on her phone and has a quick conversation while pacing her front lawn. When she ends the call, she crouches down and drops her face into her hands. I can't be sure, but it looks like she's crying.

Fuck.

I've never coped well when Chelsea cries, and as much as I don't want to give a fuck right now, I don't like what I just witnessed, and I don't like seeing her cry because of it.

I exit the ute and cut across the lawn to her. "What the fuck's going on with you and Hearst?"

Her head whips up and I'm met by her tearstained face. "Go away, Mason. This has nothing to do with you," she snaps.

"I don't give a fuck if it does or not. I don't like the way he just touched you."

She stands, squaring her shoulders like she's about to take me on. "It doesn't matter what you like anymore; I'm his, not yours. And you know what? I'm sick of dealing with the both of you. You both just take whatever the hell you want and leave me to deal with the consequences." She glares at me. "I'm not yours to touch or bite or fuck, and I'm sure as hell not yours to worry about anymore."

Her words fucking slap me in the face.

What the hell am I even doing? I step away from her

and nod. "Yeah, you're right. My fucking mistake. One I won't make again."

I don't wait to hear her response; I stalk back to the ute. Thank fuck Griff exits the house at the same time so I can kick the engine over and get the fuck out of here. What a clusterfuck of a fucking day.

10

CHELSEA

I sip my wine and watch as my husband talks with my father. It's Thursday night, two nights after we did that disastrous interview before dinner with Joe's friends, and we're at a small fundraiser for Dad's campaign. Small is around three hundred people. One would think that's a good size for me to try and lose Joe's attention, but he has a fucking sixth sense as to my whereabouts and always has his eye on me.

He glances up now and meets my gaze. I continue sipping wine because it will annoy him. He told me last night I should cut back on my alcohol consumption. I almost cancelled work today so I could drink all day.

We've been married just over five weeks, and it's safe to say things have taken a definite turn for the worse this week. I don't know what's caused it, but I'm arguing back with him more. Standing up for myself more. Saying no more. And he's becoming increasingly demanding, so between the both of us, there's a whole lot of tension in our relationship.

Some of that tension came to a head yesterday when he demanded I go to his office and collect some paperwork for him while I was supposed to be at work. I'd said no initially, but he'd grown insistent until I finally agreed. Then we'd had an argument on the front lawn, the one Mason witnessed. Not my finest moment, but it's been a long, hard week that I've spent alternating between fearing Joe will discover Mason's marks on me, and pushing back against his assholey ways.

I was awful to Mason, but I couldn't stop myself. Not when he's the cause of a lot of my stress this week. God damn him for biting me. And when he looked at me with legit concern after my argument with Joe, I panicked a little too. Mason's hate thawing is a slippery slope neither of us should tread. I achieved my goal of pushing him away, and then I came home later and had a screaming match with Joe before putting myself to bed in one of the spare rooms. He didn't like that, but he didn't force me back into our bed.

Tonight, he's treading much more carefully with me. Watching me silently rather than engaging in conversation. I think I prefer it when he talks more, at least then I know what his thoughts are. When he's like this, I have no idea, and that stresses me out. Wine is my coping mechanism.

"Chelsea," Dad's assistant Nicola says, "your father asked me to have you go see him. He has something to discuss with you."

I nod. "Thanks, Nicola."

I drain my glass before doing as she said. I haven't spoken to my father all week. It's the one high point of being married to Joe; my father tends to leave me alone these days, but that's only because he has Joe doing his dirty work instead.

Joe's still with Dad and he watches my approach, reaching for me when I join them. Pressing a kiss to my lips, he says, "Remember we're in public tonight."

I smile adoringly up at him. "How could I forget?"

"Chelsea," Dad cuts in. "I want you and Joe up on the stage with your mother and me while I make my speech tonight. My approval ratings have taken a fall this week with the new policies I announced. We need to step up our efforts and maintain our presence as a strong family."

I nod. "Sure." I expected nothing less, so I'm not sure why he's bothering to tell me this.

"Don't be so damn casual about this," Dad snaps, not even bothering to hide his annoyance.

"Careful, Dad, people are watching."

His lips flatten and he looks at Joe. "I'll leave you to deal with her."

He leaves us without another word to me.

"Why do you insist on pissing him off?" Joe asks, looking as frustrated as he sounds.

"Why does he insist on being an asshole to me?"

"What did he say or do just then that was rude?"

"Honestly, Joe, this is between me and my father. You don't need to involve yourself in it."

"Except I do. Marrying you put me right in the fucking middle of you two, and here I am trying to deal with you."

"Welcome to the fucking family. Aren't you glad you agreed to this marriage?"

His nostrils flare as he works his jaw. I'm saved from

his wrath when his assistant interrupts us and tells Joe he's needed across the room.

He bends his face to mine before he leaves and warns, "Don't overdo the wine. And I asked you to wear your hair out tonight. Go and fix it."

I watch the women at the table near us track his ass as he walks past them. I want to tell them they can have him. Instead, I make my way to the bar in search of another wine. As for my hair, I'll spend the time drinking my wine considering how much I want to be on his shit list later. Maybe I'll fix my hair, maybe I'll send him a big fuck you.

As I pass the ballroom door, I swear I catch sight of Mason.

Surely not.

Surely Joe hasn't put the club on security detail here tonight.

I can't help myself, though; I exit the room to see for myself. There's a lot of people milling around in the foyer, and I've made it through them all before I see him. He's outside the hotel on his phone, and before I know it, I'm pushing through the hotel doors and joining him. It's a dumb move, but I'm unable to stop myself.

His back is to me, and while I'm not trying to eavesdrop, I catch snippets of the conversation.

"Yeah, I know, Mum, but I'm worried about you. Do you need someone to come sit with you at the hospital while you have your chemo? I can probably swing the time off," he says.

Alexa told me their mother has cancer. I wanted to reach out to Mason to see how he was but decided against it. Hearing the worry in his voice makes me regret that decision.

He listens to what his mother says before saying, "It fucking pisses me off that Dad isn't supporting you through this. I'll be there." He pauses briefly before saying, "This isn't up for negotiation. I will be there." He turns, coming face to face with me. "Fuck," falls from his lips. And then to his mother—"I have to go, Mum. I'll see you tomorrow." He stabs at the phone to end the call, his eyes firmly on me. "What the fuck are you doing out here?"

"Wow, I really love the way you speak to me now, Mason."

"You made it really fucking clear yesterday that you don't want anything to do with me, so I'm just wondering why the fuck I'm looking at you right now."

He's right, I did make that clear to him yesterday, but good God, his hate makes it hard to breathe. I push through, though. "I didn't mean to listen to your conversation, but I heard bits of it. Are you okay?"

His eyes blaze with disbelief. Or maybe it's distrust. "I'm good, but if I wasn't, I sure as fuck wouldn't need your concern or help, Chelsea."

I swallow my hurt, but damn, it slides down like razors. Unsure whether to push the point and try to make him see I genuinely care, I stare at him for another long, few moments during which he watches me with a filthy look. Taking into account his stubborn streak, I nod and turn to leave. However, at the last minute, I look back at him and say, "When you love, you love like no other, Mason, but when you hate, it's merciless."

He doesn't respond; he simply glares at me like he wishes he wasn't looking at me.

I slip back into the ballroom, having made my decision to fix my hair for Joe. I can't withstand two assholes in one night.

11

GUNNAR

"**G**unnar, can you please help me in the kitchen?" Harlow says about fifteen minutes after I arrive at her and Scott's place on Saturday. Scott invited the club over for a barbecue lunch, and by the looks of it, there are about thirty people here so far. I'm not really in the mood for this, but I always show up for club get-togethers.

"Sure," I say while wondering why the fuck she asked me. I'm not known for any special cooking talents.

She blasts me a huge smile. A fucking suspect smile if you ask me. One that indicates she's up to something. "Thank you."

I follow her into the kitchen where she puts me to work chopping salad. Yep, fucking suspect. She's never asked me to do shit like this before.

Madison joins us, looking at Harlow and saying, "I can take over for you, honey."

"I'm okay, but can you grab the mince out of the fridge and help me make the rissoles?"

"Sure, but don't overdo it, okay?"

Harlow nods, but it's clear even to me that she has no intention of sitting this out. Fuck knows why. If I was as pregnant as she is, I'd sit on my ass all day.

Madison gets to work on the rissoles. Looking at me, she says, "I saw your brother was in town last week. How is he?"

Fuck, these chicks love Hayden. His last four movies were blockbusters, and now every woman and her cat wants a piece of him, Madison included. She's not as bad as most, because she's actually hung out with him a few times over the years and knows he farts and burps like every other guy, but she follows the news and always knows when he's in Australia.

"He's good. Back in LA now to start work on a new movie."

"Oh, is that Hayden?" Nash's old lady asks as she comes into the kitchen carrying bags of chips.

"Yeah," I say.

"I just watched his latest movie last week," she says. "I loved it."

"I fuckin' loved it, too," Nash says, coming in after her, "because it got me laid when I didn't think I had a chance in hell of getting some that night."

Velvet shoots him a dirty look. "You were being a dick that day."

"No, I was doing what you asked me to do that day."

Velvet dumps the chips on the kitchen counter and rolls her eyes at her husband. "Nash, you were being a dick. I asked you to do the laundry. You proceeded to just wash your shit. Huge dick. I wish I didn't fuck you that night now that I'm thinking of it."

Madison shakes her head at Nash. "I agree, that's a dick move."

A chick I've never met sticks her head in the kitchen, looking lost until she spots Harlow, at which point she smiles and says, "Hey, Harlow."

Harlow grins at her and motions for her to come in. "Louise! You made it. Everyone, this is Louise, a friend of mine from the gym." She goes around the kitchen, rattling off our names for the chick. When she gets to me, her smile grows, and she says, "Louise, this is Gunnar. Can you please help him with the salads?"

Louise smiles at me. "Hi." Then to Harlow, she says, "Sure, and I brought some pasta salads too."

Harlow nods at the fridge. "There should be enough room for them in there, but if not, we've got more room in the fridge on the deck."

Louise makes room in the fridge, bending over and giving me an eyeful of her ass. She's my type, brunette with curves for days, and that ass is one a man could get a good hold on, but my dick isn't interested in the least. And neither am I, but I've clued on to what Harlow's game is here: she's playing matchmaker, which means the afternoon ahead is going to be hell. When Harlow gets an idea about two people she thinks would be perfect together, she's fucking relentless.

"You're a member of the club?" Louise says when she joins me to help with the salads.

"Yeah." She already knew the answer; she's just making small talk.

She smiles. "How long for?"

"Full-patch for nearly two years."

She reaches across me to grab the tomatoes, her eyes

meeting mine. "So full disclosure, Harlow told me about you. She said you're single and that she thinks we'd get on, and I know she's trying hard to throw us together, but I'm not into this kind of thing. I just wanted you to know that in case she's told you the same thing about me."

This might be the best fucking thing I've heard today. "Good to know, and for the record, I'm not into this kind of shit either."

Relief washes across her face. "Oh, thank God." She gets to work on the tomatoes.

We settle into an easy silence for a few minutes. When I finish chopping the cucumbers, I say, "How much did you not want to come here today?"

She looks up at me and grins. "A lot, but I promised Harlow I would, and I try never to break my promises, so here I am."

Fuck, I respect that. Someone who honours a fucking promise. "You met Scott yet?"

She shakes her head. "I haven't met any of Harlow's friends or family. I've only known her for a few weeks."

The door to the back deck slides open and J enters, his eyes coming instantly to me. "You joining the sewing circle, Gunnar?"

Madison takes Willow, their daughter, from him and says, "You could learn a thing or two yourself if you joined."

He grins, bending his face to kiss her. Then, smacking her ass, he says, "I know everything I need to know, baby."

She rolls her eyes. "Trust me, you don't."

"I've gotta head out for a bit and check on something.

I'll be back in about an hour or so," he says before kissing the top of his daughter's head.

"Okay." She nods.

J eyes me. "Need you with me, brother."

Harlow's head whips up. "He's busy, J. Can you take someone else?"

I catch the quirk of Louise's lips as her eyes meet mine. I give a quick grin in return.

"No, I need Gunnar on this one, Harlow," J says.

I bend my mouth to Louise's ear. "Save me a seat next to you. We can trade stories of being set up over the years."

The smile in her eyes is one of the most genuine I've ever seen. "She's done this to you before?"

I nod. "Fuck yeah."

"Oh, I can't wait to hear those stories," she says, the smile from her eyes reaching her lips.

I grab my shit and follow J out to our bikes. "What's going on?"

"Wilder's got some trouble at the restaurant we need to take care of." He looks at me before getting on his bike. "You owe me, brother."

"What the fuck for?"

"For saving your ass from Harlow."

"You knew about that?"

"Yeah, Madison mentioned it."

"You could have fucking warned me."

"Nah, I like to see you squirm for a bit."

I shake my head. "Fucking asshole."

"You gonna pursue that?"

"I'm taking a break from women for a while." A fucking forced break because my dick's on vacation.

"I didn't ask if you wanna commit for fucking life."

I grab my helmet. "Are we gonna take care of shit or stand around here and talk all fucking day?"

"I shoulda left your ass in there to deal with Harlow," he mutters, but I know he doesn't mean it. J might be an asshole at times, but he always looks out for me. Always has. He's the one who brought me into the club.

As we take off in the direction of the restaurant, I think about Louise. It's a fucking shame that the minute I do, my brain instantly goes to Chelsea. It's been a hell of a couple of weeks running into her all the damn time, but our last encounter at that fundraiser was the fucking worst. I'd only stopped by briefly to drop something off to Moss, who was in one of the hotel suites; I'd done my best not to see Chelsea, but there she fucking was. And she was asking if I was okay after hearing me talk to my mum. That fucking threw me. I wanted to tell her no I wasn't fucking okay. I wanted to tell her I needed her. But she made it crystal clear the day before that I wasn't hers anymore, so I told her to fuck off instead. That was after spending every day this week waking up thinking about being inside her, battling to get through the day without thinking about her again, and then closing my eyes to images of her at night. I should never have fucked her on Monday. Touching her and tasting her has brought her screaming back into my head, twisting shit right up.

∼

"Thanks for your help, brother," Wilder says an hour later, after we've helped him sort out the assholes who turned up to Trilogy looking for trouble. It was a guy and a bunch of his friends there to give his ex and her new boyfriend grief. She cheated on him with the new guy, and he seems hell-bent on revenge. It all hit too fucking close to home for me; I wanted to take his side.

"You heading over to Scott's after you're finished here?" J asks him.

"Wilder, we need to talk," Scarlett says, entering his office, interrupting us.

"Christ, what now, Scarlett?" Wilder mutters.

She scowls. Nothing new there; she spends most of her time scowling at him. "Don't be a dick. I told you two hours ago that we had a problem with the reservations and you said you'd deal with it, and you didn't, and now we've got a family of ten pissed off because it's their daughter's birthday and we don't have a table for them to celebrate it."

Wilder runs his fingers through his hair. "Fuck."

Scarlett arches her brows in an "I told you" expression. "Yeah."

"Have you tried to rearrange shit to make it work?" he asks.

Her brow arch turns into the kind of expression every man knows means imminent death. "Do I look like a fucking idiot?"

He works his jaw. Wilder's in charge here, but Scarlett gives no fucks about authority. She challenges him often. I like her, but fuck, I'd want to kill her if I had to work with her. How Wilder's survived her this long is beyond me. "I'll deal with it."

"Good." With that, she stalks back out to the front of the restaurant.

"Have fun with that," J says. "And by that, I mean Scarlett."

"I doubt I'll make it to Scott's later," Wilder says. "It's been a long fuckin' day here and I'm not feelin' in the mood for people."

"Yeah," J says. "I wouldn't either if I had to work with Scarlett."

"Jesus," Wilder grumbles. "She'll be the fuckin' death of me, brother."

My phone sounds with a text.

Alexa: I need your help. Stat! Call me when you get this.

I look at J. "I've gotta make a call."

He nods, and I head outside to call Alexa.

"Oh my God, thank you for calling!" she says, sounding like I've just saved her life or some shit.

"What's up?"

"I'm down the coast for the weekend and lost my credit card last night when I was drunk. I need you to go to my place and grab my emergency card from the safe and bring it to me. Please!"

"Jesus, Alexa, how the fuck do you keep losing that card?" This isn't the first time this has happened. My sister might be more responsible than me, but she sure as shit is good at losing her credit card.

"Shut up. I didn't mean to lose it."

"You want me to drive down the coast now? Are you with anyone who can lend you some cash?"

"No, I don't want to ask anyone for money. Please. I will love you forever."

"You already love me forever." Fuck, heading down the coast is the last fucking thing I want to do right now.

"Well, I'll love you longer than forever. We're about to

go to the day spa for the afternoon. I'll be there when you get here."

"I love how you assume I'm going to do this," I mutter.

"I love you, Mace. See you soon."

She ends the call, and a moment later, a text comes through from her telling me where she is.

Fucking hell. How the hell do I get roped into this shit?

"Everything okay?" J asks, coming outside.

"I have to head down the coast. Can you let Scott know I won't be back? I'm just gonna go home after I'm finished." I feel like Wilder today, not in the mood for people.

J nods. "Yeah, brother."

An hour and a half later, I walk into the hotel Alexa's at and pull out my phone to text her.

"What the fuck?" I mutter when I see a stack of Facebook notifications on my phone.

I don't do Facebook much and never get this many fucking notifications. Opening the app, I see that Harlow has posted a heap of photos from the barbecue and tagged me in her post. The first photo I see is of Louise and me. Harlow caught us while we were grinning over something. I'm about to tap on the post when I see the next post in my feed. It's from Alexa and features a photo of her and Chelsea.

Fuck.

Chelsea's here.

How the hell did I not figure that would be the case?

Alexa mentioned the day spa, and she pretty much never goes to one without Chelsea these days.

I tap on the photo of them and blow the image up to

zoom in on Chelsea, a sure fucking sign I've lost any sanity I thought I still had. She's wearing a red bikini, and I'm helpless but to get my fill of her body.

A text flashes up at the top of my screen.

Alexa: Are you here yet?

Me: Yeah, just arrived. You at the spa?

Alexa: Yes. Just ask for me at their reception. I told them to expect you. I love you!

Me: Yeah, and you fucking owe me.

I head in the direction of the day spa and ask for Alexa when I get there. The redhead behind the counter smiles and leads me down a long hallway to where my sister is. This place is fucking fancy with its high ceilings, gold trims, and flowers everywhere. Soft music floats through the space with a backdrop of trickling water. It'd put me the fuck to sleep coming here.

Alexa appears at the door in a massive white robe. Taking her emergency card from me, she says, "Thank you!"

"Who are you here with?"

"The girls."

"Who?" I demand, feeling agitated that she's not giving me the answer I'm looking for.

She gives a quick shake of her head. "You need to go, Mason. Do not go looking for her."

I don't know why the fuck I asked her when I already knew the answer, but I had to hear it.

"Fuck," Alexa says softly, her eyes shifting to something behind me.

I turn at the same time Samantha says, "Mason. How are you?"

My head swings back to my sister and I whistle low.

"Fuck, I'm surprised you invited her." Not that I give a fuck, but I'm surprised Chelsea is okay with this.

Alexa snaps her hand around my wrist and pulls me into the room with her, closing the door to Samantha. She looks at the lady waiting inside for her. "Sorry about this. I won't be a minute." Then to me, she says, "Of course I didn't invite her. I invited Toni, who brought her. They just arrived. Chelsea doesn't know they're here, and I told them they need to leave before she sees them."

I shrug. "I don't care, Alexa."

She hits me with a dirty look. "You should. You love that girl and I fucking know it."

"No, I *loved* that girl. Past fucking tense." I reach for the door handle. "Don't lose that fucking card. I'm not coming back to bail you out if you do."

I exit the room and stalk down the hallway, running into Samantha halfway along it.

Fuck.

She smiles at me, moving closer as I come to a stop a good distance away. "Long time no see, Mason. How have you been?"

This is the woman I fucked after I discovered Chelsea was engaged. I chose her intentionally in a moment of hurt because she was close to Chelsea. We slept together once, but I'm fairly sure Chelsea thought it was an ongoing thing. I sure as fuck let her think that at the time because it gave me some satisfaction seeing the same jealousy and hurt in her eyes that she'd put in mine. Samantha called me for weeks straight trying to see me again, but I was never interested in her. I used her, and right now, I feel bad for being a complete fucking asshole for doing that.

"Hey," I say, smiling. "I'm good. You?" I need to apologise to her and then get the fuck out of here.

"I'm great. Super happy to see you here."

"Yeah, about that, I'm sorry I never returned your calls."

"It's all good. I knew it was just sex."

The door to a room just down the hall from where we're standing opens and Chelsea walks out. She comes to a halt when her eyes meet mine.

"Oh, wow," Samantha says softly. "Maybe we should get out of here."

Chelsea's lips pull together in a harsh line as she stares at me. The fact she's not happy makes my fucking day, but the fact I'm having another fucking encounter with her doesn't. I'm fucking wrecked from all the run-ins we've had this week.

When Samantha takes hold of my arm, Chelsea zeroes in on that before continuing on her way across the hall to what appear to be lockers. My feet are glued to the floor as I track her movements, not hearing a word of what Samantha's saying.

Chelsea retrieves something from the locker and then goes back into the room she came from.

"Mason, are you listening to me?" Samantha says.

I look at her. "I've gotta go."

Without waiting for her response, I leave the day spa and head to the hotel bar. I need a fucking drink. A strong one.

I order a whisky double and am almost finished it when a text hits my phone.

Chelsea: *I don't believe you, Mason. Have you fucked us all this week?*

What the fuck?

I stare at her text. It's the first one she's sent me in months, and it makes no fucking sense.

I should ignore it, put my phone away, and go home, but I've never been able to help myself when it comes to Chelsea.

Me: What the fuck are you talking about?

Chelsea: You fucked me on Monday. You were with some other woman earlier today according to Facebook, and now you're with Samantha. Were you even faithful to me while we were together?

It's that last question that does it. That causes me to shove my stool backwards, throw the rest of my drink down my throat, and stalk back to the fucking day spa. That causes me to push my way into the room Chelsea disappeared into after she saw me. That causes me to tell the staff member with her to fuck off and leave us alone.

Chelsea's eyes go wide as the woman exits the room. She jerks up out of the spa she's sitting in. I catch a glimpse of her body before she covers it with a towel, and fuck if that doesn't make me crave another taste of her.

"What the hell are you doing?" she demands, looking as livid as I feel.

My fucking chest might explode with the anger she's caused. "Was I even fucking faithful to you? Where the hell do you get off on asking me that shit?"

"For all I know, you weren't," she yells. "I mean, if you were happy enough to fuck me this week and then be with two women today, it makes me wonder—"

"What the fuck makes you think I was with two women today?"

"I fucking saw the photo of you and that woman on

Facebook! And then there you were with the woman you slept with right after we broke up."

"So automatically that makes me a fucking cheater, does it?"

"I don't know, Mason! But it sure makes me wonder."

I close the distance between us, gripping her arm. "I never once fucking cheated on you." The words breathe out of me like fucking fire. "Don't ever fucking say that to me again."

She rips her arm out of my hold. "Don't fucking touch me. I don't need any more of your marks on me."

My eyes go to her neck, and I feel immense fucking pleasure to see the faint bite marks of mine still there. It makes no sense, but I do. It also makes no sense that I move into her and take hold of her neck as I growl, "They look good on you, princess."

Heat flares in her eyes and her breathing speeds up. Her hands move to my chest as she says, "They don't belong there."

"That might be the fucking case," I say, running my tongue down her neck, getting that taste of her I want, "but that doesn't mean they don't suit you."

She grips my T-shirt as a moan falls from her lips. "Mason, no."

"No?" I bite her. "You're gonna have to try harder to sound convincing."

She brings a hand to my neck, curling her fingers around it, digging them the fuck in, exactly how I fucking like. I lift my head and our eyes meet as she drops her hand and says, "I don't want you anymore."

Fuck that. She's still full of shit.

I snap my hand out and grab hers, yanking her back

to me roughly. Her gasp makes its way to my dick, as does the way her body arches into mine. "You want me more than you want your fucking husband. Tell me that's not true." It's a demand, and it rages out of me with every beat of the anger rolling through me.

She stares at me, another lie about to leave her tongue. "I don't w—"

My lips smash down onto hers.

I need to silence that fucking lie.

My kiss is unforgiving. It's filled with every shitty emotion she made me feel by accusing me of not being faithful. If there's one fucking thing I was, it was fucking loyal.

By the time I'm finished with her lips, her hands are all over me. They're under my shirt. They're in my pants. They're desperate for more. But fuck if I'm giving her that this time.

I let her go and step back.

Running my eyes over her, I spit out, "You want me, Mayfair, but you're not fucking having me. I was faithful to you every second we were together, but you took that and fucking trashed it. Now I don't even want to look at you, let alone fuck you."

I turn to leave, absolutely fucking ravaged by this encounter.

"I deserve the hurt you're hurling at me, Mason, but I don't deserve the hate," she says as I walk away. "We're done now. I won't do this with you again."

I stop, but I don't turn back to face her.

I process what she says and then I keep going.

Yeah, we're fucking done.

12

CHELSEA

I apply sunscreen to my legs as I watch my husband dive into our pool. The November heat has been almost as unbearable as Joe the last few weeks. Between pressuring me to quit my job, signing me up for interview after interview, forcing me to attend political events, and insisting on having more control over my wardrobe and calendar than I prefer, I'm unsure how I've made it through without stabbing him in the eyes. The only answer I have for that is wine, and that's just one more point of contention between us. That, and our sex life. Joe's need for me is increasing at an alarming rate. That doesn't thrill me. But if there's one thing I'm learning about my husband, it's that fighting back does actually work at times. He doesn't win every battle, and that's the way I'm going to keep it.

After that last awful encounter with Mason at the day spa a month ago, I've tried to find a way to settle into my marriage, to make the most of a bad situation, but Joe has made that impossible. His possessiveness and need for control are suffocating. Somehow, though, I've managed to keep up the façade of a happy marriage when we're in the public eye, and while my father's approval ratings have taken a hit thanks to those shitty policies I told him about, the public can't get enough of my marriage. And of Joe. He already had a public presence because of his family; his ties to my father have magnified that presence. The only good thing about this is the fact my father is extremely happy with me at the moment. It seems my marriage has helped him more than he thought it would. Go me.

I finish with the sunscreen and relax into the sunlounger while Joe swims laps. He's a machine when it comes to physical activity, swimming and running every day as well as working out in our home gym. If I actually liked him, I'd acknowledge his muscles are impressive. Instead, all I see is the kind of strength that is beginning to scare me.

Trying to take my mind off him, I scroll Facebook. I'm not really paying attention, though, and am quickly bored by memes and photos of food.

I'm saved by a text from Alexa.

Alexa: Wanna have a girls' day next week? We could get our hair done and then go for cocktails.

Me: I'm free Tuesday afternoon.

Alexa: Perfect! I'll take the afternoon off. I'm gonna send you a hairstyle I think would look amazing on you.

An image comes through and I check it out. It's a shorter, more layered style than I have now.

Me: Ooh, I really like this.

Alexa: Right?! Your hair's so long now and it's been ages

since you had a change. I was thinking if you cut this to just below your shoulders it'd look amazing.

Me: Book it in!

Alexa: OK, what's happened to my friend? And who are you?

Me: What?

Alexa: You never make spontaneous decisions like this.

Me: A girl can change. I'm doing it. God knows I need a change in my life.

Alexa: Gah. I'm excited!

Me: Are you changing yours too or just getting a cut?

Alexa: IDK. Still looking for inspo.

Me: OK, I'll look too.

Alexa: Perfect. Lock in Tuesday. I'll try to get appointments for us at 2:00 p.m.

Me: Sounds good. I've gotta go, Joe's just come back.

Alexa: Hope you guys are having a great weekend xx

"Are you going in?" Joe asks as he joins me and dries off.

I shake my head. "I don't feel like swimming today."

Sitting on the sunlounger next to me, he faces me and runs his gaze over my body before eyeing the photo on my phone. "What's that?"

I glance at it. "Oh, a new hairstyle I'm going to get on Tuesday."

He reaches for the phone and looks at the image before passing it back to me. "I don't want you to cut your hair."

"What?" I heard what he said, but it stunned me into shock. Surely he doesn't think he gets a say in my hairstyle. I should know by now, though, that he thinks he gets a say in everything to do with me.

"I like your hair the way it is. Don't cut it." He says this so finally, like he's done with the conversation and expects no argument from me.

I stare at him. I want to punch him. I've never felt the kind of wild energy that's pumping through my muscles right now. Not even when I had my angriest fights with Mason did I feel this intensity of desire to lash out.

I'm about to let loose on him when he receives a call.

Keeping his eyes on me, he answers it. "I'm around the back of the house. Come down the side gate."

My lips press together. So much for getting into it with him.

He ends the call and moves off his sun-lounger to sit on the edge of mine. Leaning over me so he can rest one hand on the other edge, he traces a finger along the top of my bikini bottom. The shiver that runs through me is not from desire.

"That glare you're giving me leads me to believe we're going to have a problem with your hair." His finger dips under the edge of my bikini. "Are we?"

I curl my fingers around his wrist, stopping his progress. "I'm not fucking you now, Joe."

"We don't have anything else on this afternoon."

"You've got someone here to see you."

"That won't take long."

The sound of someone approaching draws my attention, and I almost jump at the sight of Griff and Mason. My heart speeds up as I lock eyes with Mason. I hate that he's walked in on us while Joe has his hand in my bikini.

I attempt to push Joe's hand away, but he fights me, keeping it right where it is as he looks up at them. "Give me a minute."

Griff nods while Mason turns and walks back towards the gate they came through.

Joe finally removes his hand and leans his face to mine. "I'll be back in a minute. I expect you to have come to your senses by then."

With that, he stands and leaves me to speak with Griff.

I risk a glance in Mason's direction. He's standing near the gate with his back to us. He's tense; I can tell by the way his shoulders look like they're carved from stone.

We haven't spoken since the day spa. I've seen him a few times when he's shown up at the house to see Joe, but I do my best not to run into him. It kills me not to see him, but we both need this. That last encounter proved that to me. The hurtful things we said to each other were awful.

I can't sit here a second longer. Not with Joe determined to come back and force his demands on me, and not with Mason's thunder rolling in over me.

Moving off the lounger, I grab my phone and cut across the lawn to slip inside the house. I run up to the bedroom and change out of my bikini into a dress before grabbing my car keys and bag, and heading out to the garage.

Five minutes later, I'm on my way to my office when Joe calls.

"Where are you?" he says, sounding less than impressed with me.

"I remembered I have some work to catch up on. I'm going into the office."

Silence for a beat. And then— "How long will you be?"

"I don't know. A few hours maybe."

Silence again, before he says, "Don't forget we have that dinner to attend tonight."

"I remember." Does he think I don't know how to use the fucking brain I was born with?

"We'll leave at six thirty."

The line goes dead and I exhale a long breath.

I wish weekends didn't exist. They used to be my favourite part of the week; now I want to cut them from my calendar.

∽

I WORK in peace for a few hours, not hearing one peep out of Joe. I pack up my work and head home at four thirty, surprised to find two cars at our house that I don't recognise. I wasn't aware Joe was expecting visitors.

When I enter the house, the buzz of people talking is the first thing I take in. The second thing is Joe's eyes as he looks up at me from the kitchen island when I walk in. The third is the hard set of those eyes and the ominous vibe surrounding him.

"Hi," the man with Joe says, extending his hand. "I'm Matthew Ronson."

I stare at him, allowing the feelings of distrust swirling all around me to settle in deep. I'm learning to go with my gut these days, and right now, my gut is telling me that none of this is good. Matthew Ronson is standing in front of me dressed in his expensive suit, with his perfectly styled hair and overpriced watch, running his gaze over me like he's assessing every inch of me, and I know not one good thing is going to come from knowing him.

"And?" I ask. I'm past being nice to these assholes.

Joe's lips press together. "Chelsea," he warns.

My eyes cut to his. "What's going on, Joe? I thought we were going out to dinner tonight."

"We are. Matt's just running through some stuff with me."

"What stuff?" I don't usually ask him about his work, but I'm not getting the feeling this is about his work. I want to know who Matthew Ronson is and why he's in my house when I was not expecting him. I mean, the last thing Joe said to me earlier was that we had nothing on today, so he wasn't intending on seeing Matthew at that point.

"We're planning for a trip next week," Joe says, and I know by his tone that there's a whole lot more about this trip that I need to know. That dark, ominous vibe won't let up.

"I wasn't aware you had plans to go away next week."

Before he can respond, a woman appears in the kitchen and looks at me. "Oh good, you're home. We're ready for you to take a look at the clothes."

I frown at her. "What clothes?"

She returns my frown. "The ones for your appearances."

My gut churns with unease. I look at Joe and find him watching me intently. I don't know what the hell is going on here, but I'm a thousand percent sure I'm not going to like it. "A word?" I say to him before turning on my heel and walking into the library.

"What's going on?" I demand once we're alone.

"I made some changes to your father's schedule. He'll be travelling up the coast next week to drum up support."

"And?" I know that's not all he has to tell me.

"And you'll be coming with us."

That ominous sensation coils right through me as I process this. As I process Joe's dark expression.

Gathering every ounce of strength I have, I say, "I have work next week, Joe. I won't be going with you."

"I've arranged for you to take the week off."

"Really? And how did you do that?" As the words leave my mouth, I know it's a dumb question. My husband has his ways to get everything he wants, and if he wants me to have a week off, he'll have found a way to make that happen.

"I called Martin." My boss. "He was more than happy to accommodate your father."

My chest fills with anger to the point I need to take quicker, shorter breaths just to get oxygen in. How fucking dare he!

I cross my arms. "I'm in the middle of a huge project at work, one I can't just take a week off from. And certainly not at short notice."

"Martin wasn't concerned."

"Well *I* am," I snap. "I won't do this. And I don't appreciate you making these kinds of decisions for me."

His nostrils flare. "These are decisions necessary for your father, Chelsea. Necessary for the family. You *will* do this and you won't fucking argue about it."

I take a step towards him. Dumb. With the way he's looking at me, I should be taking a step away from him. "I *will* fucking argue about it. I'm not taking a week off work."

He turns silent for a moment.

Just watching me.

Preparing to strike.

"Remember why you entered this marriage," he says, so low and menacingly that it makes me pay attention.

His veiled threat snakes through my veins.

I feel sick.

He means every word of what he's not saying.

My silence is my answer, and he knows it.

"You have a new wardrobe of clothes to try on. Confirm they fit and then choose one of the dresses to wear tonight." He pauses, working his jaw. "The next time you decide to leave when we're in the middle of something, don't. I don't appreciate being walked out on." He bends his mouth to my ear. "And if I want to touch you or kiss you or fuck you in front of your ex, I fucking will."

He stalks out of the library, the power he's just claimed radiating from every pore of him.

I double over after he's gone, grabbing the chair to hold myself up.

When will this all end?

And will I even survive it?

13

GUNNAR

"You look even more pissed off than the last time I saw you, and that's saying something," Louise says on Saturday night when I see her at Scott's place. Scott invited a few of us over for poker. Harlow invited the old ladies and Louise, something she's done a few times over the last month since that first barbecue where we met.

She's sitting next to me on Scott's back deck, and I look at her, taking a moment to let my eyes run down her body. Damn, she's hot, but fuck if I can get my dick interested. I've tried. My sex life is fucking ruined after Chelsea. After that night I fucked her in her library. "Nothing a few drinks won't fix," I say, not believing a word of it. The mood I'm in is gonna take more than a few drinks to shift. Seeing Chelsea with Hearst by their pool today ensured that. If I ever have to fucking watch him with his hand down her pants again, I'll fucking make it so his hands are broken and unable to fucking work.

Louise looks at me knowingly. "I think we both know

a few drinks isn't going to do it, Gunnar. You might not have told me about her, but I know what it looks like when a guy's trying to forget a girl."

I scrub a hand over my face. "It's that fucking obvious?"

She smiles. "Yeah."

I shake my shoulders and arms, trying like fuck to rid myself of the shitty energy pulsing through me. "Okay, well maybe I underestimated how many drinks it's gonna take."

She leans in close, that smile teasing me and making me wish like hell I could get my dick on board with her. "I've had a crappy day, too. Let's get fucked up together."

I jerk my chin at her. "What's your poison?"

"I'm a bourbon girl. You?"

"I fucking knew I liked you. We can start with the bottle I brought."

"And when we run out?" she says suggestively.

Fuck, this may not be my best idea. Her eyes are telling me she doesn't give a fuck if I'm still getting over another chick. I like Louise; I don't want to fuck with her, and right now, I'd be fucking with her if I took this any further.

I'm saved from answering that when Blade and Layla arrive, drawing everyone's attention.

"Hot damn, woman," Madison says to her sister-in-law. "Pregnancy suits you. You're glowing."

They announced their pregnancy last month. From memory, they were three months then.

Layla smiles, her hand going to her stomach. "I feel like I'm glowing. If this is what pregnancy is like, I'll happily do it again."

Blade watches her silently. I don't know him well, but from what I've seen, he fucking adores her.

"I didn't glow," Madison says. "I was irritable for nine straight months and felt like a whale."

"You weren't a whale," Harlow says. And then with a cheeky smile, she says, "But you were a little snappy."

"A little?" J says, earning him a smack from his old lady.

Madison looks at him. "I can't have been too bad. You're doing your best to knock me up again."

"Have you seen your tits while you're pregnant?" he says. "Baby, I'd make you pregnant permanently if I could."

Madison rolls her eyes, but she leans into him and hooks her hand around his neck before kissing him.

I push my chair back and stand. "Bourbon and Coke?" I say to Louise.

She looks at me. "Perfect. Thanks."

I head inside to make the drinks and have just located the bourbon when Scott comes into the kitchen. "I'm gonna need you to make a trip next week," he says.

"Where?"

"Up the coast. Security for Novak."

I stop what I'm doing and give him my full attention. "The fuck for?" Scott knows my history with this motherfucker; surely he knows that sending me to fucking watch over him is the worst choice he could make.

He looks regretful. "He's attending a heap of functions throughout the week, and Hearst wants extra eyes on them. He's asked me to send two men. It'll be you and Griff. And trust me, I'd send someone else if I could, but you're the best for that job. I can't afford for this to be fucked up. We've got too much heat on us, and I need Novak to keep helping us with that."

I want to say no, but I won't. Not to anything that'll help the club. "When do we leave?"

"Tomorrow. Their first event is tomorrow night. You'll need to be ready to leave with them by lunch."

"Any idea what the fuck he's tied up in that he fucking needs us as security?"

"No idea, but watch your back, brother."

I head out to the deck and pass Louise her drink. Taking a sip of mine, I say, "Change of plans. I've gotta leave after this drink."

I don't miss the disappointment in her eyes. "Everything okay?"

"Yeah, just some work I've gotta take care of tomorrow. The kind that a hangover won't be any good for."

"Maybe we could get together for a drink next week sometime."

"I'll be away all week."

"Oh, okay. Well, maybe when you get back."

I'm still fucking hopeful my dick will wake the fuck up soon, so I nod. "Yeah."

A month of no encounters with Chelsea hasn't achieved what I hoped it would. I thought keeping right the fuck away from her would help me move on, but it hasn't. The few times I've seen her while seeing Hearst hasn't helped. What I need is to get off the roster of doing his dirty work. I'll do this week with Novak and then I'll tell Griff I'm done. Thank fuck Chelsea won't be anywhere close next week; after seeing her today, she's in my veins, and I need her the fuck out.

14

CHELSEA

I slip a white camisole top over my head and pair it with a pair of eggplant high-rise wide-leg crop pants that tie in the front. Strappy nude heels finish the outfit, and I stand back to assess myself. I've curled my hair and left it out, but that's the only thing Joe's going to be happy with. He'll likely take issue with the rest, but I'm feeling like fighting this battle today since it'll probably be the only battle I'll bother with for the next seven days. And I intend to win it. I need to start this trip off with a win under my belt because God knows the rest of the trip is going to slay me.

"Are you ready?" he says, coming into our bedroom.

I reach for my purse. "Yes."

He stops and takes in my appearance. "What happened to the dress you were going to wear?"

"I changed my mind." I stand tall, refusing to shrink under his dominance.

"Change."

"I'm not changing, Joe. I want to be comfortable this afternoon before all the events start."

"Chelsea, from the minute we step out of the car at the hotel this afternoon, everything starts. I want you in that dress from that minute."

"There's nothing wrong with what I'm wearing."

He takes that in, turning silent while he does. "Are you planning on arguing with me for the entire week? Because if you are, I'd think again. There's a reason for absolutely every outfit that's been chosen, for every speech that's been written, and for every appearance we make."

I square my shoulders. "Perhaps if you didn't treat me like a fucking child, I'd argue a whole lot less. Has that ever occurred to you?"

His lips pull into a line. "Be in the car in five minutes."

He stalks out of the bedroom and I let my shoulders slump. I might have won this round, but it doesn't feel like I've won anything. It feels like I surrendered a long time ago and am now just slogging through hell.

Deep breath.

You. Can. Do. This.

I walk outside to where Joe's talking to his two security guys next to the Range Rovers we're driving up to the Sunshine Coast in. We'll swing by and pick Mum and Dad up on the way. When I asked why we weren't flying, Joe informed me that it made sense to drive considering all the day trips to smaller regional towns they'll be making.

Joe's eyes meet mine at the same time I hear the rumble of bikes. Turning, I see two motorbikes pull into the drive, my heart kicking over as I realise Mason's on one of them.

I look back at Joe and find him watching me intently. His face is like stone.

Mason and Griff cut their engines and make their way to Joe, who snaps, "You're late." He looks at Mason. "And your services aren't needed." Looking back at Griff, he says, "Replace him with someone else." Holy hell, the animosity vibrating from my husband is darker than anything I've seen from him. And Mason's standing there throwing the same back. His eyes are hidden behind dark glasses, so I can't see them, but everything else about him screams hostility and anger.

Griff's jaw clenches. "We're not fucking late and I'm not replacing him. We matched your request with the best member for the job."

"You have a whole fucking club of men, Griff," Joe says. "Find someone else."

Griff steps forward, not backing down an inch. "When someone requests security from our club, it's for a good fucking reason, so that tells me you're not tied up in anything good. You want protection, I'm gonna make damn fucking sure you get it. Mason's road name wasn't given to him by mistake."

I remember when I asked Mason why his road name is Gunnar. He told me he was given the name after the club saw him fight. The name means fighter, soldier, attacker. Or bold warrior, which is my favourite. Those two words personify Mason.

Joe's pissed off with Griff, but he doesn't argue any further. "I requested you to wear suits."

Griff nods. "We have them."

"Change in the house. Maria will show you where. And put your bikes in the garage."

I stare at my husband. Am I in a fucking alternative universe here? He's hired bikers for protection and he's ordering them to wear suits. What is actually going on?

Mostly, though, I'm trying to wrap my head around the fact Mason's going to be with us for a week. Joe might be pissed about that, but I'm anxious. With each passing second that I process this information, an increasing amount of panic is settling in. Mason and I struggle to be in the same room without wanting to either fight, kiss, or tear each other's clothes off. Throwing us together in close proximity like this, with my husband never taking his eyes off me, is a recipe for disaster.

"Chelsea," Joe says as Griff and Mason leave us to get changed. "We're in this car."

I get in the car he indicates and take a moment to calm myself before he joins me. I thought I was ready for this trip. I thought I'd mentally prepared to deal with the asshole I'm married to. That prep work is all out the window now that Mason's here. I am so far from ready for this trip it isn't funny.

Five or so minutes pass, during which I focus on my breathing. When I eye Mason exiting the house in a black suit, I practically stop breathing. He's all hard angles, thunder clouds, and raw masculinity. I'm attracted to him, end of story, but there's something about him wearing a suit with his tattoos and bad attitude that calls to me. That gets me all fucking bothered. And right now, bothered in this way is not something I need to be.

Joe directs him and Griff to where he wants them, and I track Mason's ass as he gets in the other Range Rover.

Joe slides into the seat next to me and Griff gets in the front of our car. Mason and Griff are the drivers, while Joe's security guys take the front passenger seats in each car. Again, I think of what Griff said about Joe being tied up in something bad. And I'm reminded of the conversation I overheard between Joe and his father last month where his father asked him to commit a crime.

Just who am I married to?

As Griff reverses out of the driveway, Joe hands me a folder. "Study this. It's everything you need to know for tonight's function."

I open the folder and take in the information about each of the men who'll be at the dinner tonight. "Why do I need to know all this?" He's never asked me to study this kind of information before. I've never had anything to do with convincing people to donate. My job is simply to wear a fucking dress, have my hair out, and smile all night while pretending to love the hell out of my husband and support my father.

"For once, Chelsea, can you please just fucking do what I say without asking me a thousand fucking questions."

I look at him. Like, really look at him. He's tense. Rattled over something. So unlike the man I've come to know over the last four months who's all cool and held together.

Interesting.

"Fine," I snap. "Honestly, though, if you wanted a doormat, you married the wrong girl." Yep, suddenly feeling frisky.

"I didn't want a doormat, but I do want a wife who trusts me and does what I say."

"Perhaps you should go back to school, dear husband, because you just defined a fucking doormat."

His hand clamps around my wrist tightly. "I've had enough of you today." The words fall from his lips low and harsh and contain one of his warnings that I know not to ignore. "Just read the fucking file."

I pull my wrist from his hold and bury my gaze in the file. I'll read it all right. I'll memorise the shit out of it, because if I know my husband, I know there'll likely be a pop fucking quiz on it later. And not passing his damn quiz is something I don't want to do. Not when he's on edge like this.

15

GUNNAR

Christ, this is fucked up. I don't know why I hadn't clued on to the fact Chelsea and her fucking husband would be travelling with her father this week. I'd assumed that because she works, she wouldn't be on this trip. If there's one fucking thing Chelsea's taught me, it's that I should never fucking assume anything.

We picked up her parents after leaving her place and then drove to the hotel we're staying at tonight. Hearst's security guy who I'm with is a fucking dick. He seems pissed that Griff and I are here. It's the only thing we have in common. If I make it through this week without punching him, it'll be a fucking miracle.

"Tom and I will watch from the stage while Novak gives his speech," the dickhead says to Griff and me before the dinner starts. "You two keep watch from the door."

Griff nods. He's just as annoyed to be on this trip as I

am. Not that he's said it, but I know his tells after working closely with him for years.

"You doing okay?" Griff asks after they leave us.

I run my gaze over the crowd filling the room. "Don't worry about me, brother. I can handle these assholes."

"It's not them I'm worried about."

I look at him. He's watching me closely; he knows the deal here. "Yeah, me either," I admit. There's no point trying to fool Griff.

"You think you'll last the week?"

"I'll do my fucking best."

I catch sight of Chelsea and Hearst walking our way and wish I fucking didn't. That long red dress she's wearing that hugs her tits and waist sends me close to the edge of insanity. It's Hearst's hand in hers, though, that pushes me right to the edge. The motherfucker holds her like he fucking owns her.

His eyes meet mine, and I don't miss the smug look of satisfaction. He might not have wanted me here, but he's sure as fuck making the most of it.

Chelsea doesn't look at me or acknowledge me in any way as they glide past us. She hasn't made eye contact with me since I arrived at her place earlier today. It pisses me off that she ignores me, and then that fucking pisses me off too.

We said we were fucking done. I need to get myself on fucking board with that.

Novak and his wife walk past, drawing my attention from their daughter. Griff moves next to me after Novak enters the room. "I'm gonna keep an eye on things outside."

I nod, and we move into our positions. I haven't seen

anyone suspect looking yet, but assholes can hide in suits, behind smiles, so who the fuck knows who's already here.

Three hours pass without incident. Three long fucking hours where I wonder how I'll get through more of these events. I struggle to keep my eyes off Chelsea. Every time I think I'm good, there she fucking is, popping up talking to another person here. She's got this schmoozing thing mastered. It's no wonder her father uses her at these things.

When it's time for them to leave, Griff and I follow them to the lifts, staying at the back of the group and keeping an eye out for threats.

Hearst places his hand to the small of Chelsea's back and guides her into the lift. Watching the two of them together tonight has been hell. They're sickeningly fucking sweet with each other, something the public laps up.

"I'll go up with them. You stay with Novak," Griff says. He's a smart fucking man.

Chelsea's eyes finally meet mine as the lift door closes, and I'm fucking annoyed with myself for feeling something when they do.

How fucking long will it take to stop wanting her?

~

WE'RE UP EARLY the next morning and on the road by 7:00 a.m. Novak has appearances throughout the day on the Sunshine Coast, and then this afternoon, we're heading up to Gympie for a dinner tonight.

We make it through the day without any problems

and check into the Gympie motel just before 3:00 p.m. Novak and Hearst hole up in a room together. I overhear Hearst telling Chelsea they aren't to be interrupted under any circumstance as they have a lot of stuff to go over. She appears to barely pay any attention to him. She then disappears into the room next door.

Hearst's security guys stay outside the motel rooms while Griff and I check the outside perimeter of the motel. We've been out here for an hour when he says, "I've gotta make a call. I'll be back soon."

He leaves me with my thoughts, which I'm trying like fuck to ignore. It's a good thing this week is heavy on activity; it'll help keep me focussed on something other than those thoughts.

I'm in the middle of telling myself to shut my damn brain off when Chelsea exits the motel and walks in the opposite direction of where I am. She's wearing her running clothes, and I'm fucking wondering who approved her to go running when her husband seems dead fucking set on keeping eyes on the family at all times. The fact no one is with her forces me to check in on her, something I'd rather not fucking do.

"Chelsea," I call as I head in her direction.

She stops but doesn't turn to look at me. Not straight away. I'm halfway to her when she finally turns.

"Where are you going?" I ask when I reach her.

"For a run."

"Hearst know about this?"

She scowls. "I'm not asking him. You heard him. He doesn't want to be interrupted."

I have no fucking clue why she's scowling at me all pissed off when all I did was ask her a question. "Yeah, but you can bet your ass he wouldn't want you out here by yourself."

"Well that's too fucking bad for him."

I work my jaw. "What's with the attitude, Mayfair? I'm just trying to do my fucking job here."

She looks away for a moment before bringing her eyes back to mine. "You need to go home, Mason."

I agree with her, but it pisses me off that she thinks I can just do that. If it wasn't for her fucking father and husband, I wouldn't have to be here in the first place. "Trust me, I fucking wish I could, but I can't. So how about you do me a fucking favour and go back inside?"

Her glare could kill a man. "For fuck's sake, fine," she snaps before stalking away from me, back into the motel.

I watch her go, trying like fuck to keep my eyes off her ass and failing.

It's going to be a long fucking week.

16

CHELSEA

I slam the door to my room behind me as I stalk in after leaving Mason. My body is filled with angry energy that I need to get out, and he's just killed my attempt at that. I know he's just doing his job, but still, I'm annoyed with him for stopping me.

Really, though, I'm pissed off with Joe and just taking it out on Mason. It's safer to take it out on him; Joe is far too unpredictable to keep arguing with.

Stripping out of my running gear, I find my swimmers. I'll do laps of the pool instead.

Ten minutes later, I'm in the pool and finally able to zone out and just focus on physical activity.

I don't know how long I've been swimming when I look up and find Joe standing at the end of the pool watching me. Stopping, I pull off my goggles and look at him, waiting for him to speak.

"You need to get ready for dinner. We have to leave in forty minutes." His body language and tone let me know how unimpressed he is to find me out here.

I nod and lift myself out of the pool, ignoring the way Joe's eyes rake over my body. He doesn't make a move to walk with me, and when I'm almost at the pool gate, he says, "We won't be having a repeat of last night, Chelsea."

I miss taking a breath as my feet slow.

I refused to fuck him last night and he wasn't happy about it.

Glancing back at him, I say, "Are you going to be nice to me tonight?" The fire I'm playing with is far too hot, but damn if I'm going to let him force me into this. Sex has been the one area in our relationship that he hasn't truly forced yet. Sure, I've slept with him when I didn't want to, but we've never had non-consensual sex. However, I'm no fool. Joe's edgy at the moment, and I sense he's close to breaking point with me. I'm worried the bedroom might be the place that happens, so I'm staying vigilant and trying not to show my fear. The minute he sees that is the minute every last scrap of power transfers to him.

He doesn't answer me. Instead, he closes the distance between us and says, "You're my wife and I expect you to act like one."

I bite my tongue. Like, literally bite it. That doesn't work, though. "And you're a fucking asshole. Honestly, this marriage could have gone in a whole different direction. You could have played nice and I would have too, and we could have had all the sex you ever wanted."

His eyes flash with fury. "That would never have happened. Not when you still want that fucking biker."

"Maybe I wouldn't still want that biker if my husband had made me fall in love with him."

"You're playing a dangerous fucking game here, Chelsea."

"I know. And maybe I'll keep playing it because either way, I'm screwed."

His jaw clenches. "You need to go and get ready."

"Yeah, I do."

I turn and continue to our room, taking deep, steadying breaths as I walk. God knows I need them after that. I try hard not to show my fear of Joe, but my husband scares me more than I care to admit.

After growing up with a father who hit me, I swore I'd never be with a man like him, and yet here I am. Living with a monster who I know I haven't fully met. I might tell Joe I'll keep playing this dangerous game, but deep down, in the places I've relegated my terror to, I falter every time he comes near.

My husband does not love me, and in my darkest moments when I allow myself to acknowledge it, I'm terrified of what the monster might do.

∽

THE NEXT TWO days pass by in a blur of engagements. They also pass by with me in a state of "what the hell is my life." Between my husband's moods and Mason's hostility that I can feel even though we're barely near each other, I'm all over the place, flustered and annoyed. Dad's the only one actually being nice to me, which only serves to confuse me more. It's like the universe took all my manifesting I've been doing for months and decided to send me a big "fuck you" instead. Like it decided I need to walk across fire some more before it decides which way my life should go.

Thursday rolls around and I wake up exhausted.

Physically and mentally.

I don't want to do this anymore.

Joe's nowhere to be seen, which pleases me and gives me some much-needed breathing space.

I take a long shower before dressing and doing my make-up and hair. Joe returns to the room as I'm finishing up with my hair. We've not spoken a great deal since Monday afternoon by the pool. We also haven't had sex. That actually keeps me on edge rather than making me happy. Joe acting not like Joe causes me alarm. I'm waiting for the penny to drop as to why he's acting this way.

"Change of plans for today," he says. "We've cancelled lunch so your father and I can take care of something. You and your mother will meet us in Rockhampton this afternoon."

Today is shaping up to be my favourite day this week. "Okay."

I continue fiddling with my hair.

"One other thing," he says, and I still, knowing by the commanding tone of his voice that I'm not going to like it. "Things are going so well that your father's moving up the timeline for the start of his campaign."

"And?" I hold my breath. It's what he's not saying that is important here.

The penny finally drops as he says, "He wants you full-time on this."

I stare at him. "What?"

"You heard me, Chelsea."

"You're serious?"

He looks at me like he has very little patience left for me. "I'm always serious. You should know that by now."

I feel like I'm trying desperately to suck air in through a straw. Like I can't get the oxygen I need fast enough. He's telling me I have to quit my job, and I know that neither he nor my father will accept anything less than my compliance. They'll threaten Mason and his club. Their winning card for every game we play that they refuse to lose.

I press my lips together hard as I allow my hatred to consume me.

It rages through me like a savage storm.

Howling, gusting, violent.

"I fucking hate you. I'll give you what you want because you'll only threaten Mason and the club again if I don't, but just know that this changes everything between us. *Everything*."

"This changes nothing between us, Chelsea. Don't be dramatic."

My anger seeps from my chest to my veins, to my muscles, to my bones. It fills every inch of me so deeply I won't ever be able to rid myself of it. I want to lash out. I want to pummel my fists into his face and his chest and his entire fucking body. How anyone can be so cruel and controlling is beyond me.

"It does, Joe. Every-fucking-thing." I grab my purse and phone and stalk to the door.

"Where are you going?"

I look back at him. "Out. I need to get as far away from you as possible."

"Chelsea," he starts, but I cut him off.

"No. Fuck you. I'm going out, and you're not fucking stopping me. I'll see you in Rockhampton this afternoon."

With that, I yank the door open and exit in a furious rush of energy.

I fucking hate him.

I've never fucking hated anyone like I hate him.

I blindly run past the cars parked in the motel car park, my mind in such a mess that I pay no attention to anyone or anything. It's not until I reach the road outside the motel and run smack bang into a hard chest that my awareness of the world around me returns.

Strong hands grip my biceps and steady me at the same time Mason's deep voice rumbles, "The fuck are you going in such a hurry?"

I look up at him, struggling to push my asshole husband and what he's forcing me to do from my brain. Yanking out of his hold, I try to move past him.

"I asked you a fucking question, Chelsea. I expect a fucking answer."

I spin to face him, angered that he sounds just like Joe with his goddamn expectations. "You wanna talk to me like that, Mason, you can shove your fucking expectations. You're not getting an answer."

His eyes darken and he comes closer to me. "What the fuck has gotten into you?"

I throw up my arms. "All of you! You've all gotten into me." I push him away because he's too fucking close. "So do me a favour and leave me the hell alone!"

His hand flicks out and he snaps it around my wrist as I attempt to walk away from him. Leaning in close, he says, "Leaving you the hell alone is exactly what I want to do, Mayfair. Un-fucking-fortunately I'm fucking stuck here, and if I don't keep you safe, my club'll have my ass. So get yours the fuck back inside and give me a fucking break for once."

I glare at him, anger and hate rolling through me. "I can't believe I ever loved you."

His lips smash together and his breaths come harder as he stares at me. "That fucking makes two of us."

He releases me and steps away, watching me with a hard look that roars just how much he wants me out of his sight. I hate that he's looking at me like that, and I hate the fact I hate it.

"I should just let them do what they want to you and your club," I snap before marching back into the motel.

My husband is standing on the road watching every step I take his way. His pissed-off body language and expression make it clear he watched my encounter with Mason. I don't care, though. I don't care about anything right now except showing him how fucking upset I am with his order to quit my job.

∽

IT'S A LONG DAY. Maybe the longest day of my life. Actually, no, that was my wedding day. I never want to re-live either of them.

Joe is nowhere to be seen when I arrive in Rockhampton. Neither is Mason, who left with Dad and Joe this morning. I spent the day with my mother who prattled on about some charity gala she's helping organise and a party she wants me to help her plan when we get back home. I struggle to keep up with the conversation. I want to ask her how the hell she can stay married to a man like my father. I haven't spoken to him yet about my job, but I know he's behind this decision to force me to resign. I've seen his latest approval ratings and they've improved greatly this week. It seems the public likes a close-knit family like ours. Except we aren't and never will be. If I had my way, I'd tear us apart today. I'd scatter us far and wide and never look back. But I can't do that because that would be signing Mason's future away, and as much as I tell myself I hate Mason, I don't, and I could never allow my father to do the things to him that he's threatened.

So here I am, stuck. However, something deep inside me snapped this morning, shifting my perspective. Joe might have finally crushed my spirit, but in its place is a furious need to show them they don't fully control me. I might have to play nice most of the time, but not all the fucking time.

After I dump my suitcase in the hotel room, I head back outside to Griff, who drove Mum and I here. He's leaning against the wall of the hotel corridor, on the phone. He ends his call as soon as he sees me. "You good?" he asks.

"Yeah, are you free to drive me to the hairdresser?"

He pushes off the wall. "Sure. Now?"

I nod, and we head down to the hotel car park. Griff opens the back door of the Range Rover to let me in. I really like Griff; I always have. I met him a few times while I was with Mason, and he might give off a vibe that says "careful with me," but he's always been a gentleman to me. People assume bikers don't have that in them, but I'd choose any of the Storm men as friends over most of the men I meet in my life. They might be rough around the edges and foul-mouthed, but I trust them a hell of a lot more than I trust my father and his people.

Griff settles in the front of the car and I give him the address I want to go to. Ten minutes later, he pulls up outside it and cuts the engine. Exiting the car, he opens my door to let me out.

"You don't have to wait for me," I say. "If you give me your number, I can text you when I'm finished."

"I'll wait."

"Honestly, you don't have to. This waiting around has to be the most boring stuff you've ever had to do."

With a quick shake of his head, he says, "This is what your husband is paying me to do. I'll be right out here making sure you're safe."

"Thank you," I say and make my way inside.

"Hey, darl," the hairdresser greets me, a genuine smile plastered across her face.

I give her my name and she ushers me straight through. "What are you after today?" she says as she runs her fingers through my hair. I love that she seems to have no idea who I am. I can't go anywhere in Brisbane without people knowing me.

I pull out my phone and find the photo Alexa sent me of the style she thinks will suit me. Showing the hairdresser, who told me her name is Charity, I say, "I'm thinking something like this. What do you think?"

She assesses the photo before looking back at me. "I like it. I think it'll look great on you. We could also put some foils through to give you some more depth." She reaches for one of her hair magazines and flips to a page. "Like this."

I look at the photo she's pointing at before meeting her gaze. "I love it. Let's do it."

She grins. "I like your decisiveness." She closes the magazine. "Okay, let's do this."

I take a deep breath, not that I actually need it. At this point, it's more of an automatic reaction to doing anything I know is playing with fire. However, this might be one of the first things I've done since marrying Joe that I don't feel nervous about.

I know he's going to hate it.

I know he's going to make that super clear to me in all the ways he likes to intimidate me.

I know we're going to go to war over it.

And I welcome all those things.

I've numbed myself to just how much power I've handed over to him. I've been going through the motions of life since the day I agreed to marry him, not feeling much of anything.

It's time to feel again.

It's time to wake the hell up and take some of my power back.

That day I saw Mason outside Joe's office when we fought, was a turning point. Every time we've come together since, even if only for a brief moment, has helped peel back those layers of numb. That's what Mason does to me, what he's always done to me. He makes me feel when everyone else in my life forces me to stop. It's time to embrace all these feelings. I'm going to own them and express them. Like I told Joe, everything between us has changed, and he's not going to like the real me when he meets her.

Charity spends the next two hours working her magic

on my hair, offering me champagne and strawberries while she does that. I take it all. I can't think of anything better than day drinking today.

I check in with Alexa while waiting for the colour to be ready.

Me: I miss you.

Alexa: OMG me too! How are you?

Me: Don't ask. Today has been the worst. But I'm getting my hair done and I'm here for it.

Alexa: That style I showed you that you refused to get when we went to the hairdresser?

Me: Yes. Plus some new colour.

Alexa: I need photos when you're done! Hey, I know this is awkward, but I haven't heard from Mason. Is he okay?

Me: I think so, but we haven't really spent any time together. Joe's keeping him busy away from me.

Alexa: As in Joe's jealous?

Me: I don't know if jealous is the right word. He's a possessive asshole who thinks he owns me. He doesn't like Mason simply because we dated.

Alexa switches from texting to call me. "We need to back this up, my friend. I mean, I know your marriage was arranged, but I thought you were okay with Joe. I thought you two were getting on well, and now you're telling me he's an asshole. What's going on?"

I sip some champagne. It's my third glass and I'm feeling more relaxed than I probably should be because it means my walls are down—the walls I've had to keep up for months to protect Mason.

I've never told Alexa the real truth of my marriage, and I won't give her that today, but I'm ready to share some of it. "Joe's an asshole. I've tried to make it work with him. I'd hoped we'd be able to build a relationship together, but he's controlling, and I can't do it anymore."

"As in you're going to divorce him?" She sounds as hopeful as I am resigned to the fact that won't happen anytime soon.

"I can't divorce him. I'm stuck in this marriage until Dad's not premier anymore. Then, I can leave."

"Holy hell, Chelsea, why haven't you told me any of this?"

"Because I can't change any of it, so there's no point complaining about it. I just need to get on with it."

"Have you been drinking? You're talking a little fast like you do when you're drunk."

"Yes, the hairdresser gave me champagne, and after the day I've had, I wasn't saying no."

"What happened today?"

"Joe told me Dad wants me to resign from my job so I can work full-time with them on the campaign."

She's quiet for a moment. "You're not going to, though, are you? Like, that's a big ask."

I drain my glass. "It wasn't an ask."

More silence. "What? Wait, they're *making* you do this?"

"Yes. And I know what you're going to say, that I don't have to do anything I don't want to do, but I have no say in this. It's complicated, but trust me, I can't say no."

"This makes no sense to me."

"When I agreed to marry Joe, I agreed to this without realising it."

"And you only agreed to marry him so that Mason wouldn't go to jail," she says slowly. "So if you're still going along with what they want, that tells me you still love Mason. I fucking knew it."

God, it feels good to talk about this with her. Not that I can tell her everything, but this has all been weighing so heavily on me; I didn't realise how much I needed to get it out. "This can't go beyond us, Alexa. Promise me that. Mason can't know any of this, because if he does—"

"If he does, he'll go in swinging hard to get you back, and God knows where that will end. I know, babe. I won't repeat any of this." The sadness in her voice hits me in the chest. I try never to think about this. It's too hard. Too upsetting. But I'm feeling it all now, and it just makes me want to lash out at my father and Joe more.

"Thank you," I say softly as Charity walks my way. "I have to go, sorry."

"I love you and I'm glad you told me all this. We need to talk more about this when you get home, okay? I need you to know I'm here for you."

"I know you are, and I love you too. I'll call you when I get home."

We end the call as Charity starts checking all my foils. "Oh, this colour looks great. Come over to the basin."

She rinses the colour, gives me a treatment, cuts my hair, and styles it for me. When she's finished, I stare at myself in the mirror. My hair used to reach halfway down my back; now it falls to my shoulders in choppy layers. Charity has styled it into messy waves, something I've never tried before. I love it as much as I know Joe is going to hate it. Score one to me for the night.

Griff drives me back to the hotel in silence. When he opens my door to let me out, he says, "I like your hair like that."

He catches me by surprise. Smiling, I say, "Thank you, Griff. You don't know how much that means to me."

He watches me quietly for a beat. "I think I might."

We share a moment, I'm sure of it. Griff does a lot of work for Joe, so he must see a lot, and probably hears some of it.

I nod, but I don't say anything else before heading up to my room.

I'm met by my husband, who's sitting in the armchair in the corner of the room, holding a glass of what I presume is scotch.

"Where the fuck have you been?" he demands, standing and throwing some of the amber liquid down his throat.

I drop my purse on the bed, refusing to cower from him. Gathering my strength, I meet his gaze. "I was getting my hair cut." I touch it. "Do you like it?"

He works his jaw. "You missed a meet and greet. One that was important for you to attend."

"I wasn't aware there was one. You didn't tell me."

"You were supposed to meet me here, Chelsea. I would have told you then."

"You never told me to meet you here. This is on you, not me."

"Fuck, I shouldn't have to tell you this stuff. This is your job now. You should have been here waiting."

"Oh my God, no. That's not how this is going to work, Joe. I will quit my job. I will play happy families. I will promote Dad. But at no fucking point will I sit around and wait for your instructions. I might have given almost everything up for you two, but I still have a life, and I intend to live it."

He stares at me, looking at my hair. "I see." With that, he drains his glass, slides his suit jacket on, and says, "Get dressed. Dinner is in half an hour."

I turn and watch him cut a path to the door. "What do you see, Joe?"

He looks back at me. "I see you intend to make this harder than it needs to be."

The sound of the door clicking closed as he exits is the best damn sound of the day. However, whether I won this battle or not is yet to be seen. He may not have said anything about my hair, but if there's one thing I know about Joe, it's that he sometimes takes his time punishing me for the things he's not happy about. Who knows what'll be waiting for me later.

17

CHELSEA

"Your father told me the good news about you working full-time with him," one of the guests says to me after dinner when we're mingling with everyone. "He's lucky to have such a wonderful daughter who supports him like you do, dear."

I smile at her as Joe slips his arm over my shoulders.

"Chelsea and I love working with Mark," Joe says.

The woman's eyes light up as my husband pulls her into his web. "I heard the rumours of your good news too. I'm very excited about the future of Queensland if it's true."

I frown, unsure of what she's referring to, but I don't have time to question Joe over it because he leads me to the next lot of guests waiting to talk with us.

We spend the next hour schmoozing. It's more exhausting than normal because of the tension between Joe and me. I want to punch him rather than smile at him, and I sure as hell don't want his damn hands on me, but he's insisting on putting them on me more than normal.

It's a game we're playing.

Our new battle.

This is his way of telling me he's pissed.

"Chelsea," Dad says, joining us. "I need Joe with me now. Can you make sure you're sitting with your mother when I make the announcement?"

"The announcement?" I feel like I'm missing all the pieces of a puzzle everyone else seems to know about.

Dad opens his mouth to say something, but Matthew Ronson calls out, "Joe, now."

Joe nods and looks at me. "Go sit with your mother."

I glare at Matthew. My first impression of him was right. He's spent this week ordering me around like *he's* my damn husband. We've had a few arguments, and I see many more in our future if he sticks around and works Dad's campaign.

He shoots me a filthy look back. The feeling of dislike is mutual.

I do as my husband and father directed, taking a glass of champagne from the waiter as he comes by. Joe hates me drinking at these dinners, but tonight I'm not about pleasing him. This is my second drink and I see a third coming soon.

As I move behind my mother to take my seat at our table, my eyes meet Mason's. He's standing at the door across the room, watching me. He has his usual pissed off expression on. We haven't really spoken this week, but I know he's hated every second of it. I mean, that was a given simply because he hates Joe, but I know it has to be hard for him to watch me with Joe. I've tried to lessen the fake affection I show Joe at the functions, but it's impossible to erase it completely; it's what I'm here for. And as much as Mason acts like he hates me and wants nothing to do with me, I know from my own conflicted feelings that hate sits pretty damn close to love.

"Darling, should you really be drinking that?" Mum says, eyeing my drink and drawing my attention from Mason.

I lift the glass to my lips and take a long sip. "Absolutely. It might be the only thing to get me through this god-awful day."

Her brows knit together. "I thought today was a good day."

I think I understand my mother a whole lot more these days. If I've had to numb myself to my marriage and all it entails after only a short time, I can only imagine what she's had to do to make it through decades with my father.

"I'm glad you had a good day," I say, looking at the stage where Dad and Joe are now standing.

I sip some more champagne as I listen to what Dad says.

Halfway through his speech, I sit forward, my gut on high alert. I kind of drifted off, only half paying attention to him, but I could swear he just said something about Joe entering politics.

Surely fucking not.

That would be my worst nightmare, and I thought I was already living my worst nightmare.

Joe running for premier after Dad's finished with the position would mean many more years of a man in my life having the kind of power that could fuck with Mason and his club.

Joe smiles as the crowd cheers.

Oh God, no.

No, no, no.

"I'm excited for the future," Joe says, still with that smile of his I've come to detest. He looks at me and motions my way. "My beautiful wife will be joining us too. It's a family affair, and Mark, Chelsea, and I are determined to lead this great state into a prosperous future, one where we'll always put you first. I thank you for walking this path by our side."

I stare at him in absolute horror.

He effectively just won every battle we'll ever have, in advance. There's no doubt in my mind that my husband has the charisma and drive to win an election and to become the Premier of Queensland one day. Looking back now, I see the signs I missed from the minute I agreed to marry him. They were all there to see, and yet I fucking missed them.

The waiter swings by our table again and I grab another glass of champagne.

Fuck it, I can't do this night sober.

Not now.

"This is very exciting for you and Joe," Mum says, and I know she truly means it. My mother thinks my husband is the best thing to have ever happened to me.

I guzzle my drink. All the way down in two gulps.

I know Joe's watching me, because he's always fucking watching me, but I don't care.

Pushing my chair back, I grab my clutch and leave the table without another word to Mum. I doubt she even registers the fact I've left. My mother is in her happy little numb bubble.

Striding through the room, I smile at every person I pass, but I don't really see them. I'm on a mission and I can't achieve it fast enough.

Find the bar.

Drink a lot of drinks.

Wipe myself out.

And fuck whatever Joe does to me later for this.

18

CHELSEA

I can't feel my lips. I lift my hand to my face and squeeze my mouth and pinch my cheeks. Nope, can't feel them. I drink the rest of my champagne. I've given up counting how many I've had, but I don't think it's actually that many. After not eating much today, the alcohol went straight to my head. Which I'm fucking grateful for.

My phone vibrates with another text. It's been going off for a solid half hour. Every text is from Joe. He can't find me. I've managed to enjoy one whole hour without him. It's been bliss. I'm considering how successful I could be at running away from my life. I mean, right now, it feels achievable. I've planned how I'll do it, and I'm pretty convinced I could make it happen, but even my drunk brain knows that's the alcohol talking. There's no way Joe's ever letting me leave.

Another text comes through and I check this one.

Joe: If I have to come and find you, you won't enjoy the consequences.

I click my phone off, not wanting to read the rest of the messages, and stare up at the stars. I'm lying on the roof of the hotel. I don't doubt Joe will find me soon, but for now, I just want to stargaze like I used to with Mason.

My heart aches as I think about him. I'm drunk enough to stop pretending I hate him. I could never hate that man, not even for sleeping with my friend. Well, if he did that while we were together, I might hate him, but I know he'd never do something like that. Deep down, I know why he slept with her. And I don't blame him one little bit.

I broke his heart.

I ripped it from his body and took it with me when I left.

If he'd done that to me, I'd be just as angry and hurt as he is.

Oh God.

I wrap my arms around myself.

I hate myself for doing this to the boy I've loved since I was five. He never asked for any of this. All he ever did was love me like no one has ever loved me. And I've betrayed him twice. *Twice.*

I stand and walk to the edge of the roof. Staring out over the town, I exhale a long breath. When I left him this time, I wondered if I'd ever remove him from my soul. I know now I never will.

I've loved Mason for twenty years and I'll love him for twenty more and beyond.

I'm drowning in him and there are moments I can't breathe without him.

He's what has gotten me through my marriage so far. Knowing that every day that passes is another day closer to his safety. But tonight's revelations change everything. Now, there are going to be far too many days I can't breathe properly. Mason is at risk. My husband hates him that much, and I shudder to think what kind of power a premiership brings with it will inspire Joe to do to Mason.

The sound of the door to the rooftop opening and then slamming closed causes me to squeeze my eyes closed.

Joe's found me.

I steel myself.

"Mayfair. Fuck."

My eyes fly open.

"What the fuck are you doing up here?" Mason demands, coming closer. "Your fucking husband is losing his shit downstairs because he can't find you."

I turn to him, my heart beating faster as I drink him in.

"Goddamn, you look good in a suit." The words fall from my lips without thought before I can stop them.

He slows his pace, narrowing his eyes at me. "You're drunk?"

A smile slips across my face. "Maybe a little."

"Jesus."

I stare at his neck tattoo peeking out from his white button shirt. The tattoo I can't fully see but know off by heart because it's *my* tattoo. Hearts, and stars, and wings, and Monopoly pieces, and a stiletto, and a rose with a banner across it all that says Mayfair. It spans the width of his neck and is the most beautiful tattoo I've ever seen. He got it three weeks before I smashed his heart to pieces.

I move towards him, unable to stop myself. "I'm sorry."

He doesn't respond to that, just watches me closely as I come to him. When I reach him, he says, "Which thing are you sorry for?" His words are bitter. "Or are you just apologising for causing us all a whole lot of fucking problems by not telling Hearst where you were going?"

I trace my gaze over his face, ignoring the acid flowing from him. God, I've missed him. In the kind of way I never imagined missing someone. When I meet his eyes again, I say, "You always read me perfectly. I wasn't apologising for tonight. I was apologising for breaking your heart."

His nostrils flare. "I don't want your fucking apology."

I nod. "I know, but I'm giving it to you anyway."

"You're drunk. You don't even know what the fuck you're saying."

"No, I know exactly what I'm saying. And I know you won't believe me, but I mean every word of it."

I try to take another step closer to him, needing that, but I trip over my own damn foot.

Mason catches me, his expression darkening with anger. "Fucking hell, Chelsea."

I reach out and touch his face, my whole body feeling the effect of that touch. "Please stop being so angry with me, Mason. It's killing me. I did this all for you and will continue doing it all for you. I don't care if I have to stay with him for the rest of my life; I'll do it for you."

He frowns at the same time the rooftop door opens again. Looking beyond Mason, I see my husband walking our way, a look of pure fury on his face.

Dropping my hand from Mason, I take a step away from him.

"I've got this from here," Joe says to Mason, his words falling between them with the same kind of acid Mason left at my feet.

Mason looks at me one last time before leaving us. I don't miss the confusion in his eyes, but mostly I see that hatred of his that I don't think he'll ever let go of.

Once we're alone, Joe grips my bicep and yanks me to him. He's a raging storm, and suddenly, I feel sober. "If you ever get drunk and do this at one of our functions again, I will make you regret it, Chelsea. Am I understood?"

I fight him off, pulling out of his hold. I will not fucking allow him to intimidate me again. "You're perfectly understood, Joe. You're a fucking asshole, but I've understood that about you for a little while now."

His eyes are as hard as his voice when he growls, "Do not fucking test me tonight."

"Are we done here?"

He forces out a harsh breath as he glances out at the night. Looking back at me, he says, "Go to bed. We'll discuss this in the morning."

"There's nothing to discuss, Joe."

"There's a whole lot to discuss. Your new schedule for one."

"I have no doubt my father has packed it full."

A look passes through his eyes. "You think your father's in charge here?"

My breathing slow as I stare at him.

"He hasn't been in charge for a long time," he says with more of that acid. "Your father's involved in too much shit to be in charge. Those approval ratings you're seeing now are thanks to me and Ronson spinning the fuck out of your father's messes. We'll get him elected again, but the bigger picture involves me and you. The future belongs to us, so you need to get yourself on board, and you need to do that soon, or so fucking help me God, I'll find a way to make you get on board."

I married the devil.

That's the last thought I have as I rest my head on my pillow.

That and the fact I need to get my shit together so I can figure out a plan to outsmart the devil, because I'll be damned if Joe Hearst is going to dictate how I live the rest of my life.

19

GUNNAR

I *don't care if I have to stay with him for the rest of my life; I'll do it for you.*
What the fuck did she mean by that?

I spent half the fucking night thinking about my conversation with Chelsea on the roof, and I'm no closer to figuring this shit out. She apologised to me for breaking my heart and I told her I didn't want her fucking apology. I don't. I fucking want *her* even though I fucking hate that I do. But I sure as fuck don't want that apology. And then she told me she's done this all for me and will continue doing it for me, staying with him for life if she has to.

I should take it for the drunk talk it was.

I should forget every word she said.

I should not fucking want to know what the hell she meant by it all.

But I want to know, and I want to fucking know now.

"Where are you going in such a fucking rush?" Griff

asks as I stride towards the door of our hotel room early the next morning.

"Out." I keep moving.

"Gunnar," he says, and something I hear in his voice stops me. "Don't do something you'll regret, brother."

Griff saw me come back from the roof last night. He saw the filthy mood I was in. The same filthy mood I've been in all week. He doesn't miss a fucking beat; he knows what's up.

I look back at him. "What time are we needed this morning?" I'm not getting into this with him.

He shakes his head and mutters, "Fuck," before giving me the information I'm looking for. "Hearst has meetings all morning in the hotel. His guys are with him for them. We're free until lunch."

"I'll be back in time for that."

I exit the room without another word and reach for my phone. I then do something I swore I'd never fucking do again; I send Chelsea a text.

Me: We need to talk. Now. Where are you?

When I don't get a reply within a few minutes, I send her another one.

Me: Tell me where you are or I'll make it clear to everyone I need to know where you are.

The dots go up and down as she types a reply. She takes her sweet fucking time to type the short message she sends back.

Chelsea: In the gym.

Me: Don't move. I'm on my way.

One of Hearst's security guys is standing outside the gym when I get there. He lifts his chin at me as I enter; he must think Hearst sent me.

It's early, just before 6:30 a.m. and she's the only one in the gym. On the treadmill.

She looks at me the instant I step through the door. Stopping the treadmill, she gets off it and meets me halfway.

"What are you doing here?" she asks, her voice filled with uneasiness.

"You don't seem happy to see me, Mayfair. Where's the girl who's sorry for breaking my heart?"

Regret flashes in her eyes, and I fucking hate how that makes me feel. I fucking knew she didn't mean a word of what she said last night. When the fuck will I learn with this woman?

"I was drunk last night, Mason," she starts, and I cut her the fuck off.

"Yeah, you were. But you know what? As much as I'm standing here telling myself I should have known better than to believe you, I did fucking believe you. And I want to know what the hell's going on."

Her eyes drop to the floor and I feel the bullshit before I hear it. "I am sorry for breaking your heart, but whatever else I said to you—"

I snake an arm around her waist and take her with me as I move us to the wall. Caging her in, I say, "Don't fucking act like you don't remember what you said. You fucking do. I see it in your eyes and hear it in your voice. You're not a fucking liar, Chelsea. Don't start that shit with me now. Give me the truth. What did you mean when you said you'll stay with him for the rest of your life for me?"

Her eyes search mine frantically. "You caught me in a bad moment, that's all."

"What bad moment?"

"Joe and I have been fighting," she starts and then stops herself. She's looking at me like she's weighing what to tell me.

"And what's that got to do with me? What the fuck are you doing for me?"

"I was just referring to the fact I agreed to marry him so Dad would help you after you were arrested."

"Bull-fucking-shit. Stop fucking lying."

Her eyes flare with the fight she's about to unleash. "I'm not fucking lying, Mason."

I bend my face down closer to hers so I can look directly into her eyes. "You might not be lying, but you're fucking keeping something from me. I shouldn't expect any different from you, though. I'm always the last fucking one to know, aren't I?"

More of that fight flashes in her eyes, right before she presses her hands to my chest and attempts to push me away. I don't budge, though. I stay right the fuck where I am and keep my eyes firmly on hers. I fucking hate discussing her marriage. Hate thinking of her with that asshole. But this is a long-overdue conversation and we're fucking having it.

"Let me go," she says, still pushing against me.

I keep blocking her. "We're not finished talking."

"We are. Trust me, we fucking are."

Fuck I love her fight, even when I hate the reason for it.

"Tell me about it," I demand.

She frowns. "About what?"

"About your fucking marriage."

Her breathing slows as she stares at me like I've lost

my mind. "You don't want to know about it," she says softly.

"You're fucking right about that, but humour me. Tell me why you married that prick."

"Mason," she breathes, gripping my shirt. "No, don't do this."

I bring my arms up to rest against the wall either side of her head and lean my face down close to hers again. Every fucking cell in my body is wired. Anger, jealousy, hate. It's all in there, a fucking mix of straight-up danger. "Fucking. Tell. Me."

Her eyes widen. Her breathing picks up. Those breaths of hers are coming in a panic now. We're finally fucking getting somewhere.

Still gripping my shirt, she says, "You know I married him so that Dad would help you."

"And you fucking know that's not a conversation we ever had."

"We did have that conversation. I told you it was the only solution after you were arrested."

"Yeah, you told me that and I told you I'd find another way. And then next fucking thing, I'm hearing about your engagement on the fucking news. *We* didn't fucking have that conversation. I would have fucking liked for *you* to have told me."

She swallows hard. "I know, and I'm sorry."

"So what was the agreement when you married him?"

"For you?"

"For me, for you, for fucking everything."

"Dad agreed to help keep you out of prison. I agreed to stay married to Joe for as long as Dad is premier."

"And for as long as Hearst is premier?"

Her eyes plead with me to end this conversation as her hands shift from gripping my shirt to gripping my chest. "Yes."

I don't know if it's the fact her hands are on me now, curving over my muscles, or if it's the way she just breathed out that one word that tells me just how fucking long she's bound to Hearst for that does it, but I'm fucking pissed off. She's telling me this is all arranged; she has her hands on me like she used to; she's looking at me like she fucking cares about me; and yet every fucking time I see them together, she's doing the same fucking things with him. Hands on him, eyes on him, looking at him like she fucking loves him.

But then there's that one part of my heart and brain that stumbles over the fact she did this for me.

"Fuck." I drop my arms and step back. I'm all fucked up over her and can't think straight.

"Mason, you need to go."

I hate the urgency in her voice because I know exactly where it fucking comes from. She's worried Hearst will find us. She's fucking telling me to leave because of her husband.

I close the distance between us again and take hold of her hip with one hand while sliding the other one through her hair. Angling her head back, I growl, "I'm not fucking going anywhere, Mayfair. We're not finished yet."

She curls her hand around my forearm as I watch desire come to life in her eyes.

Fuck, it's always like this for us.

Fucking always.

I'm hard as fuck for her, too.

And I know I'm about to make another bad choice.

But fuck me, I can't help myself.

I never can with her.

The moan that escapes her lips as I bring mine down onto them hits me fucking everywhere. My dick, my gut, my heart.

I kiss her with the full force of every emotion I'm feeling.

I hold nothing back.

The love, the hate, the jealousy; it's all there, and it's all leading us into dangerous fucking territory.

I try like fuck not to put my hands all over her body, but that was never going to happen. The second my brain decided it was a good idea to kiss her was the second everything else was decided. Chelsea still owns my fucking heart, and along with that, she owns every part of my body. And right now, my body wants what it fucking needs. What it's been starved of for months, because even though I fucked her a month ago, that didn't even come close to what I need.

I tear her tank top off and then her bra before bringing my hands and mouth to her tits. She threads her fingers through my hair, gripping it hard while I suck and bite.

"Oh God, yes," she moans.

Looking up at her, I demand, "Tell me you've fucking missed this."

Still with her fingers in my hair, she says, "I've missed this."

Fuck.

Those three words send me over the edge.

If I ever had any shot at walking away from her, it's gone now.

I move my hands to her hips while I lay a trail of kisses down her stomach. Her tights are the next to go, and then I'm on my fucking knees with my hands on her ass and my nose pressed to her cunt.

Fucking hell, I'm desperate for her.

I pull her panties down. Slowly. Fuck knows how I control myself, because I want them the fuck off, but I also want to taste this moment before tasting her.

If I never have her again, I want to fucking remember this.

She steps out of them and I part her legs. Placing my hands on the front of her thighs, I slowly run them up her legs while my eyes find hers. Keeping our gazes locked, I dip my face closer and run my tongue over her clit, loving the fuck out of the way she tilts her cunt towards me.

Still with my eyes on her, I slide my tongue inside her.

Jesus fuck.

I've fucking missed her.

Her taste is locked in my memory, but being deprived of it has driven me crazy. A memory only goes so far. A man needs to get his fill and I intend to get my fucking fill today.

She watches with heated eyes as I fuck her with my tongue. When I add my fingers, her eyes flutter closed and she moans. I fucking love that sound, and it drives me to work her harder and deeper.

"Oh God. Fuck," she says, her hands hitting the wall beside her as she moves with the pleasure I'm giving her.

Her cunt pulses with her orgasm and fuck if that doesn't push my dick over the fucking edge of needing inside her.

Standing, I reach for my belt, but Chelsea's hands are more frantic than mine and have my belt and jeans undone in a few seconds. Curling her hand around my neck, she pulls my mouth to hers at the same time she hooks her leg around my body and lifts herself into my arms.

Our bodies move without us even having to think about it. Like magnets made for each other. I've never had this with anyone else and fuck it if I never fucking want it with anyone else. This woman in my arms is the only woman I ever want there. Proof I'm hell-bent on my own fucking destruction.

I thrust inside her, growling with satisfaction as her cunt and arms and legs clench around me.

Pulling out, I meet her gaze and hold it while slamming inside her again.

"Fuck," she says, tightening her arms around me.

"You want it like that?"

"God, yes." Her fingers dig into me.

I don't wait a second longer. I fuck her exactly how we both want it.

We're skin on skin.

Need on need.

A mess of danger, and trouble, and desperate desire that's only going to end in more fucking pain.

But hell if I can stop myself from taking what I want.

"Oh my God, oh God," Chelsea pants as her nails pierce my skin and she comes. "Fuck, Mason. *Fuck*."

Her pleasure and her filthy words are my final undoing and I come too.

"Fuck!" I roar as my orgasm hits and lose myself in her. Finally and completely. And for one fucking moment

I forget everything we've been through. I forget how she broke me, shattered me, ruined me. In this moment, she's mine again. Mine to love and give everything to.

I kiss her, my tongue sliding over hers, still losing myself in her.

The moment is trashed when she puts her hands on my shoulders, pushes out of my embrace, and says frantically, "Mason, stop. We need to get dressed."

Of course we fucking do.

Before her fucking husband finds us.

I pull out of her and let her go. Snatching her clothes up, I throw them at her. "Yeah, we fucking do."

I put my dick away and zip my pants. What the fuck was I thinking? She might have told me she missed me, but she's not fucking choosing me. She never fucking chooses me.

I cut a path to the door of the gym, looking back at her as I reach for the handle. "The next time you want to get drunk and tell me how fucking sorry you are, don't. I don't want to fucking hear it."

As I stalk out of the gym, I tell myself I hate her.

I tell myself I'm finally done with her.

I tell myself a whole lot of fucking lies, because the truth is, I don't hate her, and I'm not done with her. Not by a long fucking shot.

20

CHELSEA

My heart cracks as I watch Mason exit the gym. Letting him think the worst about me is slowly killing me, but I can't let him think anything else. I need to start putting my plan into place with Joe so I can get us to the point where Mason is safe again. Once Joe's out of the way and once my father is dealt with, then I can tell Mason the full truth. I don't expect him to wait around for me, but I at least want him to know that what he thinks about me isn't true. I want him to know I'm not the monster in all of this.

I quickly dress and leave the gym. I have to shower. The last thing I need is for Joe to catch me after I fucked Mason. That won't help my plan at all.

Thankfully he's not in our room when I get back. I manage to shower and dress before he returns. I'm finishing styling my hair as he walks through the door.

He doesn't greet me before going to the safe and opening it, so I quietly finish with my hair and spray some perfume on. I then reach for my earrings and say, "What do you want me to do today?"

He's busy looking through some papers that he pulled out of the safe. Glancing up at me, he says, "You're free this morning. We need you at the lunch today. Griff will come by and collect you at twelve."

I nod. "Okay. Is there any information I should brush up on before lunch?"

He watches me like he's not quite sure about me, so I move to him and say, "You told me to get on board with this. I'm fucking getting on board. Tell me what you need and I'll make it happen."

Joe doesn't like it when I swear, and today is no different. That vein in his neck pulses, but he keeps his thoughts to himself. "I'll get Matthew to email you some information. Go through it before lunch."

"Done."

He watches me silently for another few moments before going back to his papers. Five minutes later, he packs them up and walks to the door. "I much prefer it when you're like this, Chelsea."

Fucking asshole.

"I know" is all I say. I need to maintain some hostility while I transition us to where I want us; Joe will sense something's up if I suddenly become sickly sweet to him.

I sag to the bed as the door clicks closed.

I still want to run away. Leave him far behind. Pretend none of this exists.

I can't do that, though.

The feel of Mason between my legs keeps me going. Reminds me why I'm doing what I'm doing. One day, Joe won't hold any power over either of us. I'm going to make damn sure of it.

∼

I SPEND the morning going over the information Matthew emails me. I also research it all further, learning facts that aren't in the documents he sent. I then spend time researching my husband and his business. I was so naïve when I married him, not seeing a need to learn all there was to know about him. Now, I'm going to the ends of the earth to dig everything up that I can find.

When Griff knocks on my door to collect me, I feel more prepared to face Joe than I've ever felt. It's true what they say knowledge is power. The other thing that's true? Nobody gives you power; you have to take it. And fuck, I'm taking it. Even if it takes me a long time, I'm fucking taking it.

Joe is all charisma and charm when I arrive for lunch. He's invited about fifty men and their partners, so I slip into the role of the perfect wife to help him sell the story of his campaign. Because I've realised now, this isn't my father's campaign we're running here—this is Joe's campaign.

"Hello, darling," I greet him with a kiss to his lips, a hand to his cheek, and a smile that screams love.

He actually looks pleased as his hand snakes around my waist and he kisses me back.

Matthew moves closer to us before Joe can say anything. "I trust you received that information," he says. He looks at me like he thinks I'm nothing. He'll regret underestimating me one day.

"I did, thank you, and I studied it all. I'm impressed by the figures on the mine and what it would contribute to our economy, but I have some questions that I think the public are going to want answered. I know I want them answered."

Matthew's eyes turn flinty. Cold. "You don't need to concern yourself with that, Chelsea."

Another fucking asshole.

I'm surrounded by them.

I catch sight of my father coming our way and smile at him. "Dad, is Dwayne Moss attending the lunch today?" It's his mine we're here to talk about after all.

He frowns, not used to me involving myself in any of this. "Not that I'm aware of." He looks at Joe for confirmation.

Joe shakes his head. "No."

"That's a pity," I say. "I think it would pay for us to talk with him about the need to do some work on his life-of-mine plan. I don't believe he's identified suitable future land uses with regard to community views. This is the kind of stuff that will help him get this development approved, don't you think? Getting the community on board is important."

Joe looks at me like he's never seen me. Dad, too. Matthew just looks annoyed by me.

"Let's discuss that some more later," Joe says before glancing around the room. "For now, I need you to go and work your magic with the wives."

"Of course you do," I say, making sure to inject annoyance into my voice.

When his lips press together, I know I've achieved my goal.

I lean forward and kiss him. "Never fear, dear husband, I've got you covered."

With that, I make my way to the first of the wives I need to schmooze, almost 100 percent certain my husband is watching me and wondering what the fuck is going on.

Score one to me today.

∽

"I didn't realise you knew about mine rehabilitation," Joe says that night when we're getting ready for the dinner we're attending.

I look at him as he takes a sip of his scotch. He's sitting in the armchair watching me while I fix my hair. He has the same look on his face he's had every time I've caught sight of him this afternoon. It's a mix of confusion, surprise, and curiosity.

Lunch was a huge success, and I know both Joe and Dad were more than happy with the way I worked the room. I mean, hell, even I was impressed with myself. It's hard work faking love for those two, and I managed to do it for a full three hours, not slipping once.

"You might be surprised at what I'm capable of."

"I'd like to see what you're capable of, Chelsea."

I nod. "I know."

He places his glass down and stands. Moving behind me, he runs his hands down my bare arms. Dropping his mouth to my shoulder, he murmurs, "I like you like this."

A shiver spreads across my skin. Not a good one, but he doesn't need to know that.

Our eyes meet in the mirror. "I'm trying, Joe."

"I can see."

He kisses my neck and I fight the urge to push him away. It takes everything inside me, but I succeed in tilting my neck so he thinks I like what he's doing. When one of his hands moves to my breast, I hold my breath and wonder if I actually have the balls to see this plan through. But all I have to do is think about Mason and I know I'll find the balls. I'll do whatever it takes to find them.

Joe turns me so he can kiss me.

He reaches his hand under my dress to slip his fingers into my panties.

I close my eyes and kiss him back while my mind disconnects and I think about the stars. I think about gazing at them with Mason, lying on our backs, staring up at the night sky. I think about rolling over and kissing him while he tells me which constellation we're looking at. I think about him pushing my hair off my face and telling me he loves me.

Joe makes me come while I think about those stars and the man I love.

I hate that he makes me come.

He loves it. It makes him feel powerful, which is what I'm banking on, and the only reason I allow it.

At the sound of someone knocking on our door, he brings his mouth to my ear and says, "I want you tonight."

I know what I have to do tonight, and I've been readying myself for it, but when I see Mason's face at the door, I stumble with it. I feel dirty and ashamed. I've never been the kind of girl who cheats. The kind of woman who sleeps with two men in one day. And yet here I am. Mason and I are no longer together, but I feel so deeply that I'm cheating on him. Especially when he looks at me the way he does when Joe takes his eyes off him. Like he doesn't completely hate me and like he's thinking about what we did this morning.

Joe comes back to me and kisses me while circling his hand around my neck. "Don't be late." He slowly uncurls his fingers from my neck and trails them down to my chest. It's all for fucking show, for Mason's benefit, and I have to work hard not to push his hand away.

"I won't be," I promise, counting down the seconds until he leaves.

"Good."

I don't look back at Mason as Joe exits the room. I can't. I don't want to see the hate I know will be blazing from him.

21

GUNNAR

Alexa: *When will you be home?*
Me: *Monday.*
Alexa: *Oh good.*
Me: *Why? What do you need?*
Alexa: *Pfft, maybe I just miss you.*
Me: *Spit it out.*
Alexa: *Fine, I need you to fix my shower. It's leaking.*
Me: *You know you can pay a plumber to do that.*
Alexa: *I'm on a budget.*
Me: *You don't even know what the fuck a budget is.*
Alexa: *I know. I'm practicing.*
Me: *So part of that is using me to fix your shit?*
Alexa: *I'll make you dinner.*
Me: *I'll be over Monday night. I want steak.*
Alexa: *You always want steak. Let me cook you something different.*
Me: *It's steak or nothing.*
Alexa: *God, you can be so boring, Mason. Live a little. Try new things.*

My gaze locks onto Chelsea, drawing my attention completely. She's proof I don't like new things; I like what I know.

Alexa: Mason?

Me: I've gotta go. See you Monday.

I shove my phone in my pocket as I track Chelsea leaving the function she and Hearst just hosted for lunch. We haven't spoken since I fucked her in the gym yesterday, but we've exchanged glances enough for me to know she's as confused by the encounter as I am. When I fucked her at her house, that was a pure hate fuck. That was me wanting to fucking claim her while her husband sat in the next fucking room. Hell, I wanted him to walk in on us that time. And while I was down with being caught with her yesterday, that was no hate fuck. That was pure fucking need. And what I need now is more of her. And that confuses the hell out of me.

"Gunnar," Griff says, his tone causing my senses to kick right in. "We've got a situation."

He's already on his way out the door, and I follow him. His pace picks up and we jog past Chelsea to the fire exit stairs. Running down the two levels to the ground floor, we exit, and I follow Griff outside to the front of the hotel where I can see Hearst in a heated argument with two men who look like they stepped off the *Sopranos* set.

"Christ," Griff mutters, slowing. "That's what he's tied up in."

"This should be fun," I say, drawing a shake of his head. Grinning, I say, "At least it gives us something to do other than fucking driving Hearst around."

We join Hearst and his two security assholes who are useless as fuck. "There a problem here?" Griff asks.

The Sopranos dudes eye him. "Yeah, one that doesn't fucking concern you."

"That's where you're wrong," Griff says. "If you have a problem with Hearst, you have a problem with us."

"And who the fuck are you?" one of the guys snarls.

"Storm," I say. "And we're fucking ready to play if you are."

"Fuck," the guy says, glancing at his mate like he's looking for confirmation they should continue.

His mate looks at me and I know it's on. This one's not fucking backing down, so I go in hard with a punch designed to knock him flat on his ass. He's a fucking fridge of a motherfucker, too, so it takes some fucking force to achieve my goal, but I do.

The other guy is straight into it, throwing punches at Griff, who blocks them all. Hearst's security guys take a step to get in on the action. I look at them and give a shake of my head, letting them know to leave this shit up to us.

The fridge gets himself up off the ground and comes at me with both fists flying.

"Come on, motherfucker," I say, motioning with my hands for him to come at me. "Make it fucking hurt. I could do with the distraction from other shit."

I let him get one punch in. On my cheek. The crack of his fist connecting with my bones settles in deep while the pain radiates through me. And then I deliver that pain ten-fucking-fold back to him.

I smash my fists into his face and body. He puts up a good fight, but I beat the utter shit out of him until he's a bloody mess on the ground, curling his legs up, trying to defend himself from me.

Bending down, I yank his legs and arms out of the way and roll him onto his back. Standing over him, my feet either side of his body, I grip his face, squeezing hard. "Don't fucking come back here. You won't fucking like what you find." I then smash my fist down onto his face one last time.

Straightening, I find Hearst watching me. I can't see his eyes because they're hidden behind his sunglasses. "What the fuck are you tied up in?" I demand, doing my best to tell myself I'm not asking because of Chelsea. That I'm not fucking worried for her safety.

His lips curl up in a snarl. "I pay you to do what you just did. I don't fucking pay you to ask questions."

I take a step towards him, but Griff pulls me back and says, "Should we expect more from them?"

Fuck, I'm fucking wired now, and Hearst throwing his bullshit at me only fills me with more angry energy I'll need to work off.

"I don't expect this will fix the situation," Hearst says.

"So that's a fucking yes, then?" I snap.

He shoots me a foul glare but doesn't answer. The asshole thinks he's fucking above answering to anyone. He stalks into the hotel without another word.

"Fucking hell," I say, looking at Griff. "The sooner this job is done, the fucking better."

He nods. "Right there with you, brother."

∽

I MAKE it through the afternoon without taking to Hearst with my fists even though that's exactly what I want to do. I have to drive him out to some fucking shitty town where I then have to spend two hours standing around in the heat while he sits in air conditioning inside. And I have to listen to him talk to me like I'm the shit on his fucking shoes. By the time we return to the hotel, I'm unsure if he'll survive the night or if I'll finally lose all sense and choke the life out of him.

It's just after five when we get back. Hearst goes straight up to his room and I head to mine after he tells me his security guy will take over for a couple of hours. He needs me back for his dinner, but that's not until 7:30 p.m.

I change out of the goddamn suit he insists we wear and into my gym clothes before heading down to the gym. The punching bag and I have a fucking date.

An hour in the gym doesn't come close to ridding me of the wild energy consuming me. And it sure as fuck doesn't take my mind off thinking about the fact Chelsea's married to a motherfucker who can't fucking protect her himself. And I'm fucking pissed off that after everything she's done, I'm still over here worrying about her.

I head back up to my room and shower before dressing in a clean suit. If I never see another suit after this week, it won't be too fucking soon.

After deciding I need some fresh air, I exit the room and head for the lifts. My legs slow as I see Chelsea waiting at it.

She turns and looks at me as I come closer. As I run my eyes over her body, I take in the sparkly silver sleeveless top and long emerald green skirt she's wearing. I never liked green until I started dating her. It's her favourite colour, and fuck she looks good in it.

"What happened to you?" she asks, eyeing my face where the *Sopranos* dude got some punches in.

"You sound genuinely concerned, Mayfair."

"Because I am."

"Don't be. The other guy looks worse. Do you know what shit your husband's involved in?"

Her eyes widen. "Was this because of him?"

"Yeah."

"Oh God." She reaches out to touch my face before I can stop her.

I remove her hand even though I fucking like it there. "You don't know what he's into?"

"No. I have no idea."

I didn't expect her to, and I believe her. "You need to be careful, Chelsea. Watch your back at all times."

Surprise flashes in those beautiful eyes of hers and she moves closer to me. "Careful, Mason, or I'll start thinking you don't really hate me."

Fuck, her scent hits me; her voice hits me; everything fucking hits me. My arm goes around her waist and I move her back against the wall between the two lifts before bringing my mouth to hers. I kiss her as I grind myself against her, and when her leg coils around mine, I fucking grip it and hold it there.

It fucking belongs there.

It doesn't fucking belong around Joe Hearst.

Sliding my hand along her leg, I reach under her skirt and bring my hand around to her cunt. As I push two fingers inside, I lift my mouth and growl, "I need to taste you."

She wants this as much as I do, but she shakes her head and tries to push me away. "Joe's on his way up."

That just pisses me off. Gripping her waist harder, I reach deeper inside her and rasp, "I don't fucking care."

She puts her hands to my chest and pushes me away. Her eyes are wide with worry. "He'll be here any minute. And besides, we're in the fucking corridor for anyone to see."

"And. I. Don't. Fucking. Care." With that, I drop to my knees, lift her skirt, tear her panties off, and bring my mouth to her cunt. The moan that escapes her lips as my tongue enters her causes me to lose my fucking mind.

Those moans of hers should all be mine, and the fact they aren't drives me insane.

Fucking. Insane.

I inhale her scent deeply as I fuck her with my tongue. She tries to resist me—I feel that in the way she tenses up—but it doesn't take her long to submit. And it doesn't fucking take her long to come.

She might have tried to push me away, but she's fucking into this. She's all frantic fingers in my hair and foot on my shoulder while pressing herself against my face like she can't fucking get enough of me.

When I'm done, I stand and wipe her from my beard while she straightens her skirt. The lift indicates that Hearst is two levels away. I fucking wish he'd stepped out of the lift while my tongue was buried the fuck inside her.

"Where's my underwear?" she says, sounding panicked and looking just as panicked.

I slip her panties inside my suit, pocketing them.

She makes pissed-off eyes at me. "Mason," she hisses. "I need them."

The lift reaches the level below ours.

"You don't fucking need them."

Still with the pissed-off eyes. "You are an asshole."

I press myself against her, bringing my hands to her face. "Yeah, baby, I fucking am." I kiss her, letting her taste herself until she pushes me away.

When the lift opens, she's doing her best to appear calm and like she hasn't just had my tongue and fingers inside her. Hearst glances between the two of us, his eyes narrowing with distrust.

Yeah, motherfucker, you should be looking at us like that.

Fuck, and now I'm fucking pissed off that he gets to put his hands on her, and guide her into the lift, and take her downstairs.

I might have just made her come, but he's the one with her on his fucking arm.

She's his, and I need to fucking remember that.

22

CHELSEA

"I like this style of dress on you," Joe says at dinner on Sunday. It's our last function for the week. Since I started working on our relationship two days ago, the tension between us has eased and Joe acts much more civilly to me. Still, it's not real; it's him getting what he wants and me doing all the submitting. But I go along with it because it's what I'm after.

I smile. "Thank you." God, this week can't come to an end fast enough.

He spreads his arm across the back of my chair and leans closer to me. "I have to spend some time tonight talking with Rob Burke. We could be gone for an hour or so. I need you to spend the time while I'm gone talking with his wife, getting her on side."

My eyes lock with Mason's across the room as I listen to my husband. I catch the way he works his jaw before looking away. I hate that he has to watch this.

Turning to Joe, I nod. "Is there anything in particular you want me to say to her?"

He smiles. It's only a flash of one, but it's one, and it's something I don't make him do often, if at all. "Good girl," he murmurs, and I want to fucking stab him in the eyes for being so fucking condescending. He then proceeds to give me a rundown of exactly what he wants me to say to her.

I sip some of my wine as I watch him exit the room with Rob Burke. I then stand and make my way over to Rob's wife, where I spend half an hour talking to her about all the things Joe told me to. I'd make an amazing politician with all the spin that comes out of my mouth. Rob's wife is easy to engage and even easier to convince that my story is right. She tells me we should catch up when she comes to Brisbane next week, and I agree that I'd love that too. When she says she has to go to the bathroom, I cheer on the inside that my job here is done, and I can escape for some time by myself before Joe comes back.

I grab another wine on my way out of the room, taking a long sip as I find a secluded spot at the end of the corridor outside the function room.

Sliding down the wall, I sit on the floor, kick my heels off, and exhale a long breath.

We're going home tomorrow, and I can't wait. There's something comforting about being in your own space. Also, going home means I can spend some time with Alexa, and God, I need that.

"Mayfair."

My eyes blink open and I find Mason standing in front of me.

"You shouldn't wander off by yourself," he says.

I sip some more wine, processing the fact his hate

towards me seems to be thawing. Yesterday he told me I needed to be careful. Now he's telling me I shouldn't wander off. Patting the floor, I say, "Sit with me for a moment."

"I'm working, Chelsea. I'm not fucking sitting and chatting with you."

I push up off the floor and stand. "So it's okay to fuck me while you're working, but not to sit and talk with me?"

"I didn't fuck you while I was working. I did that on my own fucking time."

My eyes trail over his suit before coming back to linger on his neck tattoo. Reaching out, I trace my fingers over it. I'm surprised he lets me. I know he's affected by me when he swallows hard and brings his hand up to curl around my wrist.

I meet his gaze. "I figured you'd cover it up," I say softly.

"I will." The words crash into me with their force, but there's something in his eyes and his voice that makes me doubt that will happen anytime soon.

My breathing turns shallow as I move closer to him. Dropping my gaze, I run my eyes over the tattoo again. I'm fixated on it. It's me on his skin, and the fact he hasn't covered it up yet means something.

I undo the top two buttons of his shirt. Slowly. So very slowly.

"Mayfair," he says, his voice low and full of gravel. Oh God, how I've missed that gravel. It works its way through my veins, setting me on fire for him.

I find his eyes again as I stand on my toes. "Please don't stop me."

He watches me intently, sliding his hand around my waist, not stopping me.

My fingers graze his neck as I wrap my hand around it. Bringing my lips to his skin, I press a kiss to his tattoo.

"Fuck," he groans, his fingers digging into my waist.

I move against him, into him, and bring my other hand up to his face as I move my lips along his neck and keep kissing his tattoo.

"Fucking hell," he growls, taking hold of my face and directing my lips to his.

I tell him everything I can't put into words in this kiss.

I whisper secrets I can never say out loud.

I beg for his forgiveness for every hurt, every betrayal, every ache I've caused.

He feels it all. I know he does.

It's in the way his touch is more gentle. In the way he deepens the kiss rather than forces his hate down my throat. In the way his body moves with mine rather than demands control of mine.

And it's in the way he looks at me when the kiss ends. Like he used to look at me.

He drops his hands and steps away from me. The turmoil in his eyes slays me.

"I can't fucking do this," he says. His voice is filled with a new level of torment. It slays me too. I've done this to him, and I will loathe myself forever for that.

"I'm sorry," I start, but stop talking the moment I see his reaction.

"Stop fucking saying sorry." His eyes flash with anger. "I don't need your apology. What I fucking needed was for you not to walk the fuck away. I needed you to trust I could fix things." He jabs his finger in the air. "*That's* what

I fucking needed, and you couldn't give it to me, so don't fucking try and give me anything now because I don't fucking want it."

Before I can say anything else, he turns and stalks away from me. I stare breathlessly after him, every piece of my heart shattering into tiny pieces.

He will never be mine again.

I was born to be Mason Blaise's girl, and I will never be that again.

23

CHELSEA

Alexa: I'm sorry, babe, but I have to cancel our lunch today. Mum's just been admitted to hospital.
Me: Oh my God, is she okay?
Alexa: They're running some tests. I mean, I didn't think she was any worse than usual, but the doctors are saying the cancer treatment is affecting her kidneys. Or something like that. Honestly, I'm finding it hard to keep up and understand everything going on.
Me: Do you need me? I'll come if you do, but I get it too if you would prefer me not to be there.
Alexa: I love you and I always need you, but not at the hospital. I'll call you tonight and we'll reschedule lunch.
Me: Okay. I'm always here if you need to talk. Love you xx

I place my phone down on my desk and think about Alexa and her mum, which then leads me to thoughts of Mason and how he's coping with all this. Mason hasn't been close to his parents for a while now, but I imagine his mum being sick would have stirred a lot of emotions up for him. After hearing his phone call with her when he told her he'd come and be with her at the hospital, I know he's struggling with this; I heard that in his voice.

"Chelsea," Joe says, coming into the office he had set up for me next to his, "I have to go to Sydney tomorrow, so I'm going to need you to attend a lunch I was supposed to go to with your father." He places a file on my desk. "This is the information you need to know for it."

We arrived home yesterday from our trip and are straight into the campaign today after taking yesterday afternoon off. I resigned from my job the day Joe told me to and wasn't surprised in the least when my boss told me I didn't need to give any notice. I suspect Joe had a hand in that. He's got what he wants now—me settled into an office right next to him so he can keep an eye on me and boss me around.

Joe really did marry the wrong woman.

I'm determined to show him that.

I pick up the file. "I'll go through it today. Is there anything else you need me to do while you're away? When will you be back?"

"I'll be home on Friday. I'll email you what needs to be done before then."

He exits the office, and I spend the next hour going over the information in the file. It's more about the mine that Dwayne Moss is trying to gain approval for and that Joe and Dad are trying to help him with. All so very above board when the premier is doing dirty deals behind doors to push a mine through that half the state doesn't want. I don't have an opinion on it either way; at this point, I can only focus on what *I'm* trying to achieve.

Closing the file, I push my chair back and stand to go

in and tell Joe I'm going out for lunch. I'm almost at the door between our offices when I hear his angry voice. Slowing, I stop and eavesdrop on his conversation. This is the only good thing about working so closely with him, and I intend to make the most of the opportunity to snoop.

Although he's talking angrily, he's doing it in hushed tones, so I can only make out some of what he's saying. By the sounds of it, he's discussing some financial investments he's made on behalf of a client that don't sound like they were legal. If I'm not mistaken, he's involved in money laundering and insider trading. Thank God for my degree in finance; it'll help me figure out Joe's dirty secrets.

He abruptly ends the call and I dart back to sit at my desk in case he comes in.

A minute later, he appears in my office looking stressed. "I have to go out for the afternoon. I'll see you at home tonight."

I watch him leave, thinking about this new information I have on him. I know what I'll be doing while he's away: going through his files looking for proof of his illegal activities.

∼

JOE COMES HOME SUPER LATE that night. I'm already in bed, so I'm spared having to spend time with him, and then he leaves early on Wednesday morning to fly to Sydney. The universe appears to have come to its senses and decided to play nice with me. It starts my morning off well and this continues for the rest of the day.

I attend the lunch Joe asked me to and impress my father again with my knowledge of the mine. I then spend time trying to crack Joe's password on his computer so I can take a look at his files. After two hours of trying to do that and also rifling through his paperwork, I admit defeat. I've found nothing in his paperwork and can't figure out his password.

By the time I arrive at Alexa's for the dinner we rescheduled from lunch yesterday, I'm frustrated and annoyed. And I'm ready to have a drink with her to take the edge of that frustration.

"How's your mum today?" I ask as we walk into her kitchen, where she's making tacos for dinner.

"They sent her home this morning. She needs to keep being monitored, though."

"On a scale of one to ten, how worried are you?"

"Nine, but this is me we're talking about."

I smile. This is why I was adamant about making sure we caught up sooner rather than later. Alexa is a worrier when it comes to her family. A nine for her is the equivalent of a five for most other people. "I bought a bottle of your favourite wine." I hold it up.

She opens her fridge to show me two bottles of the same wine sitting in the door. "I think we're good for tonight." She grabs two wine glasses. "We have a lot to talk about tonight, my friend. And just let me say it, I fucking love your hair. I knew that style would suit you."

I take a sip of wine after she passes me a glass. "I love the length. It's so much easier to manage."

"Okay, spill. Tell me all about your week away and your new job, and don't leave anything out."

Oh, I'll be leaving a whole lot of it out. Last week was

a fucked-up mess of epic proportions, and she doesn't need to know about half of it.

I share what I can with her while we eat dinner and work our way through a bottle of wine. The alcohol goes to my head pretty fast because wine always does that to me, so when Alexa suggests we open another bottle, I'm all for it. Drinking more always sounds like a good idea when you're already drunk.

We sit on her couch and talk about my marriage, her mum, and her work before moving onto discussing the guy she's been sleeping with. We're laughing our asses off as she tells me how her cat bit him on the ass while he was going down on her when Mason's voice cuts through our laughter.

"Your door was unlocked," he says, his eyes firmly on me, instantly causing desire to pool low in my stomach. "Any-fucking-one could have come in while you two were in here fucking about."

Alexa moves off the couch, stumbling a little on her way to him. "Good God, do you ever stop worrying and bossing people around? You need a drink is what you need." She comes to a stop, pointing her finger at him. "Oh, and you really need to look at my showerhead since you didn't get to do that the other night."

He looks at her. "Yeah, that's why I'm here."

I run my eyes over him while they discuss her leaking showerhead. He's wearing jeans and a white T-shirt tonight. I miss his suit, but I've always loved him in a white shirt. With his tanned skin, beard, and muscles that are distracting as hell, he makes a white shirt look better than I've ever seen one look on a man.

"Chelsea," Alexa says. "Did you hear what I just said?"

I blink and stop staring at Mason, who's looking at me like he's thinking about all the things he did to me last week. "S-Sorry," I stutter, tripping over my words, feeling all bothered by him. "What?"

She gives me a knowing look. "I asked if you were ready for another wine?"

I nod. "Please."

She pours our drinks and hands me mine before saying, "I'll be back in a minute."

I take a big sip of wine as I watch her walk to the bathroom. Being alone with Mason is dangerous, and while it's all I want, I know it's a bad idea. A very bad idea. I'm doing my best not to look at him, but without Alexa in the room, I'm struggling.

He places the toolbox he's carrying on the kitchen counter, opens the fridge, and bends to search for what he wants. A moment later, he retrieves a beer and closes the fridge. Twisting the cap off, he takes a long swig before coming to me. His eyes reach deep inside me as he says, "You need to be more careful, Mayfair. I told you to watch your back. Not locking that door isn't fucking watching your back."

His concern causes my stomach to flutter more than it already is. This is Mason not hating me completely, and it reminds me of the Mason who loved me with everything he had.

I sip some more wine. "Thank you."

He frowns. "What the fuck for?"

I smile. "For caring enough to remind me of that."

He takes another long swig of beer, not shifting his attention off me.

I watch as he swallows it down, waiting for his reply,

but Alexa rejoins us, ending our conversation.

"You hungry?" she asks him. "We've got leftover tacos if you are."

He watches me for another few seconds before looking at her and nodding. "Yeah, I could go some tacos."

She picks up her glass of wine and walks back to the couch as she says, "Last person to eat cleans."

Mason gives a shake of his head and mutters, "Of course they fucking do."

I smile. I've missed being around these two together. We had some good times while I was with Mason.

Taking my wine, I go back to the couch where Alexa tells me about some new make-up she's discovered that she loves. Mason potters around in the kitchen, making his tacos, and comes and sits with us while he eats.

I wasn't expecting him tonight and am not prepared for him. Last week was a hot mess and has left me a little bewildered about what we're doing. I want him with every fibre of my being, but it feels all kinds of wrong to do what we've been doing. It's not fair to him. But I can't deny how good it is to know his touch again, to talk to him again, to have his eyes on me again.

"Did you speak to Mum today?" Alexa asks him after we finish talking about make-up.

"Yeah. I'm gonna spend the afternoon with her tomorrow," he says.

"Dad's home with her this week. Just so you know."

Mason nods. "I know." His words are as tense as his shoulders. There's no love lost between Mason and his father. It was because of his dad that he walked away from everything his family and their wealth offer. He might still be close to his siblings, but he wants nothing to do with the Blaise power and money.

Alexa takes a long gulp of wine. "Promise me you won't get into it with him. Not while Mum's going through all this."

He works his jaw. "I can't guarantee anything. He wants to be a motherfucker, I'm gonna check him on it."

Alexa shakes her head, looking exasperated with her brother. It's an expression I've seen a lot of with these two. Alexa prefers to manage people in a subtle way; Mason is all in their face and unyielding. They love each other fiercely, but they piss each other off just as much. "I hope you have a son one day and he's as frustrating as you are."

The thought of Mason having a child that's not mine makes me trip over my thoughts.

It physically hurts my chest.

When his eyes meet mine, filled with the same turmoil they held three nights ago after we kissed, I know he's feeling it too.

He stands abruptly and walks into the kitchen. I don't watch him, but I hear him in there. I hear the sound of a bottle or glass slamming down onto the kitchen counter, and then another one, and the sound of him unscrewing a lid and pouring liquid into a glass, and of him stalking back to the couch.

He brings a bottle of rum, placing it roughly on the coffee table between us.

He doesn't look at me.

When he drains his glass of rum in two long gulps, I know he's settling in to drink the entire bottle.

Mason's hate is back, and I shudder to think where this night will end up.

24

GUNNAR

Thank fuck I left an almost-full bottle of rum at Alexa's the last time I had a drink with her. I fucking need it tonight.

It's been three long fucking days of never-ending thoughts of Chelsea since she put her hands all over my tattoo and I fucking kissed her. It was that kiss that fucking did it. I might have kissed her, and fucked her, and tasted her before that night, but that kiss was different. It was fucking intimate and it's fucking screwed with me. And now, after Alexa mentioned me having a son earlier, I'm sitting here fucking thinking about the fact the only woman I wanted to have a child with is a woman I can never have a child with. And I'm fucking pissed off again.

I'm halfway through my bottle of rum and it's not coming close to easing my mood. Alexa and Chelsea have spent the last hour talking shit about make-up and music and TV shows and other bullshit I'm not fucking interested in, but I can't bring myself to leave. Chelsea has that kind of pull, she always has, and I'm fucking incapable of walking away when I should.

"Alexa," Chelsea says, poking her. "Are you falling asleep?"

"Ugh," Alexa groans and wiggles on the couch so she's lying on her side with her head on the armrest. "I so tired," she mumbles while her eyes open and close lazily. "Can't keep my eyes open."

I'm surprised she's lasted this long. She's drunk most of the wine they've been sharing. Chelsea might have been drunk when I arrived, but she's slowed down since, while Alexa kept going hard.

I move off the couch and scoop my sister into my arms. "Time for bed," I say as I carry her into her bedroom.

"Macey Mace," she mumbles, flinging her arm around my neck. "I love you, but you too angry with her. She loves you so much.... Be nicer, 'k?" With that, she passes out on her bed, leaving me thinking about the shit that just came out of her mouth. She doesn't know what she's talking about; if Chelsea loved me, she wouldn't be fucking married to another man.

Chelsea's in the kitchen when I go back out, bent over the dishwasher trying to rearrange it to fit more dishes in. I rest my ass against the kitchen counter and cross my arms while running my eyes over her body. She's wearing the fucking shortest red dress known to man tonight. It's distracted the hell out of me all night, allowing me to get my fill of her legs.

Straightening, she looks at me. "I'll just finish cleaning up and then I'll go home."

"You're in no state to drive."

"I know. I'll call an Uber."

"No." I jerk my head towards the hallway. "Stay here."

She looks at me like I've just suggested the absolute worst thing ever. I probably have, but fuck if I want her out there where Hearst's enemies can get at her. She mentioned during her conversation with Alexa that he's away for a couple of days; I don't want her home alone, especially not when she's drunk and not fully alert.

"I'm not staying, Mason. I'll—"

I push off from the counter. "You are staying. It's not fucking safe out there for you to be on your own, and since your fucking husband didn't make sure of your safety, I'm making sure of it."

Her eyes widen, but she doesn't say anything.

I grab my toolbox and stride out of the kitchen, needing to put some space between us before I do something stupid again.

I work on Alexa's showerhead while trying to stop thinking about Chelsea and that damn kiss. If I could shut that shit off, I'd have half a chance of stopping my thoughts from constantly circling back to her. For now, though, my brain is hell-bent on keeping that kiss on repeat.

I'm in the bathroom for a good forty minutes before I finish what I'm doing and have just turned the shower on to confirm the leak is gone when Chelsea comes in. The look in her eyes causes my gut to tighten. And when she speaks, I know for fucking certain that we're doing this all over again.

"It wasn't that I didn't trust you to fix things," she says with what I know is fake confidence. I know this because of the way her eyes hold all the hesitation in the world. I also know this because I fucking know this woman. I only have to take one look at her to see she desperately wants me to listen to what she's saying and that she's nervous I won't. And fuck knows why, but I give her this.

"What was it then?" I ask, the shower still running behind me.

She takes a step closer to me, that hesitation in her eyes intensifying. "You couldn't have fixed it, Mason."

"Why? What the fuck was so bad that I couldn't fix it?"

"My dad would have ruined you."

"I would have gone to prison and done my time for you. That's what you're not fucking getting. I would have preferred that than you fucking marrying another man."

More fucking hesitation in her eyes. "And what if you'd been in prison for decades?"

"Fuck, Chelsea, I wouldn't have. Not for what they were trying to charge me with."

"You don't know that."

"I do fucking know that."

She comes even closer, right to me, her hesitation shifting into that fight of hers I love. "You don't fucking know that!" She jabs me in the chest, her eyes now blazing with determination. "I was so fucking scared for you and what they'd do to you. That's what *you're* not getting."

It's what I hear in her voice that does it. That grabs my fucking heart and squeezes all the hate from it. This is the Chelsea I fucking love. The Chelsea I never stopped fucking loving.

My hand hooks around her neck so I can pull her lips to mine. She stumbles as I pull her, and we end up under the running shower. Neither of us gives a fuck. We're all lips and hands and desperation, oblivious to the water soaking us.

Our last kiss was intimate; this one's frantic with need.

Chelsea pushes herself against me, her fingers clawing at my hair, while her tongue tangles with mine. She's making the kind of noises that intensify my desire for her, that drive me fucking wild.

I tear my mouth from hers, trying like fuck to think this through. That's impossible, though. I don't think with Chelsea; that's not how we work. We just fucking feel. And we might not be together, but we're buried so fucking deeply in each other that we're connected for life. That's why I haven't covered her tattoo and why I'll never fucking cover it.

Chelsea's the girl I've loved since I was five.

She's the girl who owned my heart before I even knew it.

She's the girl I'll always love.

"Fuck," I say as she grips my shirt and looks up at me through the water with an expression that tells me she knows my thoughts and is waiting for my decision. I claim her lips again in a savage kiss that she gives right back to me. When I end the kiss, I rasp, "I know how this fucking ends, Mayfair, and I still can't stop myself from fucking wanting you."

My mouth is back on hers without wasting another second, and we're a frenzy of clothes coming off, skin on skin, and the kind of sex I've only ever known with her.

Chelsea comes in my arms as I fuck her against the shower wall with water cascading over us. I come right after, and when I pull out of her, I hold her eyes and say, "I want you tonight."

She frowns, not understanding, so I say with force, "I want you in my arms while I sleep. I fucking want to wake up with you tomorrow."

"Mason," she says, her voice full of misgiving, "I don't think that's a good idea."

"I agree, it's not, and yet I fucking want it, and you're gonna give it to me."

Her eyes search mine for what feels like a long fucking minute, and then she nods and says softly, "Okay." And not for the first time, I think about how this woman was made for my destruction.

25

CHELSEA

I slip into the bed in one of Alexa's spare rooms, and Mason slides in after me, his strong arms coming around me and pulling my body against his.

What the hell are we doing?

My heart is beating so fucking fast that it almost feels like it could beat its way out of my damn chest.

"Breathe," he murmurs against my ear, his chest pressing to my back.

I bring my hand up and curl it around his arm that's holding me tightly to him. "I'm not sure I can," I say. It's barely a whisper, but he hears me.

"It's just one night, Mayfair."

"I'm not sure you and I can do just one night."

He kisses my neck. "You might be right there."

Oh God, I *am* right. And yet, I want this as much as he does. I just don't want to admit it.

I turn silent while he continues pressing kisses to my neck and shoulder. His mouth on my skin feels so good and I never want him to stop. I never want this night to end. I never want to go back to my real life.

Tightening my grip on his arm, I say, "Do you remember that time in grade twelve when you got drunk at that party, and I was freaking out because you got in a fight with a guy and his machete?"

His kisses slow, but don't stop altogether. "Yeah. Why?"

"Jenny Parish was going to tell you she liked you that night, and I told her she shouldn't. I told her you and I had fooled around and were getting together."

He chuckles, lifting his lips from my skin. "I know."

I wiggle in his arms so I can roll over and face him. "How do you know that? I never told anyone that." Hell, I was going to take that secret to my grave because I was so horrified that my desperation not to see Mason with another girl had caused me to lie to a friend.

"Jenny told me when she kissed me at a party the next weekend."

My eyes go wide. "You never told me you kissed her. And why'd you never ask me about it?"

He grins, and it causes butterflies in my stomach. It's so good to see the real Mason rather than the angry, hateful Mason I caused. Curving his hand over my waist, he says, "I didn't tell you about every girl I ever kissed, Mayfair. I figured you just didn't like Jenny enough for me to date her, so you told her some bullshit story to keep her away. You sure as hell never let on that you liked me like that. Why are you telling me this now?"

"I don't know. I was just thinking about where this all started."

"Where what all started?"

"Us." I pause, unsure of whether to say what I really want to say, but then decide we're way past pretending there's no us in this world. Because even though we're not together, there most definitely is an us. "Me wanting you so desperately I can't think straight sometimes."

He presses himself against me as heat flares in his eyes. "That party was where it all started for you?"

I smile, running my finger down his cheek. "No, it started in grade eleven, but that party was the first time I felt super possessive of you and jealous of any girl who got close to you. How many girls did you kiss that I didn't know about?"

He grins, dropping his gaze to my lips. "I don't think you wanna know."

I smack him playfully. "Seriously. How many?"

Brushing his lips over mine, he says, "I can't remember, but there were a few."

"We both know your idea of a few is not the same as what a few actually is, so I'm guessing maybe ten?"

"Give or take," he says, moving his mouth down my neck to my collarbone while he slides his hand over my hip and down my leg to take hold of it and bring it up over his.

I take hold of his face and stop him. When I have his eyes, I say, "You're being very evasive, Mr Blaise."

The smile dies on his lips as he turns serious. "I don't like to think about you with your lips on anyone else, so I'm not going to help you think about my lips on someone other than you."

This is why I love this man with all my heart.

I want to tell him that, but I don't. That's not fair to him. Instead, I say, "Tell me a favourite."

His eyes flash with gratitude at my change in subject, and even though playing our favourites game isn't something he loved to do while we were together, I can tell he's happy to do it tonight.

I started the "tell me a favourite" when we first began dating because I wanted to know all his favourite things, the things I didn't know he'd found a love for in the eight years we weren't friends. Mason would grumble and complain and tell me he'd rather fuck me than tell me all his fucking favourites, but I would force him into talking because sometimes a girl just wants to talk. And sometimes she just wants to know everything about the man she loves.

"I'm pretty fucking sure we've covered all my favourites," he says, rolling onto his back.

I move so I'm lying next to him on my stomach with one arm spread across him. The familiarity and intimacy of tonight are causing all kinds of feelings I'm not sure what to do with. Feelings that will create all sorts of havoc for both of us after tonight. "We've got eight years to cover. I'm sure we haven't covered them all."

He thinks for a few moments. "Okay, Brantley Gilbert. I started listening to his music."

"What? Really?" I scramble to a sitting position. "This is huge. How did you never tell me this?" My mind is blown. Brantley Gilbert is one of my favourite singers, and Mason always hated his music. Mason hated all country music while it's my favourite.

"I never told you because I only just started listening to him."

My breaths slow as I process what he's saying. "You started listening to him because you were missing me?"

Keeping his eyes firmly on mine, he nods. "Yeah."

With that one word and the look in his eyes, Mason makes me fall in love with him all over again while also chiselling a new crack in my heart. A crack all of my own making.

I reach for his hand, interlocking our fingers. I want to tell him again that I'm sorry, but he's made it more than clear he doesn't want to hear those words from me, so I don't. Instead, I pull his hand to my mouth and kiss it before putting it around my waist and crawling on top of him.

"I want you inside me. And I want it slow," I say, needing to feel his love. I like rough sex just as much as he does, but I want to remember what it's like for Mason to take his time with me and to do it with love rather than hate.

His hands slide through my hair and he brings my face to his so he can kiss me. Slow and deep, he gives me exactly what I've requested.

He then spends hours kissing every inch of my body.

Touching me.

Slow fucking me.

Showing me the love he still feels deeply for me.

Mason's preferred way of showing his love is with physical action, whether that be sex, or fighting for those he loves, or doing things for loved ones. Tonight, he shows me unequivocally how much he loves me, and I wonder how we'll go on from here.

26

GUNNAR

Chelsea was right: spending a night with her was a bad fucking idea. I woke just after 5:00 a.m. and spent an hour watching her sleep before leaving the bed more fucked up than when I arrived at Alexa's last night. I didn't wake her even though fucking her was all I wanted to do, because each time I have her makes it fucking harder to walk away again.

I don't know what the fuck we're doing here; all I know is I'm not going to survive it.

"Mason." Chelsea's voice cuts through my thoughts as I shower.

Turning, I find her joining me. Her hands are on my waist before I can stop her. Fuck, not that I want to stop her. That's fucking evident in the way my hands automatically go to her body too.

"Tell me what you're thinking," she says right before her lips find mine.

Our kiss quickly grows urgent, and I push her up against the shower tiles as I begin to take what I need from her. When I finally drag my mouth away, I rest my forehead against hers and say, "The only thing I'm thinking is that this is a fucked up mess."

Her fingers dig into my waist and she nods. She doesn't say anything, though. There's nothing fucking to say, because I said it all.

Fucked. Up. Mess.

And yet, I know I'm going to keep taking every stolen moment she offers because I only want her, and I'll take her any way I can get her.

Fuck.

Too much fucking thinking about shit I can't change.

I just need to fuck her.

Lifting my head, I growl, "Turn around." When she frowns, I take hold of her hips and turn her myself. Then, sliding a hand between her legs, I say, "I need to fuck you, Mayfair, and then I need to get the fuck out of here."

"Mason," she starts, but I cut her off. I don't want to hear anything she has to say today.

"No," I throw down between us, harshly, "We're not fucking talking anymore. We did enough of that last night." Fuck, we talked for fucking hours, and while I want decades more of talking with her, I'm not going to get that, so I don't fucking want scraps of it from her.

I push two fingers inside her. She's already wet for me, and while I usually like to take my time with her, I don't have that in me this morning.

I fucking need to be inside her, and I fucking need that now.

"Fuck!" I roar as I slam my dick as far as I can in her. "Fucking hell."

Chelsea presses her hands to the tiles and takes every

thrust, every ounce of fury, every shred of hate I give. I love her so fucking much, but she's not mine to give that to.

This is all I have left to offer.

After, I pull out of her and exit the shower without looking back. I find my clothes, dress, and get the fuck out of Alexa's apartment, wondering how many days it'll be before I'm back looking for more. Back begging her to dig around some more in the fucking hole in my chest she put there.

∽

"You look like shit," J says at lunch when he takes the stool next to me at the clubhouse bar.

I drink some of my beer. "I feel it, too."

"What's going on, brother?"

I look at him. "Should we call Madison and the girls? Maybe have a fucking sewing circle with them."

He arches his brows. "You're a moody motherfucker lately, Gunnar."

"Yeah, and I don't see that coming to an end any-fucking-time soon."

"Fuck, how long since you've been laid?"

I suck back some more beer. "That's the problem, brother. I had some this morning and I fucking shouldn't have."

"What shouldn't you have had this morning?" Nash asks, joining us.

"Pussy," J says.

Nash frowns. "I can't, for the fuckin' life of me, think of one time I had pussy when I shouldn't have."

J takes a swig of his beer. "Me either, brother."

"Gunnar!" Griff calls from the doorway. "Need you for a minute."

Thank fuck for Griff.

I eye J. "Thanks for the pep talk. It was real fucking enlightening."

"What the fuck is wrong with him?" Nash says as I walk away.

I tune them out as I head towards Griff. "What's up?" I say when I reach him.

"Got a stack of jobs I need you to pick up tomorrow. We'll need to start early so I'll need you to be here at six in the morning. You good with that?"

I nod. "Yeah." I'm more than good with that. Anything to take my mind off shit.

He checks his watch. "Okay, good. I'll see you then."

He heads down the hall towards the office and I make my way out to my bike. Scott okayed me to take the afternoon off to spend with Mum.

She's in bed when I arrive. My father lets me in and tells me to take my boots off before coming in. I tell him I fucking know his house rules before leaving my boots at the front door and stalking to their bedroom. With the mood I'm in today, we'll be lucky not to go a fucking round.

"Mason," Mum says, turning her head on her pillow to meet my gaze as I enter the room.

I walk around the bed and sit on the edge next to her. "How are you feeling?" My chest tightens as I trace my eyes over her face, noting how weak and exhausted she looks. I can't fucking lose her to this shit, and as much as I don't believe in imagining the worst when someone's sick like she is, I'm fucking worried.

She smiles, but it's not a full-throttle smile. Not even fucking close. Reaching for my hand, she says, "Don't worry about me, darling. Let me do the worrying. That's a mother's job, not a child's."

"Fuck, Mum, you don't need to waste your energy worrying about me. You need to keep all your energy for getting better."

"Please don't use that language. You know I don't like it."

She's been telling me this for a good fifteen years, and still I fuck up. I always was the son who couldn't get shit right.

"Tell me what the doctor said." Alexa told me she was seeing him this morning.

A look passes in her eyes, the kind of look that I know means she's hiding something from me. "He didn't say much, just that he wants to keep an eye on me still."

"Don't lie to me, Mum. What is it?"

She watches me silently for longer than I know is good. Finally, she says, "I have nerve damage from the chemo. It's just started, but the doctor says it can last for a long time and that it can get worse. He's started me on new medication to try and help with it."

If I thought my chest was tight before, I had no fucking clue. Now it's fucking tight. "What does that mean? Nerve damage? How does it affect you?" It doesn't sound fucking good, that's for damn sure.

"I'm having trouble gripping things and am dropping things. My feet go numb and sometimes I have trouble walking too." She squeezes my hand. "Please don't worry about this. It's common from what the doctor has said."

"Fuck, it doesn't matter if it's common or not, the fact is *you* have it, and I don't fucking want you to have it."

She doesn't bother to mention my language. Not this time. She's my mother, after all, and she knows every piece of my soul, so she knows I'm fucking struggling here. "I know, darling, but I have faith in my doctors. I trust they know what they're doing and will get me through this."

I want to punch something. Someone. Any-fucking-thing. And I sure as fuck want that doctor to take back this diagnosis. It's bad enough that she has cancer; she doesn't need to be dealing with this shit as well.

I stand and pace beside her bed. My entire body is crowded with the kind of wild energy I need to get out, and since punching her walls is out of the question I'm left with pacing.

"Mason." She sits up. "Please come and sit with me. I want to hear about what you've been up to."

If my mother knew what I've been up to, she wouldn't be asking me to tell her. I know that for sure. She raised me hoping I'd turn out to be a far different man than I've become, and while I am more than fucking good with who I am, I don't share much of what I do with her.

I sit and talk about the one thing we both love: her children. "Alexa got smashed last night while I fixed her showerhead that was leaking. And apparently, Calder's still being an ass to her at work. You really need to have a word with him about that. She won't stick around working with him if he keeps that shit up."

Her eyes widen. "Alexa got drunk on a weeknight?"

I chuckle, my goal achieved. I'll do anything to help take her mind off what she's going through. "Don't be so shocked, Mum. It's not the first time and it won't be the last."

"You kids will be the death of me," she says, not realising what she's saying. I fucking hope we're the death of her, when she's in her nineties, rather than this cancer taking her out.

"Have you heard from Hayden? He was supposed to call me last week but didn't." I'm fairly fucking sure he's too busy fucking his co-star to bother picking up the phone and calling me, but she doesn't need to know that.

"Oh yes, he called me last night," she says before launching into a long story about how his movie is going.

Mum likes the details in shit, so a story that takes her half an hour to tell is one that could be told in less than ten minutes, but I don't give a fuck. I'll sit here and listen to her for hours. And I do. By the time she falls asleep next to me, we've been talking for almost three hours.

I move off the bed carefully so as not to wake her. After covering her with the blanket, I exit out into the hallway and head for the front door. I've got a head filled with a clutter of thoughts over her and am not thinking straight when Dad stops me halfway down the hall and says, "She doesn't need you coming over and confusing her."

My eyes lock onto his. "The fuck does that mean?"

"It means that I don't want you coming over to see her."

I stare at him. How the fuck did I come from him? "You're a piece of fucking work," I snarl. "I'm coming over to see her. You're not fucking stopping me."

"I wasn't the one who stopped you coming to see her in the first place, son. That was your choice, and now you'll see the consequences of your actions."

"What fucking consequences?"

"Did you ever wonder where the cancer came from?"

This is what my father does to me. What he does to all his children. He uses lies and manipulation to get what he wants, and often what he wants is to make his sons feel worthless. He may have achieved that goal often enough when we were kids, but since becoming men, not one of us buy into it anymore. However, we've each had to figure out how the fuck to deal with him and his bullshit, and my way was walking away from him. Unfortunately, that also meant I didn't see my mother for a long time, and that, I fucking regret, but no fucking way am I going to stand here and take the blame for her cancer.

"You're a fucking doctor, are you now, Dad?" I shake my head at him. "Save the bullshit. I'm not fucking interested in hearing it."

His lips pull up in displeasure. "If there's one thing I regret in my life, it's bringing you into this world, Mason. You are not a Blaise as far as I'm concerned. Your mother was too damn lenient with you, allowing you to run wild all over the place when you were a kid. And with that girl too."

Every muscle in my body tenses. "That girl?"

"Chelsea," he snaps. "I imagine she's as bad as her father. God only knows what her influence over you did. It's the only thing I can put your bad behaviour down to because your mother and I did our damnedest to fix you and make you a real man."

I advance on him, my fists clenching by my side. "If

you ever say another bad word about her, I will fucking make it so you don't."

His nostrils flare. "I don't know why you're defending her. She showed you the whore she is when she left you and married Joe Hearst."

My fist is in his face before my brain catches up. He stumbles back before coming at me with his own fist. I block it before it connects with my face and hold it as I say, "I'm gonna walk the fuck out of here now before I do something I'll regret." I shove his hand away. "But if you ever fucking say something like that to me again, I won't hold myself back again. And trust me, Dad, you might think you didn't turn me into a real fucking man, but I sure as fuck fight like a motherfucker. There won't be much left of you if I get my way."

I stalk out of the house, regretting the fact I let him off the fucking hook. I did that for my mother. Next time, all fucking bets are off.

By the time I get home, I'm worked up over both of them. Mum's news today has rattled me while Dad has angered me.

I reach for the bottle of rum in my kitchen and pour myself a drink. Throwing it down my throat, I drink it all in two gulps. I pour another, and another. I'm a quarter of the way through the bottle when I place my hands on the kitchen counter and drop my head. Squeezing my eyes closed, I suck in some deep breaths.

She's not going to fucking die.

I won't fucking let her.

Fuck.

I push off from the counter and stride out to my

garage. Ripping my shirt off, I punch the punching bag I've got set up in here.

Again and again.

Over and over until I can't fucking breathe.

It was light outside when I started; it's now dark.

And I don't feel any fucking better.

I can't think straight. I can't even begin to process one thought, let alone all of them.

I go back into the kitchen and pour another drink. It's sliding down my throat when I know what I fucking need. And fuck if I'm making shit happen before stopping to think it fucking through.

27

CHELSEA

Mason: I need you.

I stare at my phone, re-reading Mason's message over and over.

He has never sent me a message like this, so I know it's big, whatever's causing him to tell me he needs me.

Me: Where are you?
Mason: At home.
Me: I'm on my way.

I take a moment to steady my thoughts.

He was so angry with me this morning that I wasn't sure when I'd see or hear from him again. I've spent today wondering if last night would be our last time together. I know it should be just as much as I know I'm not ready for that. We're in a cycle now, and I don't know how we're going to get ourselves out of it.

I grab my keys, purse, and phone, and head out to my car to drive to Mason's place. I'm almost there when a call comes through from Joe. I want to ignore it, but I know he'll keep calling until I answer.

"Hi," I say. "What's up?" He's not the kind of husband who calls me each night he's away to see how my day was. He only calls when he wants to tell me to do something.

"I need you to go into my study and locate some paperwork and email me a copy."

Shit. "I'm not at home, Joe."

"Where are you?"

"I'm out at dinner."

"Who with?"

"Alexa."

He's silent for a beat. "How long until you'll be home?"

"I don't know. We've just sat down."

"Chelsea, your job is to be by my side in everything I do. I need this paperwork." He's annoyed, that's clear in his tone. But fuck him. My job isn't to sit around and wait for orders.

"It's going to have to wait. I'm not going home yet." I'm not letting the man I actually love down. Not tonight when he needs me.

"Let me know when you're home." He ends the call without another word, and I think about how much I truly despise him and how I really need to figure out his damn computer password. I tried again today, still with no luck. I'm going to dedicate hours to the task tomorrow before he comes home in the afternoon.

I arrive at Mason's house five minutes later, the familiarity of it rolling through me as I walk up the five stairs to his front veranda.

I count each step, taking them slowly, my heart beating faster with each one.

I remember the first day I visited him here. It was

three days after the night we got together. I walked up these stairs that first time with butterflies in my stomach. Being with Mason was everything I ever dreamed of, from when I was younger and all the way through those eight years we weren't friends. He was the boy I could never forget, the boy I still stalked on social media. I dreamed of a life with him in it, never actually thinking that would happen, and then there he was, in it.

He was my everything.

We talked about getting married, having kids, and growing old together.

He told me he would never look at another girl ever again.

I told him we would be buried together for eternity.

We planned all the countries we would visit, all the bucket list items we wanted to tick off together, all the ways he'd fuck me when he was eighty, and still couldn't get enough of me.

We weren't supposed to end up like this, with me walking up these stairs as anything but his girl.

I reach his front door and knock, hating that I have to do that.

We weren't supposed to end up with me having to knock on this door.

He opens it and I inhale sharply at the look of pure torment on his face.

"Mayfair." My name falls from his lips on a ragged breath, and I move without thought.

I step inside and wrap my arms around him. I don't know what's happened, but I know this man needs me more than he's ever needed me.

His arms go around me and we cling to each other for

what feels like forever. When his hold loosens, I look up at him. "What is it? What happened?"

"It's Mum's cancer."

Mason's not much of a talker, so I know it'll take him a little while to give me the full story. I don't push him for more now; he'll talk when he's ready. Instead, I say, "Have you eaten dinner?"

He shakes his head. "I'm not hungry."

I close the door behind us and walk past him towards his kitchen. "You need to eat."

He follows me. "I don't need to fucking eat."

I ignore him. He needs me to take charge tonight, and that's exactly what I'm going to do. "You do. Don't argue with me."

"Chelsea," he says, his tone letting me know he's about to argue.

I look at him as I point at one of the kitchen stools. "Sit your ass down and let me cook you dinner."

I'm not sure what response to expect with him. It could go either way. He might be amused enough at me bossing him around to do what I've said without argument, or he could become pissed off. I'll take my chances; he needs me to. The more I look at him, the more I see how ravaged he is.

"Fuck," he mutters, shoving his fingers through his hair. "This was a bad fucking idea. You should go."

"I'm not going anywhere, Mason. You've never told me you need me like you did in that text. That means something to me, and while I know I've let you down in so many awful ways, I'm not letting you down tonight."

That quietens him. Completely, for a good few moments. Finally, he pulls the stool out and sits his ass on it. He doesn't say anything, but he doesn't need to. His actions do all his speaking for him.

"Any requests for dinner, or should I just go through your fridge and see what you have?"

"Good fucking luck finding anything in there that will make an actual meal."

"You haven't been shopping in a while?"

"Baby, I haven't been fucking shopping since you left."

I stare at him in silence, hating this fact. I internalise it as all my fault to start with but then decide there's only so much blame I can take. At some point, he's going to have to get his shit together. "You need to go shopping, Mason," I say with some force before turning to the fridge and taking a look.

He wasn't joking; there's not much food in here that'll make a meal. However, he does have eggs and bacon, which doesn't surprise me; Mason's go-to breakfast to cook me was bacon and eggs.

Holding up the avocado I also find, I say, "This is random. I've never known you to buy avocados."

He eyes it. "Yeah, Harlow gave it to me the other day. She picked them up for cheap and handed them out to some of us at the clubhouse."

I smile. "I really like her. Always looking out for you guys."

Locating the utensils and pan I need, I cook us bacon and eggs. Mason sits quietly, watching me. I'm usually a talker and will happily take lead on a conversation, but right now with him, everything I want to discuss feels off limits.

I want to talk about this morning. About last night.

About us. But none of those things can lead anywhere good because they can't lead anywhere, end of story.

And I want to ask him about his mum, but I don't want to force him to talk about her until he's ready.

So, I cook. And I hope that just by being here it's helping him in some way.

"I can't remember the last time I ate bacon and eggs," I say as I sit on the stool next to him, trying to find safe ground for a conversation while we eat.

Mason looks at me. "No one cooks it for you, princess?"

His attitude blazes from him, and I don't know what causes it, but I realise I'm done with taking his hate. Placing my fork down, I say, "I know you're angry with me, Mason, and I understand why. Up until now, I've taken all of it. I've let you throw your hate all over me because I know you're hurting, but I'm done. I won't take it anymore. I *can't* take it anymore. It hurts too much. One minute, we're kissing and having sex, and the next, we're back to this. It's too much to bear. I want to be here for you tonight to help you, and I'll stay as long as you let me, but after tonight, I won't be back if all you're going to serve up is that anger and hate. I love us too much to completely ruin what we have."

A myriad of emotions flash through his eyes while he sits silently processing that. When that silence continues past the point where I expect him to speak, I wonder if he will actually say anything. And then he shows me the boy I fell for all those years ago and the man I love with all my heart.

"I'm jealous and possessive, and I feel like you've locked me in a fucking fire and left me to burn on my own, but I don't hate you, Mayfair. I could never fucking hate you. Not when I love you more than I know what to do with." He takes hold of my stool and pulls me to him. Curling his hand around my neck, he says, "I don't know what we are now, but I sure as fuck know I need you in my life. And I don't want to completely ruin what we have either."

His lips come to mine and he kisses me. There's no hate in sight. Or anger. There's only love and a plea for me to stay and fight for this together.

When he lets me go, he rests his forehead against mine. "Mum's cancer treatment is causing nerve damage."

"What does that mean?"

He lifts his head and meets my gaze. "I don't know the full details. She only told me this afternoon and she didn't say much, but it doesn't sound good."

I reach out and cup his face. My beautiful, broken man. I'll do whatever it takes to help him get through this. "Let's eat, and then I'll do some research. You can watch *Game of Thrones* while I do it maybe." Mason isn't one for details, so I can't imagine him spending time researching this. And watching TV is how he relaxes and switches off, so this is a good option for him tonight.

He nods. "Yeah, sounds good."

Looking down at the stool, I say, "You need to push me back."

He eyes the stool, which is pushed right up against his. "Fuck that," he says, reaching across me and pulling my plate across the counter to me. Then, placing his hand on my thigh, he jerks his chin at my food and says,

"Eat up. We've got a date on the couch for the rest of the night."

Butterflies.

In my stomach.

So many butterflies.

I really need to crack that fucking password on Joe's computer because I really need this man back in my life. I need to drag him from that fire I left him in and put us back together.

28

CHELSEA

I wake up with a start, not knowing where I am for a moment. It's Mason's arm tightening around me that helps me remember.

I'm at his house.

In his bed.

With his arm and leg over me, and his body pressed hard against mine. It's like he doesn't want to let me go, and I don't blame him. I don't want to go either. My phone sounding with text after text brings me crashing back to real life.

"Fuck," I mutter, trying to push Mason's arm off me so I can reach for my phone. When he refuses to budge, I say, "I need to check my messages."

"Motherfucker," he grumbles, letting me go. I know he's referring to Joe, and I'm more than okay with it. I agree that my husband is a motherfucker, but what I'm really okay with is the fact that while Mason's complaining, his hate isn't directed at me.

I grab my phone and scroll the messages. Joe came

back to me last night just after 8:30 p.m. and told me not to bother sending him any paperwork, but now it seems he wants it.

"Fuck you, asshole," I mutter, sitting and pushing the sheet off so I can leave the bed.

Mason has other ideas, though. Before I can move, his arm comes around my waist, and he slides me back to him. Sitting up, he brings his mouth to my ear. "I fucking like it when you call him an asshole."

I still in his arms. We've barely discussed Joe or my marriage except for the conversations we've had about how it was arranged. It seems like a terrible idea to start now, mostly because I know it will stir up Mason's jealousy, but also because I don't want to give him the chance to push me for more information on why I stay in the marriage. I'm worried he'll take matters into his own hands if he knows how truly horrible Joe is, and that's a place I can't let him get to because Joe will destroy him. I used to think it was my father who would do that, but all along it was Joe who dealt the cards.

"He is an asshole," I say. "He's a motherfucking asshole."

Mason chuckles against my shoulder. "That filthy mouth of yours turns me the fuck on, Mayfair."

I place my hand on his arm that's around me. "I have to go."

He kisses my neck. "Why? I was just getting started."

"I know, but I have to get home."

He removes his mouth from my neck and lets me go. When he doesn't say anything else, I stand and look at him while reaching for my clothes. He's lying on his back with his hands resting under his head, watching me. "I can't get a feel for your mood. Talk to me," I say.

"You sure you wanna know?"

Yes.

No.

I nod as I do up my bra. "Go easy, though, okay? We're still getting the hang of this."

"I'm pissed off that you have to leave. I'm pissed off that he snaps his fingers and you go running. And I'm pissed off that I can't fuck you before you go. But I'm a selfish asshole that you should just fucking ignore."

A smile spreads slowly across my face. Crawling across the bed to him, I kiss him. "I like this honesty. We should keep it up."

As I move to leave the bed again, he reaches for my wrist. "What is this, Chelsea?"

I know what he's asking and I don't have a good answer. Not one that he's going to be okay with. But I try to answer him, regardless. "This is us figuring out how to be together again."

His brows furrow. "How the fuck can we be together again if you're fucking married?"

"I'm working on that."

"You're talking, but you're not giving me much, baby. What are you working on?"

I finish dressing and say, "I have to go. We'll talk about this later, okay?"

"Fuck," he mutters, waving me off. "Go, but this is a conversation we will be finishing."

I have no doubt. Mason isn't the kind of man who can be easily distracted from a conversation. Not even with the promise of a blowjob. He's fucking relentless when it comes to some things, and I know this will be one of them.

~

I MANAGE to get Joe's paperwork to him without having him completely lose his shit at me. He's pissed, though, and I know I'll hear more about that when he arrives home this afternoon.

I shower and dress for the office. When I arrive, Joe's assistant is in a flap over a glitch with his computer. Staring at it, at the fact it's turned on and working, I say to her, "Why are you in Joe's computer?" I try to sound authoritative, like I give a shit that she's at my husband's computer, but what I really am is excited that she's at it. She must know the fucking password.

She frowns at me. "He asked me to log in and send him some files that are on it."

I walk around the desk to stand next to her. "Oh, that's right. He mentioned this. What's happening with it?"

"Ugh," she complains and proceeds to show me how it keeps crashing whenever she attempts to open one of the files. She then adds, "I've got a million things to do this morning before he gets back. I don't have time for this."

"Why don't you leave it with me? I'll figure it out."

She looks at me with relief. "Really? You have time?"

I wave her off. "I'll make time. I don't want you stressed."

"Thank you so much, Chelsea." She walks to the door and looks back at me. "Marrying you was the best thing Joe ever did. He used to be so, ahh, difficult before you came along. I hope you don't mind me saying that, but he's so much nicer now he's with you."

And here I was thinking she didn't like me. She barely smiles. It turns out she suffers from the same problem I do—knowing Joe.

I smile. "I don't mind you saying that at all. Us girls need to stick together."

After she leaves, I settle myself in his chair.

Okay, dear husband, where do you keep your secrets?

First, I figure out the glitch and send the files to Joe that he's requested. Then, I start my digging, and holy hell, my asshole husband is in some shit with the mafia. I was right about him being involved in money laundering and insider trading. Going by the files I find, he's been working for them for three years. I locate a USB stick and start copying the files across. I'm about a quarter of the way through when I'm interrupted by two men who force their way into the office. Joe's assistant apologises profusely for allowing them in, but I tell her not to stress. I only need to take one look at these men to know no one would have kept them out.

Standing, I say, "Good morning, gentlemen. My husband isn't in until around lunchtime. Is there anything I can help you with?"

Both these guys look like they've stepped in a boxing ring a time or two. They have that smooshed-nose look I always think boxers have.

The blond guy trails his eyes down my body, giving me not-so-nice vibes before saying, "The thing is, sweetheart, we're not leaving here until your husband comes out and talks to us. So keep this charade up if you want, but our patience won't last forever. And once it's gone, there's no telling what we'll do in order to get what we came for, if you catch my drift."

"I'm not lying. He's not here. Honestly, he'll be here in about an hour, so feel free to take a seat and wait for him."

The guy with the black hair steps forward and leans in close. "Babe, you're not getting it. He owes us and we're here to fucking collect. And we don't fucking wait around for anyone." He tries to intimidate me a little more when he barks, "Go fucking get him."

I fucking hate all these motherfucking assholes I'm surrounded by. My father, Joe, Matthew Ronson, these assholes.

Dragging my balls out, I say, "You know what? My husband threatens me enough, so if you think I feel scared by you assholes, think again. Do whatever the fuck you want to me, but I'm telling you he's not here. Trust me, if he was, I'd shove him your way faster than you can blink because I'd be hoping you might take care of him for me, if you catch my drift."

With that, I walk back around Joe's desk and take a seat and continue transferring files across to the USB. Files that I am almost certain are tied up with the men who employ the assholes standing in front of me.

I don't chance a look at them. I just pray they fuck off.

They don't. However, they do as I suggested and take a seat and wait for Joe. That actually makes my heart happy. I want him to have to deal with them.

I'm almost halfway through transferring the files when the office phone rings, and Joe's assistant tells me there's a delivery I need to sign for.

Standing, I eye the two men sitting on Joe's couch. "I'll be back. Don't touch anything."

The black-haired guy scowls at me while the blond one looks at me with amusement. They don't say anything, though, and I hurry out to sign for the delivery.

I've signed and am making my way back into Joe's office when his voice sounds from behind me. He's talking with his assistant, but his eyes meet mine as I turn to glance back at him.

Holy fuck.

He's back earlier than I thought he would be.

I've got a USB stick sitting in his computer transferring financial files that I want to use to force him to divorce me and leave Mason alone, and he's about to fucking go into his office.

Panic swirls in my gut, causing some light-headedness as I try desperately to figure out how the hell to stall him and fix this situation.

"You don't look pleased to see me," he murmurs when he comes to me.

That's because I'm fucking not.

Oh God.

God, God, God, where the hell are you today and why aren't you on my side?

I smile, but even I know it's a tight smile that won't convince him. "I'm not feeling the best today, Joe."

He frowns. "What's wrong?"

"My stomach. I have cramps and I feel like I'm going to vomit." Jesus, why didn't I learn how to be a better liar? I feel like that's a life skill I could do with.

His gaze drops to the box I'm carrying. The one I just signed for. "What's that?"

I have no idea what's in the box. All I know is that Alexa sent it to me, and knowing her sense of humour, I should do my best not to let my husband see what it is until I confirm it's safe for his eyes.

Good fucking God, I may just die from severe anxiety today.

"It's make-up that Alexa sent over for me to try."

I swear Joe has a bullshit detector for me. He narrows his eyes and says, "What the fuck is really in the box, Chelsea? And why are you lying to me about not feeling well?"

Those balls I found earlier for the mafia men? They just fell off. I can't juggle balls while also juggling an asshole. One has to give, and unfortunately, the asshole isn't going anywhere soon.

I shove the box at him. "Take a look for yourself. And thank you very much for being a prick. For your information, I'm not lying. My stomach is twisting up like it wants to exit my body. And I could vomit all over you right now I feel that ill."

The fact that what I just said is the actual truth goes in my favour. Joe doesn't detect any bullshit, so he refuses to take the box and says, "I see we're going to have one of those days."

When he moves past me to walk towards his office, I almost literally throw up all over him.

Scrambling to come up with something—*anything*—that will distract him from going in there, I blurt, "And here I was actually fucking missing you while you were away. So much so that I bought you something, but you know what? I don't think I want to give it to you now."

Every part of me holds its breath, waiting for his

response. I'm hopeful he'll take the bait and run with it so I can try to drag him to the office kitchen, pretending the gift is in there before telling him to wait while I go get it. I'm fully aware this is the worst plan in the entire history of dumb plans, but I'm fucking desperate here.

He stops. "What the fuck is going on?"

My eyes widen at his tone.

He's not buying a word I'm saying.

And I'm pretty sure I'm about to discover just what a monster he is. I'm under no illusions that if Joe figures out my plan to save Mason, I'll learn that anything he's done to me so far doesn't come close to the devious shit he'll dream up in response to this.

When I don't answer him, he barks, "Get in my office now. We need to discuss the fact you didn't come home last night."

He turns and stalks into his office before I can get another word in. I can barely process the fact he knows I didn't come home because I'm still trying to process the fact he's going to punish me for snooping on him and trying to blackmail him.

I consider running away. Like seriously consider it. And then I think about the power I'm trying to claim and realise running away isn't claiming anything. It's hiding and it's admitting defeat. I need to go in there and stand tall against him. I don't think I can salvage this, but I sure as hell can stand proud that I tried to improve mine and Mason's life. I'm not going to give Joe the satisfaction of thinking I'm scared of him.

But hot damn, the steps I have to take into his office are some of the hardest steps I've ever had to take in my life. And if I thought I wanted to vomit before, now I know what it truly feels like to want to vomit.

I reach his office door and take a deep breath.

Showtime.

I step through the door and am almost knocked over when Joe meets me. He's on his way back out with the two smooshed-nose men right behind him, and he doesn't look pleased with me.

Huh. I should have just told him he had visitors. I suspect he would have left the building without further argument.

I race around his desk and remove the USB and close down everything I had open before turning his computer off. I then stash the USB in my bag and sit at my desk, sucking in deep, calming breaths. Not that they're very fucking calming. I don't even think if I was to meditate all day, have a massage, and drink an entire bottle of tequila that I'd feel calm.

That was fucking close and I need to be more careful in the future.

29

CHELSEA

Alexa: We still haven't discussed the fact you slept with Mason at my place on Wednesday night. When are we getting together to do that?

Me: He told you?

Alexa: Hell no, but I woke up and heard you guys. And Jesus, you two are noisy AF. I was worried you were gonna ram a hole through my wall.

Me: LOL you should be worried. Your brother is hardcore.

Alexa: Oh god, you did not just say that.

Me: Well you're the one who wants the goss.

Alexa: Not the details, girlfriend. Just the goss on what's happening with you two. Jesus.

Me: Honestly, I don't know when I can swing some time. Joe's home and all over me. We've got a fundraiser tonight, a dinner tomorrow night, something the next night, and then dinner with his parents the night after. And don't even get me started on the days. He's filled my damn schedule right up. He's punishing me.

Alexa: I won't even ask what for, but see if you can make room for me, even for a quick lunch or coffee one day. Tell him to fuck off with not allowing time for your friends.

Me: I love you. I'll try. Gotta go xx

Alexa: I love you too.

Alexa: PS I love that you and Mason got it on. I hope this continues. You know I'm secretly hoping you two get back together.

Alexa has no idea of the man I'm married to. After the visit from the smooshed-nose men, Joe came back angrier than I've seen him in a while. Unfortunately, they didn't take care of him how I'd hoped they would, so he came in and let me know in no uncertain terms how pissed he was. Two hours later, I had a new schedule on my email. One he oversaw himself. One designed to fill every available minute of my day for the next week. God only knows what the week after will look like. And on top of that, he informed me he's put hidden cameras in our home for security. What he was really saying, though, is that he can see when I'm not home when he thinks I should be.

"Chelsea, I need you to bring your A-game tonight," Matthew Ronson says, coming up to me as I exit the Range Rover outside the hotel where the fundraiser is being held tonight.

I hate this asshole almost as much as I hate the one I'm married to. "I always bring my fucking A-game, Matthew." I don't bother being polite to him anymore.

"I honestly don't know what the fuck Joe sees in you," he says, hatred blazing in his eyes.

"That's because you're not actually smart; you're just

an asshole who gets what he wants through lies and manipulation."

He opens his mouth to respond, but Joe joins us and cuts in. "Chelsea, go and find your mother and sit with her." He's all snappy and snarly like he's been since he arrived home yesterday.

"Yes, dear husband."

His fingers curl around my bicep, digging in hard as he leans his mouth to my ear. "You keep giving me attitude and I'll wash your fucking mouth with soap tonight after I fuck it."

The fear of my husband I've been pushing away for weeks slams into me. I know he has so much more inside him that I haven't seen yet, and I can't help but think he has a violent streak I should be doing everything in my power to avoid stirring. But my attitude has a way of falling out of my mouth where he's concerned, and as much as I know I should rein it in, I fail more times than not.

When he jerks me away from him, I walk inside the hotel, find my mother, and sit with her. She's sitting at the table assigned to our family for this dinner, looking as blank as usual.

"Are you happy, Mum?" I run my gaze over her, taking in her perfect hair, flawless make-up, expensive dress, and trim figure. My mother looks like she has the world at her feet, but I know she doesn't, and I want to know how she really feels about it. She and I have never had a truly honest and raw conversation in our life, and I doubt we will now, but people still sometimes surprise me; maybe she will.

She turns and frowns at me. "What kind of question is that, Chelsea?"

"The kind I really would love to know the answer to."

Still frowning, she says, "No, I'm not happy that we've been made to sit at this table. It's in an awkward position, and the light is shining in my eyes."

"I mean in your life. Are you happy with your life?"

She opens her mouth to speak but snaps it closed before flattening her lips. "Really, darling, that's not a question that can be answered."

"Why not?"

"Because there is so much going on in my life that makes it impossible to answer. Some things are good, while others are not as good."

I lean forward, my eyes boring into hers. "Yes, I get that, but surely you have an overall sense of your life and whether you like it and are happy."

She stares at me like I've lost my mind. "One doesn't just decide if they're happy, Chelsea. That's not how this works. We just get on with the things we have to do and take the good with the bad. We don't get to choose happiness in life; life chooses it for us."

I have my answer and it makes me sad. That a woman can get to her age and not have a clue about whether she's happy or not saddens me greatly. And that she thinks we don't have the power to create our own happiness hurts my heart even more. If there's one thing I've learned from Joe and Dad, it's that, yes, life can dictate a lot, but it's how we choose to work with life that is the key to happiness.

I take a wine from the waiter as he comes past, and as I

sip it, I think about my life. I think about the choices I've made and the consequences of those choices. I think about being my mother's age and decide here and now that I will do everything in my power to know deep happiness. I will own the power I have to create the life I want. I do not want to look back on my life and regret a second of it.

I sip some more wine and consider a new approach for getting those files off Joe's computer.

I also think about my father and how I'm going to bring him down.

It came to me earlier.

I've figured out how to force my father's hand. After all this time, I've finally figured it out.

Now, I just need to sort out my husband.

Unfortunately, I think he's going to be a handful. But nothing good in life comes easy, and Mason is worth every second of pain I'll have to endure.

30

GUNNAR

"Tell me again what the fuck we're doing here," I say to Griff as we enter an office building on George Street. It's just after 8:00 p.m. and I'm not having any good feelings about this job Moss sent us on.

He jabs the button for the lift and looks at me. "You know why the fuck we're here."

"Yeah, and it feels off."

The lift doors open and we step in to go up to level twenty.

"That's because of your situation with Novak and Hearst."

"Yeah, it fucking is, and it's also because I don't fucking trust these motherfuckers."

Moss and Hearst have sent us here to threaten one of the engineers who has been consulting on the mine approval he's trying to push through. Apparently, this guy has decided he wants Moss to pay him a fair chunk of change before he'll sign off on his part of the process.

"That makes two of us, brother, so let's just keep our shit together, get through this, and then go the fuck home."

My VP is in a mood today. Fuck knows why, because he keeps shit to himself, but I'm picking up the vibe he's putting down, so I know it's time to pull my head in and just get shit done.

We exit the lift and make our way to the guy's office. He appears to be the only one here, which makes sense; it's Saturday night, and most sane people are busy drinking, fucking, or zoning out in front of the TV.

Griff doesn't bother to knock. He tries the door first, and when it's locked, he kicks it in. The guy we're here to see looks up from his desk with panic, and when he sees us coming towards him, he madly reaches into his drawer, searching for something. Something that I just fucking know isn't going to be anything good.

Knowing this, I don't take my fucking time stalking around his desk. And I sure as fuck don't take my time getting my fist in his face. He lands on the floor, at which point I reef him up and slam him back down in his seat. Pressing my hands to his chair armrests either side of him, I get in his face and demand, "Do you know why we're here?"

His lips curl up. "My guess is Dwayne Moss sent you."

"He sure as fuck did," I say. "You're gonna sign some paperwork for us."

"I'm not signing anything, asshole. Not until I get my money from Moss."

I push up off the chair and punch him again. Then, gripping his neck, I steady him in the chair and say, "There's not gonna be any more money from Moss."

Griff produces the paperwork we need signed and shoves it across the desk at the guy with a pen. "Sign that and don't waste our fucking time. We all know how tonight's gonna end. I'd rather just cut straight to the end now."

The guy eyes Griff, and snarls, "I don't think you're gonna like how tonight ends."

My fist connects with his face and he ends up on the floor again. As I reach down to hoist him back up, the motherfucker pulls a move and grabs a fucking knife he had stashed around his ankle. He then tries to fucking stab me with it.

"Are you fucking kidding me?" I bellow as I fight him off and jerk him back up to a standing position. I'm fucking ropable now. All fucking bets are off. "You sit at a fucking desk all day and you sling a fucking knife around your ankle? Who the fuck are you? Crocodile fucking Dundee at a desk?" I jab him in the face, hard and snappy. His head bounces back and then forward, at which point, I punch him again, this time hard enough to lay him flat on the floor.

This asshole thinks he's the shit, though. Instead of lying down and accepting his fucking fate, he keeps fighting against me and is back up in my face fast. We go another round of punches, and Griff steps in to help, pulling the guy away from me and holding him around the neck.

Tightening his hold on him, Griff roars, "Sign the fucking paperwork or I'll let Gunnar go to fucking town on you, and that is the last fucking thing you want. Mark my fucking words."

The guy shows us just what a dickhead he is when he

struggles against Griff. "I want my fucking money before I sign anything!"

I look at Griff. "And here I was thinking this'd be a quick, easy job." Jerking my chin at the guy, I say, "Hold him for me."

Griff holds him steady and I smash my fist into his face. Fast. Repeatedly. Until I'm punching a bloody mess that I can't fucking make out as a face anymore.

"You ready to sign yet?" I ask when I take a breather.

The guy shakes his head. It's hanging from his shoulders like it could roll off at any time and looks like something out of a horror movie, but still, he fucking manages to shake the fucking thing.

Griff shoves him forward, letting him fall to the floor, while I eye the room, surveying it for things I can use to hurt this motherfucker. I didn't expect this to be so fucking difficult, so I didn't come prepared.

"Fuck," Griff says as I'm poking around the room. "I think he's had a fucking heart attack."

"The fuck?" My head snaps back to eye the dickhead on the floor, and sure as fuck, he doesn't appear to be breathing.

Griff bends over him, checking his pulse, before straightening. "No fucking pulse."

"Well, that just fucking pisses on our party."

Griff rakes his fingers through his hair. "It does more than that." He pulls out his phone and makes a call to Hearst. After a quick conversation, Griff puts his phone away and says, "It's too risky to move the body due to where we are, so we're gonna clean the room and get the fuck out of here. I'll pull the surveillance on the building and wipe us from it. Hearst is gonna make sure this doesn't come back on us."

I don't argue with my VP, but I don't fucking trust Hearst. If anything, I'd trust him to ensure it did fucking come back on us.

We clean the room and exit the building, keeping our heads down and moving fast. Twenty minutes later, we're back at the clubhouse so Griff can pull the surveillance.

Scott's in the bar talking with Blade. He glances up as we come in. "All done?"

Griff gives a shake of his head. "No." He fills Scott in.

"Jesus," Scott says. "You trust Hearst to make good on that?"

"I don't fucking know," Griff says.

"I'm not convinced," Scott says. "I think the three of us need to have a conversation with Novak over this."

"When?" Griff asks.

"Now," Scott says, ruining the rest of my fucking night. "You take care of the surveillance while I line up a meet."

The two of them take care of their shit while I change my shirt, and thirty minutes later, we're on our way to some hotel in the city where Novak's attending a fundraiser. He wasn't fucking happy to hear from Scott and tried to say no, but Scott pushed the point and made it happen.

We wait outside the hotel when we arrive, and Scott lets Novak know we're here. Novak directs us as to where to wait for him, in a hidden alcove around the corner of the hotel. I expect Hearst to be with him when he comes out, but he's alone.

"This better be fucking important," he says, throwing

some heavy pissed-off vibes our way. "I'm in the middle of a fucking dinner and I don't appreciate being interrupted."

Scott steps towards him, his shoulders like stone walls, his face the same. "You know what I don't fuckin' appreciate, Novak? Taking care of your dirty work and not knowing if we'll be backed up when something goes wrong."

"What the fuck went wrong?"

"Hearst hasn't told you?"

There's something in the way Novak scowls that causes me to sit the fuck up and pay attention. "My son-in-law doesn't run to me with everything, Mr Cole, no. Please enlighten me."

Scott gives him a rundown on the events of the evening, to which Novak says, "If Joe said he'd take care of it, he will."

What he says is too fucking dismissive for me, and I can't hold myself back any longer. "I don't fucking trust him," I say.

Novak glances at me and I fucking hate the smug look in his eyes. "Trust me when I tell you that we have our ways of keeping your club out of trouble. You of all people should be aware of that, Mason."

Scott cuts in. "You need to know that if we do end up going down for shit, you'll be going down too."

Novak turns to him, looking less than fucking friendly. "I suspect you're alluding to sharing with the world the fact you've done some work for me."

"I'm not fuckin' alluding to anything. I'm fuckin' stating it loudly," Scott says. "You fuckin' take our back or you won't be premier anymore."

I watch as Novak walks away from us and think about what was just said. For the fucking life of me, I can't figure out what my brain is latching onto, but it's fucking latched onto something Novak said.

You of all people should be aware of that.

I am aware of that. I'm fucking aware of that. But the way he said it makes me feel like there's something else to it. Something I'm not fucking aware of.

Chelsea told me that her dad helped keep me out of prison in exchange for her marrying Joe. So what the fuck did he mean when he said I should know he has ways of keeping the club out of trouble?

"You coming?" Griff asks as he looks back at me when I don't make a move to leave.

I shake my head and reach for my phone. "I've got something to do. I'll see you back at the clubhouse later."

They leave me and I send Chelsea a text.

Me: I need to see you. Now.

She takes a good five minutes to come back to me.

Chelsea: I can't now. I'm busy.

Me: I'm outside the hotel. We need to talk.

Chelsea: Mason, I can't.

Me: I don't give a fuck what you need to do to get out here, but I need you to come out and talk to me. Don't make me come inside.

The dots go up and down for a long time before her reply comes through.

Chelsea: You're busting my fucking balls here. Give me five minutes.

Fuck, I love her fire.

She takes a good ten minutes to come out, but she does, and I struggle to take my eyes off her. She's wearing a silver dress that is hell on a man's ability to think straight. Since I need to fucking think straight for the conversation we're about to have, I force my eyes back up to her face and keep them fucking there.

"What is so important that I just had to fake sickness to Joe for and risk his wrath for the rest of the night? And if you tell me it's just because you want to get your hands on me, I swear to God, I will—"

"What else did you get in exchange for marrying that motherfucker?"

Her mouth snaps shut, all her words swallowed. I watch as her brows wrinkle, her forehead wrinkles, and her thoughts wrinkle. She's trying to figure out how to get out of telling me the truth, but fuck if I'm allowing that tonight.

"You need to start talking, Mayfair, and you need to start fucking doing that now. And *I* swear to fucking God, if you don't give me the truth, this will be it for us. I will walk the fuck away from you and never come back."

Those beautiful blue eyes of her look at me so wide and so scared that I can't help but feel the pull to her that is always there. She hasn't told me she still loves me, but she did tell me she loves us enough not to ruin us, so as far as I'm concerned, that's her telling me she loves me. But I don't need to hear what I can plainly fucking see— Chelsea never stopped loving me, and I think she made a deal with the fucking devil for me. A deal she's refused to tell me about, even when I've been hell-bent on shoving my hate in her face. And I want to fucking know what it was and why the fuck she made it.

Moving into me, she grips my T-shirt. "I got your safety. You know that."

"What the fuck else, Chelsea? Tell. Me."

Her eyes frantically search mine, and I just fucking know I'm not going to like what I hear when she finally gives me the truth. "Please don't make me do this, Mason. Please."

I'm on the edge here. Every muscle is straining while my heart beats so fucking loud I swear they could hear it in fucking Perth. "You're doing this. You're going to tell me and then I'm going to fucking take care of this shit like I fucking should have when it all started."

Her face twists and she shakes her head. "No, you can't. They will ruin you." She grips my shirt harder. "I have a plan and am almost ready to—"

"Fuck, Chelsea, no. I'm not spending another fucking second watching you be with that motherfucker. I want him gone and I fucking want that now. Tell me what the fuck they're holding over you to keep you married to him."

"Mason, stop. No. You're not thinking straight."

"Baby, this is the first time I *am* fucking thinking straight since this mess all fucking started." I take hold of her neck and pull her to me. "I should have fucking known you wouldn't walk away from me willingly. I fucking hate that we had to go through all this to get here, and now I need to fix it, and you need to fucking let me."

"It's not that I don't want to let you fix this. Please believe me." Her eyes plead with me as much as her voice does. "I've figured out how to stop Joe, and I've almost got everything I need to do that. Please let me see this through. Please let me make this right between us after I broke what we had."

Fuck.

Fuck.

When Chelsea's standing in front of me, looking at me the way she is, begging for me to let her do something for us like she is, I'm fucking helpless but to give her what she wants. I will always fucking give this woman what she wants.

"How long is this going to take?" I say.

"I don't know, but I'm hoping not long."

"I'm putting a time limit on it. One week, Mayfair. If it's not sorted by then, I'm fucking taking over and you won't fucking argue with me."

"Thank you," she says, and I feel every ounce of her gratitude and relief.

Her phone sounds with a text, and as she glances down at it, I say, "They threatened the club, didn't they?"

She looks back up at me and nods. And so fucking softly I can only just hear her, she says, "Yes, they threatened the people I know you'd die for."

Fuck me.

I've spent all these fucking months hating her and treating her like shit when she was going to her own grave in her own way for me because of the people *I'd* go to my grave for. I really am a fucking asshole.

I tighten my hold on her neck and pull her body against mine. Kissing the top of her head, I say, "I fucking love you and I swear I will make this up to you."

I will spend every day of the rest of my life doing that.

I will also make these cunts pay for what they've done to her.

31

CHELSEA

I squint as the sun beats down on me, blinding me for a moment. Reaching for my sunglasses, I slide them on. I also put my hat on before walking the path from the house to the pool where I intend to spend most of today. A lazy Sunday by the pool in the sun sounds like heaven to me. Especially since Joe has locked himself in his office for the day. He told me he has a stack of work to get through, so not to expect to see him anytime soon.

I survived the fundraiser last night and I also survived Joe after the fundraiser. After he threatened to wash my mouth out earlier in the night, I wasn't sure what to expect from him, but he'd been distracted by something and didn't come near me after we arrived home.

Sitting on the sunlounger, I apply sunscreen and think about Mason. He gave me a deadline last night and I'm a little stressed by it because I know he meant every word he said. If I don't take care of Joe, he'll go in guns blazing and do it. But what he doesn't realise is that dealing with Joe once and for all will require a lot more than brute strength. This isn't something Mason can beat out of him. We need to be smarter about how we handle this situation.

An hour of blissful peace and sunshine passes before I decide to go for a swim. I'm about to dive in when Joe's voice sounds from behind me.

"You've been fucking your biker."

My entire body tenses as I still.

It's not just that he knows this that causes my reaction. It's the malice in his voice. The malice that slips into my veins and slides through them like an angry snake.

I don't want to look at him, but I do.

Bile hits my throat as I take in the menacing storm that is my husband.

He comes closer.

"I knew you were spreading your legs for him."

My fear lies trapped in my lungs while I struggle to breathe. "I'm not spreading my legs for him, Joe."

His hand is across my face before I see it coming. "You fucking are. Don't fucking lie to me."

I press my fingers to my cheek where he's left the kind of sting I'll feel for hours.

"I've had a guy watching you since I got home on Friday. He caught you with Mason last night."

"So talking to a person automatically means you're fucking them, does it?"

He strikes me again. Harder this time. "I'm not blind. You're fucking him. And I'm putting an end to it. I'm also putting an end to his club. I'll fucking take everything he cares about."

I don't know exactly what he means by that, but I

know just from looking at and feeling his dark energy that I'm not going to like it.

Still running with denial, I say, "I'm not going to stand here and listen to this. I've given you everything since I married you. *Everything*. My life, my body, my fucking soul. Don't you dare come here and throw accusations in my face that aren't true."

I try to move past him, but he stops me. Squeezing his fingers around my throat, he says, "By the time I'm finished with you, you will know never to lie to me again. And you will know that I am the only man who touches you."

His fingers are cutting off my oxygen and my attempts at prying them from me are unsuccessful. He watches me gasp for breath, exerting more pressure, almost choking me.

My head spins, my lungs wheeze, my fear roars to life.

The monster I live with is finally rearing its head.

My fingers claw at his.

"Joe," I choke out. "Stop."

"We're just getting started, Chelsea," he says, his voice as dark as his eyes.

He shoves me away from him and I stumble backwards on the paved area of the pool while sucking air in and trying to refill my lungs.

I need to run, but my legs are weak and every part of me is slow after being deprived of oxygen. But I push myself because I need to get far, far away from Joe.

As I take steps backwards, he advances towards me. When I run into a chair and almost trip over it, his hand is across my face. This is more than a slap but not quite a punch, and it causes me to crumple over the chair.

Joe's hands grip my waist and he lifts me back to my feet. "How many times have you fucked him?"

Still trying to get my breath back, I look at him. I don't want to answer him. The truth will enrage him even more than he is—a lie will do the same. When I don't give him an answer, he hits me again. This one knocks the breath out of me.

You need to run.

He's going to kill you.

Panic oozes through me as what he's doing to me now collides in my mind with what my father did to me when I was younger.

I want to take my power back and stand up against Joe, but all that baggage weighs me down.

It makes me feel weak and unable to defend myself.

It keeps me small.

That's what these assholes want, Chelsea.

To keep you small so they can be big.

Stand the fuck up and fight.

I force myself to straighten and to push my shoulders back.

I force myself to look my husband in the eyes.

And then I force myself to stand up to him even though it's the scariest thing I've ever had to do.

"I love him, Joe, and I will never stop loving him. And you can keep hitting me all you want, but it's not going to look good when the media sees how you manage your wife, because trust me, I will show them."

"You won't have the chance to show them, because I won't let you near them without me. Everything you do from here on out will be monitored. I gave you space to begin with, to see if you could be trusted, and now I know you can't be. Things will be very different now."

Run.

You need to fucking run.

I stare at Joe, horrified at the man I married, and I know I'm right. I need to fucking run.

So I do.

I run towards the front yard.

I need to find other people because Joe won't chance touching me in public.

He comes after me, but I have an advantage. I'm lighter and I'm a runner, so I'm faster than him.

The problem is the gate to the front yard. I have to stop to unlock it and that gives him time to catch up.

As I madly fumble with the lock, I glance back at him. When I see how close he is, I kick my leg out at him, aiming for his balls. He anticipates that, though, and stops my leg before my foot connects with him.

"You can't win here, Chelsea," he says, breathing his evil all over me.

I keep working the lock.

Why won't it unlock, goddam it?

Fuck it.

I give up and push my hands into Joe's chest as hard as I can.

He's almost unmovable, but I do manage to force him back a couple of steps. I take the opportunity to scramble up the gate. If I can't fucking go through it, I'll go over it.

I'm almost at the top when Joe's hand latches around my foot. I kick out, trying to dislodge his hand, and I succeed, but not for long. Joe's hands grip my calves and he yanks me down with every bit of strength he possesses.

My body slides down the gate, smacking my chin in the rush, and I land on the cement path with a loud crack.

The pain that shoots through my body is what I imagine an earthquake to be like. Radiating waves of agony and terror.

Reaching to touch my head where it hurts the most, I find sticky liquid, which I confirm is blood when I pull my hand back.

I don't have time to think about this, though, because Joe steps over my body and bends over me to bring his face to mine. The pure rage I see in his eyes makes me shudder.

"I will teach you how to be a wife if it's the last fucking thing I do."

He raises his hand and brings it down on my face and I see black.

32

GUNNAR

"I haven't seen you for a couple of weeks," Louise says at Scott's place on Sunday when I rock up for the barbecue lunch Scott invited me to. "How was your trip?"

I take the seat next to her. "Let's just say I'm glad it's fucking over. How have you been?"

She smiles. "I've been good. Busy with work, but good." She pauses. "How are you going with getting that girl out of your system?"

I know what she's asking, and I'll give her a straight-up answer because she needs to know there's no chance at anything happening between us. "It turns out she's in there for life."

She keeps smiling and surprises me when she says, "I'm glad you've figured that out. I mean, I'm disappointed for me, but happy for you. I hope I get to meet her one day."

"You know what? I think you two'll get on well."

"Who'll get on well?" Harlow asks, sitting next to me.

"Louise and Chelsea."

Harlow's eyes widen a little. "I thought Chelsea was out of your life."

"She was, but now she's not." I lean towards her. "So I no longer require your matchmaking services." I eye Wilder across the table and grin. "Maybe move on to Wilder. He needs all the help he can get."

Harlow appears confused, like her brain is taking its sweet time accepting what I've told her. She looks at Wilder, though, and waves her hand as she says, "Oh he's already sorted. We all know who he's going to end up with."

I frown. "I'm out of the loop on that."

She looks back at me. "So you and Chelsea are back together?"

"We're working on it, but let's go back to Wilder. Who's he gonna end up with?"

Harlow looks at me like I'm an idiot, but before she can answer my question, Scott calls out from the other end of the table, "Gunnar, need you for a minute."

He pushes his chair out and walks inside. I follow him, more than happy to put an end to the conversation with Harlow. I'm not ready for her interrogation over what's happening between Chelsea and me. Once I've made Chelsea mine again, I'll fucking talk about that as much as Harlow wants, but not until then.

Griff is with Scott inside. "The cops have started an investigation into that guy's death last night," he says. "We're keeping an eye on it and may need to pay Novak another visit."

Scott looks at me. "Watch your back at all times,

brother. It looks like the cops have stepped up their efforts."

"How?" I ask.

"I woke up to their eyes on my house this morning," Scott says. "And they were watching Griff too. You notice anything today?"

"No, and I checked." I'm always fucking checking.

Scott nods. "Okay, well stay vigilant. I don't know what the fuck's going on, but it doesn't feel good."

Griff receives a text and says to Scott, "I've gotta take care of something."

"You coming back after?" Scott asks.

"Yeah. Even if this takes longer than I think it will, I'll swing back and pick Sophia up."

After he leaves us, Scott eyes me. "You still good working the jobs Hearst gives us?"

I know what he's asking: How close to losing my shit am I? And should he assign another member to this work?

"I'm good."

"You sure?"

Scott's my president, and I have more respect for him than for most of the people I know. I trust him completely. At various times over the years, he's given me the kind of advice that helped me more than I knew it would. He's been there when I didn't even fucking know I needed someone to be there. And right now, I fucking need to get some shit off my chest, so I say, "Chelsea's leaving him."

"Fuck. When?"

"I've given her a week to make it happen."

He frowns. "You've given her a week?"

"Yeah. She says she needs to do it in a particular way. If she can't make shit happen, I'll take over."

Scott turns silent for a moment before saying, "Sometimes we need to give our woman the space to find her feet, Gunnar. We can't always be the one to make shit happen."

"Scott," Harlow says, joining us. "Sorry to interrupt, but your mum just called. She fell down the stairs and needs someone to go help her. I think she might need to go to the hospital."

Scott nods. "J and I will go. How did she sound?"

"Like she needs some strong painkillers."

"Call her back and tell her to get an ambulance so she can get painkillers faster. J and I will leave now." To me, he says, "Keep your eye out and let me know if you feel any heat."

My phone rings as I watch Scott and Harlow walk away. When I see it's Chelsea, I answer it straight away.

"Mason." My name strangles out of her and my gut roars to life with alarm. "I need you."

I don't know what the fuck is going on, but I'm not going to stand the fuck around and ask her questions. Not with the torment I hearin her voice.

"Where are you?"

"At home," she breathes out on an agonised whisper. "Hurry."

Fuck.

I stab at the phone to end the call and shove it in my pocket, and without wasting a fucking second, I get on my bike and speed to Chelsea's house. Thank fuck I don't have any cops watching me like Scott and Griff do.

When I arrive, I don't bother to knock; I kick the fucking front door in and stalk inside.

I don't know what the fuck I'll find, but I'm ready for Hearst if he's here. If he's fucking hurt her, I will kill the motherfucker.

Chelsea's house is huge, and I move fast, searching for her. When I don't find her inside, I head out the back. My fucking chest almost explodes when I see her lying on the grass, beaten and bloody.

"Fucking hell," I say as I drop to my knees. "He did this to you?"

Her face is a swollen mess of blood and gashes and bruises. She can barely open her eyes, but she manages to open one and look at me. "Yes." Her answer rasps from her, barely loud enough to hear, but I fucking hear it. It's like a fucking roar to me and it causes a shitshow of emotions to course through me.

"Where the fuck is he, Mayfair?"

Her hand curls around my ankle and she grimaces from the pain of making even that small move. "Please, we need to go. Before he comes back."

She's right. I need to get her the fuck out of here.

"I'm going to scoop you up and it's going to hurt like a motherfucker," I say.

She nods but doesn't say anything. From what I'm seeing, I'm surprised she's even still conscious. Hearst has almost beaten the fucking life out of her.

"We'll need to take your car. Where are the keys?"

"Kitchen," she says, her face contorting in pain as I lift her into my arms.

I move swiftly, locating her car keys and getting her into the Range Rover in her garage. Chelsea fights against the pain that every step delivers. I know this because I hear every anguished breath she takes.

Once I've settled her in the back of the car, I reverse out of her driveway and make the drive to the cabin the club owns at Mt Nebo.

I keep my eyes peeled for cops and I keep them on Chelsea as much as I can. She's pushing through her pain like the fucking badass she is, but I've taken enough beatings in my life to know exactly how much she's hurting.

Joe Hearst will fucking pay for this.

I will track that motherfucker down and exact more pain from him than he can ever imagine knowing.

No one hurts my woman and lives to tell the fucking story.

33

GUNNAR

"You free this afternoon?" I ask Wilder over the phone while I watch Chelsea on the bed.

We arrived at the cabin about half an hour ago, and I managed to get her inside and to the bed, but fuck, that killed her. I've given her some painkillers that I located in the bathroom, but she needs stronger ones that I'll organise for Wilder to bring if he's free.

"Yeah, why?" Wilder says.

"I need your help." I detail what's happened and that I need him to come and stay with Chelsea while I take care of Hearst. I also ask him to bring those painkillers.

"I'm on my way," he says, not letting me down.

"Thanks, brother."

I end the call and crouch next to the bed. "Wilder's bringing you some stronger drugs."

She cracks an eye open. "Thank you."

I want to touch her, but I don't dare. "Baby, we're done working your plan with Hearst."

"I know."

"What happened today?"

She swallows, making a pained face as she says, "I need water."

I stand and get her a drink. I then help her drink some, hating every tortured sound she makes doing it.

"He knows I've been with you. I thought he was going to kill me. After he finished, he got a call and left me. He thought I'd passed out." She pauses, looking at me like she has more to say. "I can't be in this marriage anymore, Mason, but I'm scared of what he'll do to you and your club."

"When I said we weren't working your plan with him anymore, I meant I'm fixing the problem once and for all. He won't be able to do anything to me or my club. And he sure as fuck won't ever be able to hurt you again." Unable to stop myself a second longer from touching her, I gently stroke her hair. "You need to tell me what threats they made against the club that caused you to marry him."

She nods, swallowing again like she needs water. After I help her take a few sips, she says, "They have stronger legislation drafted that is far worse than what they've already brought in. Your club won't survive it. They also have evidence ready to plant in order to convict you of two murders. Strong evidence that will lock you up for life. They made threats against the families of club members too." She slowly slides her arm across the bed so she can touch me. "Joe told me today that he's putting an end to your club. I'm worried he's already made a move on this."

I clench my jaw, willing my fury to calm the fuck

down. But I know it won't. And that's okay for later, when I take care of Hearst, but for now, I don't want to let any of it out in front of Chelsea. She doesn't need that. She needs me to step the fuck up and let her know I've got her.

"They kept using these threats to keep you playing along with the marriage?"

"Yes." It's one word, and it falls brokenly from her, but it's the fucking nail in both their coffins as far as I'm concerned. Her father will pay for this too.

"What was your plan to get rid of him?"

She gives me a quick rundown of what she discovered about Hearst's involvement with the mafia, and I agree it was a good plan, but mine is far fucking better. Mine will deal with the problem once and for fucking all. And mine is the one we're rolling with now.

Wilder arrives and I give Chelsea the stronger painkillers. Leaving her to hopefully sleep, I close the bedroom door and join Wilder in the living room.

"What's the plan, brother?" he asks, looking concerned as I stalk past him outside.

I need to get some of this wild anger out after holding it in with Chelsea, and that's gonna involve me punching something a few fucking times.

I find a wall and let loose on it, and when I'm done, I look at Wilder. "I'm going to fucking kill the motherfucker. That's the fucking plan."

"You taking anyone with you?"

"No."

"You need to reconsider that, brother."

"I don't wanna drag anyone into this shit with me."

"Yeah, I get it, but we're already in this shit with you. Scott needs to know what he's up against."

Fuck, he's fucking right. And the fact that both Scott and Griff now have eyes on them again makes me think Chelsea's right. That Hearst has already put his plans into motion.

I force out a harsh breath and nod. "I'll call Scott."

"I'll stay here with Chelsea as long as you need me to."

"Thanks, brother."

I pull out my phone and call my president. After I detail the events of today for him, he says, "Griff and I still have heat on us, but J and Nash are clear. They'll go with you. I'll also organise for Blade to take your back. And Gunnar?"

"Yeah?"

"Don't leave this motherfucker breathing. I don't fuckin' care what he does to threaten the club; no one fuckin' threatens our women."

∼

An hour later, the four of us storm Chelsea's home and find Hearst sitting in an armchair in his lounge room waiting for us. The cunt looks smug as fuck sitting there drinking his whisky.

"Where is she?" he demands, standing.

"I have her as far fucking away from you as I can," I snarl. "And you won't ever be getting your hands on her again."

"Oh, I think we both know that's not true."

J steps forward, a feral expression on his face. "You

think you're gonna survive the fucking day, Hearst? You're fucking not."

Hearst's gaze snaps to J. "It seems we've got a trade to make."

"What fuckin' trade is that?" Nash asks, knowing full fucking well we're not here to make any trades.

"You give me my wife back and I give you your club back. If you're not aware by now, the police have stepped up their efforts against you, and tomorrow Novak will push through new legislation to assist them with that. I'm the only one who can put a stop to all of that, so I suggest you do as I say."

"You're not fucking getting her back," I say.

He eyes me. "I am, and when I do, I'm going to spend time making her regret the fact she let you between her legs." He comes closer to me. "I thought I was fucking her enough to keep her from straying. Now that I know she requires more to be satisfied, I'll be sure to fuck her multiple times a day."

I see fucking red.

It blazes in my eyes, in my head, all the fuck around me.

And it forces its way out of me in a punch that propels Hearst against the wall.

Closing the distance between us in two angry strides, I punch him again while roaring, "You will never fucking touch her again!"

He fights back, punching me, but he's outnumbered here, and since we're not making any trades or agreements, he has no hope of surviving this.

After we exchange a few punches, Blade steps in and

pulls me off him. "We need to get out of here, Gunnar. The longer we stay, the higher the risk."

I know what he's saying, and he's right. The plan is to take Hearst up to Mt Glorious and rid this earth of him. I would have preferred to take my time with him, days of my fucking time, but with the cops back on us, that's not a good plan.

Hearst wipes blood from his nose as he looks at me. "Novak's waiting for my call to assure him his daughter will be returned. If he doesn't receive that call tonight, he *will* proceed with this legislation."

I grip his neck and yank him closer. "What you're not fucking getting here is that we don't cave to fucking demands. We'll take our fucking chances with convincing Novak to leave our club alone, and to be really fucking honest, with the shit we have on the both of you, I don't think he'll be passing that fucking legislation."

Letting him go, I sucker punch him and knock him the fuck out.

Blade looks at me. "Your woman must be made of fucking steel to have put up with this motherfucker."

Yeah, she fucking is.

∼

WE GET Hearst in our van and I follow them on my bike that I left at his place earlier. An hour and a half later, J, Nash, and Blade dig his grave while I take the breath from his fucking lungs.

With his hands and feet tied, I slam him up against a tree and take to him with my fists. I pound them into him while thinking about what he's done to Chelsea. I don't know all the ways he's abused her over the last few months, but I can take a good fucking guess, and I make him hurt for every one of those wrongs.

Every blow I deliver works its way deep into my soul.

I won't ever fucking forget what my woman endured on my behalf, and I won't ever let her go another day not knowing I love her for everything she did to save me and my club. But this piece of motherfucking shit will feel the anguish *I* feel over what she gave for me.

I surrender to my darkest needs.

I allow myself to torture how I've never tortured.

It's bloodshed and brutality and carnage like I've never known.

I use my hands.

My knife.

My gun.

I carve his heart from him.

I carve my hatred into him.

I carve his death. Over. And over. And fucking over.

It's not enough.

It'll never be enough for what he's done.

And when I'm finished, I sit back and stare at the man who took too much from my woman, and I want to fucking start all over again.

"Gunnar," J says, drawing my attention his way. "We need to bury him and get out of here, brother."

I nod.

I know.

I don't fucking like it, but I know.

Pushing up off the ground, I start moving Hearst's body into the grave, piece by fucking piece. I've butchered him so completely that he's unrecognisable.

Once he's all in the ground, I stare down at him and lock the sight into my memory. This is a fucking memento I want to carry with me for life.

Joe Hearst will rot in hell for what he's done, and anyone else who comes after my woman will fucking join him.

34

CHELSEA

I listen to Mason on the phone with his club president and my gut twists with worry. They've been on the phone for the last fifteen minutes discussing how to handle my father and his refusal to back down on some legislation he's going to push through today. I don't know what conversations have taken place between them and Dad because I slept through most of yesterday afternoon and last night thanks to the painkillers Mason gave me, but I've worked out things are tense for the club.

It's just after 5:00 a.m., and Mason doesn't know I'm awake. I'm sure he wouldn't be having this conversation in here if he knew I was. My man doesn't like to worry me with things. He likes to handle stuff so I don't have to even know it was a problem to begin with. Well, this is a problem I helped cause, so I want to know about it, and I want to help them.

When he stabs at his phone to end the call, I say, "Mason."

He's already up off the bed and halfway to the door, but my voice halts him, and he turns back to me. "I didn't realise you were awake."

"I know."

Coming back to the bed, he looks at me with so much love, I feel it right down to my bones. "How are you feeling?"

"Like a truck slammed into me."

"Fuck." His anguish is clear in his eyes and I want to rip it out. I wish he didn't have to see me like this.

I reach for him even though it pains me to move any part of my body. "I can help with Dad."

"No." The word smashes out of his mouth and I swear I feel the impact of it.

"I know my plan is out the window. I get it. We're doing this your way. But I think I can help force Dad out of office."

"I don't fucking want you anywhere near this, Mayfair. I want you here, safe with me, where they can't fucking hurt you anymore."

"I know. And I love you for that, and I promise to go along with whatever plan you decide from here on out, but please take me to my father this morning so I can talk to him. You can stay in the room with us and make sure I'm safe, but this is something I need to do. For me, as much as for your club."

I watch him war with this decision, my strong protector. I meant what I said, I'll go along with whatever he decides, but I'm desperate for him to agree to my request. I helped make this mess. I want to help clean it up.

Mason rakes his fingers through his hair before giving me a tight nod. "I'll take you to your father this morning, but"—he jabs his finger at me—"the fucking minute shit goes south, I'm taking you out of there."

I know he's worried that history will repeat itself. That I'll do what my father demands. But I won't. I'll never do that again.

I pull myself up to a sitting position, ignoring how it kills me to do so. Bringing my hands to Mason's face, I touch him gently and say, "I'm done with making decisions without you. I know it's going to take me a long time to gain your trust back, but I promise you that from here on out, I'm yours for life, and I'll spend the rest of it showing you I mean every word of what I've just said."

The Mason staring back at me is the boy I loved as a child. The boy who showed me his hurt when his father wounded him. I'm looking at that same kind of wound, and it pierces my heart. I never want to put this kind of look in his eyes again.

I bring my lips to his and kiss him softly. I can't manage more than soft, but that doesn't matter because he knows what I'm promising in this kiss.

When it ends, he gives me his eyes. "I fucking love you, and if you ever try to walk away from me again, I just won't fucking let you."

I smile, and it's from such a deep place within that not even my injuries and the pain it causes can stop how big it becomes. "You are my greatest favourite, Mason Blaise."

"Thank fuck, because you were always mine too." He moves off the bed. "Now, let's see how fucking hard it's gonna be for you to get ready to go see your dad. I swear, if this hurts too much, I'm not fucking doing it."

Still smiling at him, because I love him and his bossy,

grumbly ways, I say, "I won't complain about any of the pain. You won't even know I'm feeling it."

"Baby, I never hear the fucking end of it when you have a headache. There's no fucking way I'm not gonna hear about this."

And just like that, Mason helps wipe away some of my pain. Just by being him. Just by being my man. Just by loving me.

∽

Mason helps me shower and dress, and I only complain about some of it. Every time he gives me that look of his that signals he's almost reached breaking point of dealing with my pain, I pull back on letting him know how bad it is.

He drives me into the city and escorts me up to Dad's office. I phoned ahead to let him know I was coming, so he's waiting for me. And he doesn't look happy.

"Chelsea," he greets me after shooting Mason a filthy look. "What the hell happened to you?"

"Your favourite son-in-law decided I wasn't a good enough wife."

Dad's eyes widen. "He did this?"

It strikes me that most fathers would have a far different reaction to their daughter turning up looking like I do. My entire body is covered in bruises. I'm black and blue and swollen. I can't open one eye. After this, Mason's taking me to the doctor to ensure I don't have any broken bones. And yet, my father just stands there staring at me like he can't quite believe I'm telling him the truth.

"Yes, Dad, Joe did this."

"Where is he? I haven't been able to reach him."

Mason and I haven't spoken about where Joe is, but I can guess. That's a conversation we'll have later, but it's not a conversation I'll ever have with my father. "I don't know. I called Mason after Joe left me beaten in the backyard, and I haven't seen Joe since." I straighten my back and shoulders as much as I can and add, "And I don't plan on seeing him again."

"You're married to him, Chelsea. You live with him," Dad says. "You can't not see him."

"And you seriously think I'll choose to stay with him after he did this?"

He looks between Mason and me. "We have an agreement for that, yes."

Mason has been standing next to me quietly, even though I can hear his thunder slowly building. At what Dad just said, he snarls, "This voids that fucking agreement, Novak."

I place my hand on his arm and look at him, sending him a plea to let me handle this. Misgiving flashes in his eyes, but he begrudgingly turns silent again.

"I'm divorcing Joe, Dad, and you're not going to stop me." He doesn't need to know a divorce won't be needed. All he needs to know is I'm done with the marriage.

Fumes of anger billow from my father. "Over my dead fucking body are you divorcing him. I will not allow you to walk away from what we've been building. Between Joe and me, we will run this state for decades, and you, my girl, will not jeopardise that."

Mason practically growls by my side. I take his hand in mine and squeeze it as I say, "You know, you and Joe threatened me and forced me into doing things I didn't want to do, and I allowed that because the one thing you instilled in me growing up was fear. I was so scared of what you'd do to Mason and the people he cared about that I couldn't see what was there right in front of me all along." I let go of Mason's hand and step closer to my father. "I had the power all along. I know where yours and Joe's bodies are buried. All I have to do is share those secrets with the world, and your power disappears. All I have to do is decide that I won't let you bully me anymore and take my power back in order to wipe yours out."

My father stares at me with a look I've seen on him a few times. Anxiety. And suddenly I realise he's known this all along too.

I don't wait for him to speak. I've got more to say, and I want to say it fast so that Mason and I can get out of here. I cannot be in my father's presence a minute longer than is absolutely necessary. "You will figure out a way to get rid of that legislation you introduced months ago against motorcycle clubs and you will push that through today. Once that's done, you will resign as premier. If you don't do these things, I will schedule interviews with the media and start talking, and with what I know about you and Joe, you will wish I didn't."

My father looks like he wants to murder me himself. "You won't."

"I will." My promise breathes from me with all the fire inside me, and Dad feels every lick of it.

He shifts his gaze to Mason. "I imagine this is all your doing. I should have ruined you the first time I threatened it."

Mason steps next to me, taking my hand in his again.

"I didn't have a fucking thing to do with this. Your daughter found her feet all by herself. I'm just along for the ride."

"I'll wait to hear from you today," I say to Dad before looking at Mason and letting him know I'm done here.

He walks me out to the lift, and once we're safely inside it, I collapse against him. His strong arms come around me and I grip his shirt. I don't know why, but tears slide down my face as I say, "I think I'm going to vomit."

He tilts my face up to his, and his thumb gently wipes my tears. "I've never fucking loved you more than right now, Mayfair. And not because you just stood up for my club, but because you are strong and soft all rolled into one. You love so fucking fiercely that it takes my fucking breath away." He kisses me before adding, "If anyone ever tells you you're not a badass, don't fucking believe them. You have more fucking balls than half the men I've met in my life."

"You did have something to do with this, Mason." I hold his eyes as I mention the thing my father said. "You love me so completely that it lets me be a badass. Thank you for giving me that."

As we exit out into the sunshine together, I know that no matter how hard it's been being apart from Mason, it strengthened us.

The fire didn't burn us, it built us.

I also know I never want to be apart from him again.

Mason Blaise is my forever favourite.

35

GUNNAR

"Just got word that the cops are pulling back on watching us and that they've stopped investigating that engineer's death," Scott says, joining me in the clubhouse bar late Friday afternoon. "Also got word that Novak just resigned."

I suck back some beer. "It's a good fucking day, brother." It's been a good fucking week. Novak did everything Chelsea told him to, Chelsea moved back in with me, and she's recovering slowly from the beating Hearst gave her. She also told me today that she's done with her father, something I'd already taken as a given. It was good to hear her say it, though. She needs to be done with him.

I'm keeping my eye on the motherfucker. If he wasn't her father, I'd deal with him the same way I dealt with Hearst. But as much as I want to wrap my hands around his throat and watch him take his last breath, I can't do that to her. She might be done with him, but that doesn't mean she wants him dead. Stripping him of his power sorted out our problem, and unless he gives me a reason otherwise, that'll be him dealt with.

"Tell Chelsea I want a word the next time she's in here. She took our back and I want to thank her for that," he says before leaving me.

My phone sounds with a text.

Alexa: Bring steak with you tonight and I'll cook it for you.

Me: Since when am I coming over tonight?

Alexa: Since Chelsea arrived an hour ago and agreed to you guys having dinner at mine.

Me: Will I always have to fucking share her with you?

Alexa: Always. But if you put a hole through my wall the next time you bang her here, I'm not gonna be happy.

Me: I'm making that my top fucking priority in life as of now.

Alexa: Bring me some wine too. You know the one I like.

"You look how I feel after being ambushed by my old lady," Nash says, pulling up the stool next to me.

"That's because I've just been fucking ambushed by mine and my sister." Not that Chelsea texted, but she would have known Alexa was messaging me.

He grins. "Welcome to the rest of your life, brother."

I drink some more beer as we settle in and watch some sport on the TV in the bar. J joins us and we shoot the shit for an hour or so before I say, "I've gotta go."

"You coming to Scott's tomorrow night?" J asks, referring to Saturday night poker that Scott started up recently.

"Yeah, we should be there."

Nash lifts his chin at me. "See you then."

I leave the clubhouse and stop off to pick up steak and

wine before heading to Alexa's. When I arrive at her apartment, I'm greeted with a "Can you please bring the chips over with you?" from Alexa, who's sitting with Chelsea on her couch.

I put the steak and wine in the fridge, grab the chips she wants, and join them. Chelsea smiles at me as I dump the bag of chips in Alexa's lap and say, "I'm expecting good fucking things with dinner after running around getting steak and fucking wine for you."

"How was your day?" Chelsea asks as she threads her fingers through my hair and pulls me in for a kiss when I drop down next to her.

I allow my lips to linger on hers for a long time before ending the kiss and saying, "Good. Yours? Tell me you saw the doctor today."

I took her to the doctor on Monday after we saw her father. The doctor said Chelsea had no broken bones, but that she wanted to check up on her healing at the end of the week. I fucking know my woman, so I know she probably didn't fucking go. She doesn't like visiting the doctor because they're always fucking running late, and she has less patience than I do for waiting around at the doctors surgery.

"Yes, I went, Mr Bossypants. And I'm fine. All is healing well, so you can stop worrying about me now."

"Baby, you know that's never gonna fucking happen. I was put on this earth to fucking worry about you."

Her smile is sexy when she leans in close and kisses me again. "I love you."

"Okay, you guys," Alexa says, "let's focus. I need your advice."

Chelsea eyes her. "What about?"

"I met my new neighbour today. He's hot as sin and we flirted in the lift. Is it a bad idea to sleep with your neighbour? I mean, all kinds of things could go wrong, right?"

"Yeah," I say as Chelsea says, "No, I think you should do it."

Chelsea looks at me. "Why is it a bad thing?"

"Because he might be a needy fuck. He'll always know when the fuck she's home, and she'll never be able to fucking escape him."

"You're assuming it goes bad. What if he's her soulmate?"

"And what if he's fucking not?"

Chelsea shakes her head at me and looks back at my sister. "Ignore him. If he turns out not to be the one for you, surely you can just ignore him."

Alexa looks between us. "Well, that helped."

Chelsea laughs and I say, "Ask Calder. He slept with his neighbour and look how good that turned out for him."

"Oh God," Alexa says. "I'd forgotten about that. You're right. I can't do it. He might be a nutcase."

"Did you see Mum today?" I ask, changing the subject.

Alexa nods. "Yeah, she was better today than yesterday. The new medication the doctor started her on seems to be helping." She stands. "I'm going to get wine. Do you guys want a drink?"

"God yes," Chelsea says.

I glance down at her as I say, "No, I'll drive home." After Alexa leaves us, I say to Chelsea, "What's going on, Mayfair? Is your pain worse today?" It's been gradually easing throughout the week, but I know she's still feeling the beating she took.

She looks up at me and shakes her head. "No, it's not too bad today."

"So what gives?" I can tell there's something going on with her after the way she practically just begged for a drink.

"I seriously can't keep anything from you, can I?"

"Seriously, no. Now spill."

She sighs. "I had to endure Joe's father today, grilling me over where he is. If I never have to speak to either of them again, it'll be too soon." When I don't respond straight away, because I'm fucking trying to figure out how I can help her with this, she says, "And no, you can't help, so stop thinking you can. This is something I have to take care of myself."

If there's something I've learned in all this, it's that I need to give Chelsea the space to find her way sometimes. Scott gave me that advice, and she's shown how true it is, and now I need to step the fuck back sometimes and let her handle shit. It's the hardest fucking thing to do because my natural instinct is always to take care and take over, but I'm fucking trying.

"Where are you with the cops on this?" They've grilled her a couple of times this week.

"That's the weirdest thing. One of them came to see me today and told me not to worry, that the case would work itself out and that he knows I didn't have anything to do with Joe's disappearance."

It is weird, but not completely unexpected. The club has cops it works with in times like this, so I imagine

Scott has called on them. I make a mental note to ask him about it.

Alexa comes back with drinks for her and Chelsea, and they proceed to spend the next fucking hour talking make-up and hair while I zone the fuck out.

When Chelsea snuggles against me and starts on her third wine, I know we're settling in for the night. And as fucking bored as I am with the conversation, I wouldn't be any-fucking-where else. I'll never fucking take Chelsea for granted again, and I'll sit through as many hours of girl talk as I have to. This woman is worth every fucking second of it.

36

CHELSEA

"What's going on, Mayfair? You've been anxious all fucking afternoon," Mason says while I get dressed for his poker night that we're leaving for in ten minutes.

I yank the top off that I had on, annoyed at my own damn self for the mood I'm in. Mason's right, I have been anxious all afternoon. I've taken it out on him, and God love him, he's put up with it all.

"I don't want to admit to you what it is," I say. "I feel like an idiot."

His brows furrow. "The fuck? Just tell me. You're not an idiot, and I would never think that."

"I'm nervous about seeing everyone again. Like, I'm worried what they must think of me for what I did to you." God, just saying it out loud makes me feel even more anxious.

Mason slides his arm around my waist and pulls me close. "You have nothing to be worried about. Everyone knows what happened and why you did it, and fuck, they respect you for what you did for the club."

"Okay."

He cups my cheek. "You don't believe me, do you?"

"It's not that I don't believe you. I just…. I don't know. I guess it's important to me that the people who you call family don't think badly of me. And I know that sounds dumb, but—"

"It doesn't sound dumb." He brushes his lips over mine. "I fucking like how important this is to you. Trust me, they don't think badly of you."

I believe him. Mason doesn't lie. So I just need to get over my issues with this.

Stepping out of his hold and glancing around the room, I say, "I promise I'll clean this mess up when we get home." I've strewn clothes all over the place that I decided weren't good enough for tonight.

"Baby, you've trashed this room worse than this before. This is fucking nothing."

I glare at him and throw my top at him. "You are the worst, Mason Blaise. I'm having a meltdown here. I need support, not trash talk."

He grins. "If you weren't injured, I'd pick you the fuck up right now, and throw you on the bed and show you some fucking support."

Arching my brows, I say, "So you're saying I can get away with stuff thanks to my injuries?"

"Try me. See how fucking far it gets you."

God, I've missed this with him.

I moved straight back in with him on Monday after we dealt with my father and after Mason took me to the doctor. I couldn't bring myself to go back to the home I shared with Joe, so Mason collected the few belongings I wanted, and we shopped for whatever else I needed.

Being back with Mason is as easy as if we were never apart. We've been through a lot, but we haven't allowed any of it to come between us. And as much as I believe I have a lot of work to do to rebuild his trust in me, he hasn't given me any signs that's the case. I actually think we both just know deep in our souls that we'll be together forever now.

I wave him off. "You need to leave me alone so I can think straight about what I want to wear tonight." When he doesn't give me the impression he intends to leave the room, I say, "I'm serious, Mason. You're too damn distracting with those muscles and that face."

"You fucking wound me, woman. Here I was thinking it was my fucking heart that you loved, and it's just my good fucking looks."

"Nope, not your heart. I'm shallow and all about your looks." I tease him with a smile as I add, "If I were you, I'd be worried about ageing. Who knows what will happen to those looks?"

He closes the distance between us and hooks his hand around the back of my head. "I'm fucking banking on you going blind, but I'm not above begging." He kisses me, deepening the kiss until my thoughts are in shambles because all I can think about is how much I want him. When he finally lets me go, he says, "You wanna revise your statement?"

Leaning into him, I smile up at him. "It's your heart I love. It's always been your heart." Then, as his eyes soften,

I add, "I only recently realised you have muscles to die for."

He smiles and, with a shake of his head, says, "You keep me on my fucking toes, Mayfair."

"Yep, that's my job. Now, go. I need to think."

He finally leaves me, and I finally figure out what to wear. I also get my shit together over my nerves. And when we exit the house, I'm more than good, because I have Mason by my side, and that's all I need to take on the world.

~

Mason was right, no one from his club thinks badly of me for what I did. That's clear in the way they welcome me back in like I never left.

Harlow is all over me, making sure I'm comfortable. Madison invites me to the weekly session at the beauty salon the girls have. Velvet suggests we all do a yoga class together when she discovers I love it. Sophia asks me to join them all at her home next weekend for a painting get-together. At first I assume she means art, but it turns out they're all getting together to help her and Griff paint their house. Layla tells me that if I can't find a new job and am desperate, she'll hire me in her bar. And Scott's mum, who is on crutches, tells me to sit down and have a drink with them.

The guys don't say much, but I don't expect them to. They all lift their chin at me in greeting, and I take that as their welcome back.

Scott pulls me and Mason aside, though, and surprises the hell out of me.

"I want to thank you for what you did for the club," he says. "You took our back and I won't ever forget it."

"Thank you for saying that."

He nods and eyes Mason before looking back at me. "I took care of your problems with the cops."

I frown. "My problems?"

"Yeah, over Hearst's disappearance. They won't bother you about that again."

I stare at him as I realise what he's saying. And I'm so fucking grateful to him for doing this. "I appreciate that."

"If you need anything else, come see me," he says before leaving us.

I look at Mason. "I don't really need to know, but how did he get the cops to look away?"

He takes his time answering me, to the point where I don't expect him to. And I get it. Club business stays between the club. But finally, he says, "Like you said, Joe was tied up with the mafia. They're looking at two guys the mafia sent to threaten Hearst. Apparently, they killed someone for Hearst who was threatening his brother and didn't like it when Hearst tried to cut ties with them."

Oh my God.

The crime his father wanted him to commit.

That has to be it.

I really was married to the devil.

I wrap my arms around Mason and press my head to his chest, listening to his heartbeat. I find it soothing. I always have. I also find it soothing when he puts his arms around me and holds me tightly to him, which he does now. We stay like this for a few minutes. It's like he senses I need this, so he gives it to me without question. And when I finally look up at him and say, "Thank you for saving me," he simply nods and says, "I'll always save you, Mayfair."

I know he will.

Mason Blaise was born to be my saviour, my protector, my hero.

And I was born to be his girl.

37

GUNNAR

"Are you trying to kill me, woman?" I ask Chelsea when I come home from work and find her dressed in the tightest red dress I've ever fucking seen.

She smiles. "No, but I think that means I've achieved my goal."

"If your goal was to get me hard, then you've fucking achieved it." I run my eyes over her tits and down her body, deciding to move my plans to fuck her from later this evening to right fucking now.

"That's unfortunate."

I bring my hands to her hips. "The fuck why?"

"Because we're going on a date."

"A date?" Chelsea and I don't do dates. We never have.

She smacks my hands away from her body. "Yes, a date. You need to go and shower and get ready."

I arch my brows. I fucking like her bossiness, but I'm not fucking letting on about that. "Do I now?"

"Yes."

"And where are we going? Do I need to get fancy for this?"

"We're going out for dinner. Wear whatever you want."

There's something about her tonight that makes me do as she's asked.

"Are you going to tell me where we're going? I ask as I walk out of the bedroom, showered, and dressed, fifteen minutes later.

"Somewhere special," she says, giving me nothing.

"And how the fuck am I going to get us there if you don't tell me where?"

"You're not in charge of getting us there. I've hired a limo."

This night has just taken a turn I'm fucking into. However, Chelsea reads me in the way she always fucking reads me and shakes her head. "I'm not fucking you in the limo on the way to dinner, so get that thought out of your head."

It's been a month since she moved back in, and after she healed from her beating, I haven't been able to keep my hands off her. If she thinks she's got any fucking chance of keeping me away in this limo, she needs to fucking think again.

Her phone sounds with a text, and after reading it, she says, "The limo's almost here."

We head outside as the limo pulls up at our place. Five minutes later, we're on our way to wherever Chelsea's taking us, and I'm about to get her on my lap. However, my plans go out the window when she turns her body to mine and says, "Tell me a favourite." When

Chelsea wants to play this game, nothing can distract or stop her.

"This fucking dress for one."

She rolls her eyes. "Tell me a proper one, Mason. I'm being serious here."

And so the fuck am I, but I sense something going on here, something deeper that I haven't clued onto yet, so I give her what she's asked for. "Watching you read on the beach with the sound of the waves in the background and the sun on you."

Her eyes widen a little. With surprise and with pleasure. She slides closer to me and takes hold of my hand. "I like it when you give me your favourites."

"I'll be fucking honest, and it's not just because I'm a horny fucking bastard, but one of my favourite favourites is you sitting in my lap. Doesn't matter if I'm fucking you or not, I fucking like you there and I wish you were there right fucking now."

She moves before I've even finished talking, giving me what I want. As her hand slips around my neck, she says, "Do you want to know one of my favourites?"

"I wanna know all your favourites, baby."

She bites her lip as she gives me one of those sexy smiles of hers I love. "Coming home to you every night. Cooking dinner with you every night. Laughing with you every night. Sleeping in your arms every night." She presses her lips to mine and kisses me. It's slow and filled with promises I'm yet to know. But I know for damn sure that Chelsea will make good on all those promises during our lifetime. When she drags her lips from mine, she says, "I want twenty-seven thousand more nights with you. And I want my most favourite favourite to be the fact you are my husband." She pauses. "Will you marry me, Mason Blaise?"

Fuck. Me.

I fucking love this woman.

Tightening my hold on her, I say, "I would marry you right fucking now if I could, because *my* favourite favourite will be growing old with you. I don't know how the fuck you figure the twenty-seven thousand nights, but I fucking need every one of them with you."

Her lips are back on mine, and with the way she kisses me, I should be given a fucking medal for not tearing her fucking dress off and slamming my dick inside her right fucking now.

It turns out, though, that my bride-to-be is as horny as her future husband, and before I know what the fuck's happening, she's got my jeans undone and my dick in her hand while trying to wiggle her dress up

"Maybe next fucking time you decide you wanna propose to me in the back of a limo, you could plan ahead and wear a dress that's not so fucking tight," I say as I yank it up.

"You are so fucking grumbly sometimes," she says, dragging my mouth back to hers.

I take hold of her ass as she sits on my dick.

"Oh God," she says, letting my lips go again. "Fuck, you feel so good." Her fingers dig into my biceps as she starts fucking me.

"You're telling me I get to fuck you at least twenty-seven thousand more times?"

"Well, that depends on whether you can still get it up at one hundred, because that math roughly figures us living until then."

I grin. "Give me some fucking credit, Mayfair. I'll still be getting it up then."

"Maybe we should get extra in while you're younger, just to be sure."

I thrust harder into her. "Maybe you should have some fucking faith in your husband."

"Oh, fuck," she moans as I take control of this fuck. "You're not my husband yet."

"I don't give a fuck if it's not official. Calling myself that is my new fucking favourite."

She wraps her arms around me and squeezes her cunt around my dick as she says, "I fucking love to hear your favourites, but not while you're fucking me. Can you finish the damn job and then tell me all your fucking favourites?"

"Fuck your mouth is filthy these days," I mutter before getting the damn job done.

After we come, she kisses me slowly. Lazily. So damn sexily. Threading her fingers through my hair, exactly how I fucking love it, she says, "I wasn't going to propose until after dinner."

I wrap my arms around her. "What happened?"

She smiles. "You happened. You always happen. I lose my mind when I'm with you. In all the best ways."

"Can I ask now where you're taking me for dinner?"

She continues with her fingers in my hair. "I booked the room in the hotel where this all started."

"The room we got trapped in?"

"Yes. I hired a caterer to make your favourite food and I rented a hotel room for the night."

"You fucking love me."

She kisses me again before saying, "Yeah, baby, I fucking do." She pauses. "Tell me."

I bring my lips to hers and show her what she wants to hear.

I show her the love I feel so fucking deeply I might drown in it one day.

I show her the loyalty I will have for her until the fucking day I die.

I show her the commitment I'm making to her for life.

And when I end the kiss, I tell her the words I will whisper in her ear for twenty-seven thousand more nights. "I fucking love you, Mayfair."

EPILOGUE
GUNNAR

"Chelsea is positively radiant today," my mother says as I watch my wife scoop our son up off the beach and walk my way.

The sun in her eyes causes her to squint.

It causes my breathing to falter for a second.

Chelsea has never looked more beautiful to me than she does today and that's fucking saying something, because not a day has passed without her looking beautiful.

She discovered she's pregnant again today.

I don't know if that's what's done it for me. Knowing she's carrying my child again. But fuck me, she's fucking glowing, and the sun shining on her only intensifies her beauty.

Dragging my gaze from her, I look at Mum. She's been in remission from her cancer for just over two years now and divorced from my father for one year. The day she told me she was leaving him was one of the best fucking days of my life. Or as I tell Chelsea, one of my favourite fucking favourites.

"She's pregnant again," I say, even though Chelsea and I agreed to keep this news to ourselves for a little while. I know she won't mind Mum knowing, though. She loves my mother with all her heart. Tells me she's the mother she never had, which blows my damn mind some days when I think about the mother I knew growing up. She wasn't a bad mother, but she wasn't the woman she is today. She didn't love so freely during my childhood. Something happened to her during her cancer journey and she's like a new woman. One who has learned to love without conditions.

"Oh my goodness, that is wonderful news."

I nod. "Yeah."

My phone sounds with a message notification.

Alexa: I'm on my way. Should be there in an hour or so. Don't let Calder take my parking spot.

Me: Good fucking luck if he arrives before you.

Calder: I'm almost there, Alexa. I'll be sure to save you the spot next to yours.

Alexa: You suck and I will quit my job if you take my spot.

Calder: I'll accept that as your notice and find a replacement this afternoon.

Alexa: *pokes tongue*

Me: Put your tongue away. I'll tell Chelsea you want your spot guarded. She'll pull Calder into line more than I can.

Hayden: I'm just pulling in now. Tell that woman of yours to come give me a hug.

Me: I'm not fucking letting her near you after the last time you two got drunk together.

Alexa: OMG OMG OMG is she pregnant? Tell me she is!!!!

Jesus fuck, how my sister knows shit is beyond me.

Alexa: I'm taking your silence as a big fat YES and I am here for it!

Adam: I'd take his silence as his death notice. And the poor fucker didn't even announce anything he shouldn't.

Me: Maybe we could keep this secret between the five of us? Chelsea and I agreed to keep it quiet for a bit.

Calder: I'm putting a hundred on Alexa failing at that.

Hayden: No one's gonna bet against you, Calder.

Adam: True.

Alexa: I hate you all. You all suck. I can keep a secret.

Me: Fuck it, you can't. I'll tell Chelsea you figured it out.

Chelsea reaches Mum and me and leans in for a kiss before passing our son over. We're in Port Douglas for our yearly family holiday, the one we started a tradition of after giving that first Port Douglas holiday to Alexa as a birthday present. This is our third time here. This year, we're also celebrating Christian's first birthday.

"He needs his nappy changed," Chelsea says as I press a kiss to Christian's head.

"Here, let me take him," Mum says. "I need all the time I can get with my grandson this week."

Mum is one of those grandmothers who dotes like fuck on her grandchildren, and since Christian is her only one, she detests having to share him. And she has to share him, because Chelsea never went back to work after having him and also doesn't like to share him. It's a good fucking thing these two get on so well or I'd have my fucking hands full managing them.

I pull Chelsea into my arms after Mum leaves us. Resting my hands on her ass, I run my eyes down her body, appreciating the fuck out of her green bikini. "You should wear this more often at home."

She reaches up and laces her fingers through my hair. "Should I serve you your dinner in it after you get home from a long day at work?"

I grin. "See, this is why I married you. You read my fucking mind at times."

"Baby, let's be real. You married me so you'd have twenty-seven thousand guaranteed orgasms."

"And I'm fucking behind on them. You need to start putting out some more."

"You need to stop getting me pregnant then."

"You fucking love being pregnant."

She smiles. "I fucking do."

I drop my lips to hers and claim the kiss I've wanted since this morning when Christian interrupted us. I take my time and am hard as fuck when I'm done. "Jesus, I fucking need you, Mayfair. It's been two fucking days."

"I can't help it if your son wears me out. Honestly, sleep feels way more important at the moment."

I tighten my hold on her. This woman has no idea how fucking much I need her. She might think she does, but she doesn't. "So fucking long as it doesn't become your only favourite."

She brings her mouth back to mine for a long, lazy, sexy kiss. The kind I would sell my soul for. "Fucking you will always be above sleep on my favourite list."

"Mum will take Christian for the night."

Her eyes light up. "So we can sleep?"

"Smartass," I mutter, bending my mouth to her neck and biting her lightly. "Trust me when I say there won't be much fucking sleep happening. I have to make the most of this time before you have the baby. I'm pretty fucking sure that if you're tired now, you're not gonna make good on meeting those twenty-seven thousand orgasms I'm owed when you've got two kids."

"You're such a grumpy ass. Don't you know marriage is about the valleys and the peaks?"

"The fucking what and what?"

"The highs and lows. So we'll have some low years. We'll back that up with some high ones."

I kiss a trail from her collarbone back to her mouth. "Let's make our marriage about the peaks and the peaks. We'll just have high years all the fucking way around."

She smiles and it settles deep in my gut. Bringing her hands down to my face, she holds me and says, "I love you, Mason Blaise, but I didn't ask you to marry me thinking we'd sail through it on one long high. I asked you to marry me because I knew you were the only man who'd make it through twenty-seven thousand nights with me regardless of whether we were in a valley or a peak."

Fuck. Me.

My wife never fails to remind me she's the fucking shit.

"Tell me," I say.

She keeps smiling. "No, you tell me first."

I grip her like I'm never letting go. "I fucking love you."

"Yeah, baby, you do. But I love you more, and don't you forget it."

Hayden takes this moment to cut the fuck in on my time with my wife. "Pregnancy looks good on you, Chelsea."

She looks at me, her brows arched. "I thought we were keeping this between us for a while?"

"Fuck," I mutter, shooting daggers at my fucking brother.

Hayden grins. "You should know by now there's no such thing as a secret in our family."

Chelsea shakes her head, but she's smiling. "Yeah, Hayden, I do."

I lean in and brush my lips over her ear, murmuring, "Peaks and valleys, Mayfair. Peaks and fucking valleys."

She shakes her head again. "You're lucky I love those muscles of yours, Mr Blaise."

"And you're fucking lucky I keep them up for you."

The grin she gives me right before leaving me to hug my brother is sexy as fuck and hits me deep in my gut. "We both know you'd do anything for me," she says.

I watch her ass all the fucking way to my brother.

She's fucking right. I would do anything for her, because any valley with her by my side is better than any peak without her.

∽

Thank you so much for reading GUNNAR. I hope you loved it as much as I loved writing it.

My next Storm book out will be WILDER. I know so

many of you have been waiting patiently for his book. It'll be out this year! I have pre-orders up on all sites with the release date set for the end of December. I'm actually hoping to release it sooner than that. As soon as I have a confirmed date, I will email it out and post it all over social media.

You can pre-order WILDER here.
This is Wilder & Scarlett's story!

ALSO BY NINA LEVINE

Storm MC Series

Storm (Storm MC #1)

Fierce (Storm MC #2)

Blaze (Storm MC #3)

Revive (Storm MC #4)

Slay (Storm MC #5)

Sassy Christmas (Storm MC #5.5)

Illusive (Storm MC #6)

Command (Storm MC #7)

Havoc (Storm MC #8)

Gunnar (Storm MC #9)

Wilder (Storm MC #10 - coming 2020)

Colt (Storm MC #11 - coming 2021)

Sydney Storm MC Series

Relent (#1)

Nitro's Torment (#2)

Devil's Vengeance (#3)

Hyde's Absolution (#4)

King's Wrath (#5)

King's Reign (#6)

King: The Epilogue (#7)

Storm MC Reloaded Series

Hurricane Hearts (#1)

War of Hearts (#2)

Christmas Hearts (#3)

Battle Hearts (#4)

The Hardy Family Series

Steal My Breath (single dad romance)

Crave Series

Be The One (rockstar romance)

Billionaire Romance

Ashton Scott

www.ninalevinebooks.com

ACKNOWLEDGMENTS

I have my dream team for every book. They're always the same people, and I need to thank them from the bottom of my heart for contributing to this book.

Jodie O'Brien - you know I love you, but I don't think you know just how much. I couldn't do this life without you. I certainly couldn't write books without you. I never want that USB of all my files back off you, 'k? No one knows my heart like you do and maybe that's why you just get my books and know exactly what needs fixing and what needs to be left the fuck alone. You are my forever favourite.

Becky Johnson - gah! My love for you is huge. I seriously can't thank you enough for always choosing to work with me even when I keep crazy hours and deadlines. You are an amazing editor, but mostly, you are the fucking bomb. And I know you just edited my commas in your head. I give up on commas. We aren't friends. Thank God for you!

Letitita Hasser - this cover!! Thank you for making magic happen again. You are amazing and I am so thankful to be able to work with you.

Wander & Andrey - you guys!!! Holy shit, this image is epic! Thank you so much for going above and beyond to get me cover photos. I love you both!

To my amazing and loyal readers & bloggers - THANK YOU! It's been almost seven years since the first Storm book came out and you are still here by my side. I can't thank you enough for your support, your encouragement, and from so many of you, your love. You stuck by me these last few years after my mum passed away, while I re-discovered myself, and you lifted me up. You don't know it, but you helped me take back my power. I will love you forever for that.

To my mofos - you know who you are. Thank you for loving me. I love you all.

FULL PLAYLIST

Must've Never Met You by Luke Combs
All Over Again by Luke Combs
Don't Stop Now by Sam Riggs
Love Bites by Def Leppard
Don't It by Billy Currington
Love You Like That by Canaan Smith
Hell of a Night by Dustin Lynch
Gonna Wanna Tonight by Chase Rice
Trying Not To Love You by Nickelback
Fire't Up by Brantley Gilbert
She Ain't Home by Brantley Gilbert
Laid Back Ride by Brantley Gilbert
Man of Steel by Brantley Gilbert
The Black and White by The Band CAMINO
Bad by James Bay
Scars by James Bay
Slow Dancing in a Burning Room by John Mayer
The Last Time by Taylor Swift

All You Had To Do Was Stay by Taylor Swift
Naked by James Arthur
Better Together by Luke Combs

ABOUT THE AUTHOR

Nina Levine

Dreamer.

Coffee Lover.

Gypsy at heart.

USA Today Bestselling author who writes about alpha men & the women they love.

When I'm not creating with words you will find me planning my next getaway, visiting somewhere new in the world, having a long conversation over coffee and cake with a friend, creating with paper or curled up with a good book and chocolate.

I've been writing since I was twelve. Weaving words together has always been a form of therapy for me especially during my harder times. These days I'm proud that my words help others just as much as they help me.

www.ninalevinebooks.com

Printed in Dunstable, United Kingdom